LAUREL AND BARON

MARY MECHAM

LAUREL AND BARON

LAUREL AND BARON

Copyright © 2021 by Mary Mecham

www.marymecham.com

Edited by Ashley Eddy

LAUREL

$\mathcal{I}$ held Baron's hand as we surveyed the carnage laid out before us. The rather unpleasant and grisly sight of the Sheriff of Nottingham's dead body stood out prominently. The arrow I shot through his heart only minutes before was still protruding into the air from his chest. I gave Baron's hand a gentle squeeze. However horrible a person the Sheriff had been, he still was Baron's father, and I had killed him. I noticed that Baron refused to look at his father's body, and my heart ached for him. He didn't have any family left any more.

My own father, Robin Hood, was rummaging through the Sheriff's pockets. Dale and Little John, two of the Merry Men, had both been injured during the battle. Little John was coming around, but Dale was still out cold.

The rest of the Merry Men had collected all the weapons from the fallen men, and began to drag the prone bodies into a pile. I saw Lincoln beckon Alan over, and they both bent to listen at one soldier's chest. They left the man out of the pile. He must still be alive, and I recognized the face. It was one of the men who had been stationed with the Sheriff's company all during the winter while they held me prisoner. Baron had been my bodyguard back then. His job was to hold me hostage, but the more time we spent together, the harder it became to resist our mutual attraction.

Father pulled a scroll out of the Sheriff's boot, and showed it to Will Scarlet. Will was in his forties, but still had a youthful, boyish face that matched his energy level, just like Father. As their eyes flicked back and forth, both of their frowns deepened. Will Scarlet looked up and caught my eye. He motioned for me to come over. I let go of Baron's hand, stepped over several bodies that hadn't been moved yet, and approached them both. Without a word, Father shoved the scroll toward me. I didn't need to read it to know that it contained very bad news. Father's brow was puckered up with worry, Will's with eager anticipation. He never could stay away from a fight.

I unrolled the paper and scanned the writing. It was a letter, addressed to the Sheriff of Nottingham from Prince John, summoning him and his platoon of soldiers to Nottingham Castle. My mouth fell open as I read. What he had proposed was treason! When I got to the bottom of the page, I stared at Father, and he back at me, his expression full of meaning. Ever since Mother had died when I was eight years old, Father and I had developed a close bond. Often, it felt as though we could read each other's minds, and now, we both knew what we had to do. James, another of the Merry Men, approached and tugged the scroll out of my hands to read.

Father motioned for everyone to gather away from the bodies. Who knew how deep their slumber was? We withdrew a distance. Baron looked relieved to be further from his father's vacant, wide-eyed stare. The scroll was being passed around from person to person while we waited for instructions. Father waited until everyone had read the letter, and spoke in hushed tones, as if afraid to wake the few unconscious men in the clearing behind us.

"As you all know now, King Richard has been captured, and his army is still on the Crusades."

Silent and solemn nods rippled around our group. King Richard- the Lion Heart, who we respected and were devoted to- betrayed and taken prisoner by Duke Leopold of Austria. Just the thought of my king being kept in some dank prison cell in Vienna made my blood boil. I wanted to run to Vienna and fight Duke Leopold himself. I could tell many of the Merry Men felt the same way. Will Scarlet actually took several steps, as if he needed to physically show his eagerness to leap into action.

"But we can't all go," James put in. "Prince John said he is gathering his army. We are at war."

A stunned silence met this dire pronouncement. Several men shook their heads dejectedly. With King Richard's army still in the Holy Land, Prince John would have an easy time of taking over the throne. In the letter, Prince John had gloated to the Sheriff about how he had secured the support of King Philip of France, who was sending additional reinforcements. There were no obstacles for John. None, except our small band of Merry Men.

"It is hopeless," muttered Alan. He had always been such a pessimist.

"It is not!" I said firmly. "We have this information; we can plan a counterattack!" I caught Baron's eye. There was a hardened look on his face that I couldn't quite understand, so I let my gaze pass over him.

"Ten of us against two armies?! What can *we* do?" Alan's arms were crossed.

I wrenched the scroll away from Will Stutely, who had received it last, and walked among the men. "It all depends on who those ten people are and where they are positioned. For instance, no one at the Sheriff's camp will know what happened to him yet. They only know he went out looking for Baron."

It had been a month since I had convinced Baron to run away with me, on the eve of my scheduled execution. That had been my fourth escape from the Sheriff's camp, and only successful one. The other three times, Baron had tracked me down and brought me back.

I had circled our group and returned to Baron. I reached out to touch his chest, a wicked smiled crept over my face. "Just imagine their shock when they learn that Robin Hood's daughter succeeded in assassinating the Sheriff of Nottingham. Naturally, his son would have avenged his father's death. And it would logically follow that the Sheriff would need to be replaced by someone familiar with that group of soldiers. Say, a respected senior officer. They need never know his allegiances changed since he set out to bring back said hostage."

Everyone stared at us, and mischievous grins slowly widened across their faces as the plan took hold.

"Me?" Baron asked in shock.

"No, she meant me," Father said sarcastically. "They would love to have Robin Hood as their commander. Of course you! We can have someone on the inside; this is brilliant!"

His gaze flicked back to me. "I don't think any of them will be sorry to hear that Laurel was killed in the struggle. Knowing her, she caused more than a little trouble when she was a prisoner!"

Will Scarlet leaned over to Little John, who was sitting

cross-legged on the forest floor, and whispered something into his ear. Little John choked back a laugh then winced and put a hand up to his chest. His tunic was torn and bright red from where the Sheriff had slashed at him during the battle. Lincoln cuffed Will across the backside of his head. "Don't make him laugh you idiot! You want him to die like the Sheriff there?"

Then he bit his lip. "Sorry, Baron."

It didn't look like Lincoln's comment had registered with Baron.

"No one will believe that story." Baron said flatly. "Too many people died."

"Ah, but you will have witnesses!" I said, pointing out two bodies in the clearing that hadn't been placed with their deceased companions. Their chests still rose and fell ever so slightly. They were alive. Both Will Scarlet and Will Stutely moved over to examine them more closely.

"But they didn't see anything!" Baron protested.

"Exactly! They will wake up and you can tell them whatever you want them to believe! It is perfect!"

Baron's facial expressions were difficult to read. He didn't seem to be grasping the awesome genius of my plan. Baron would be perfectly positioned to feed us information from the very heart of John's army! He would become a trusted advisor to Prince John; all he had to do was lead his men to the castle and then he would be able to take over as Sheriff. The second we needed him to, he would be in a perfect position to act. But Baron didn't seem excited at all. His brow was furrowed, and he was frowning at me.

Everyone else had broken into pairs or small groups and continued to brainstorm details of the plan. Father unfurled a map, traced a path to Vienna, and mused, "Of

5

course, some of us will set off to free Richard and it would be helpful to get another person on the inside of Nottingham Castle to feed information to us as needed."

"Who?" the ever-cynical Alan quipped, "If you don't remember, every single one of us was imprisoned there for months, and Baron will be off gallivanting around the countryside."

"Not *everyone* was a prisoner," responded Will Scarlet, who had returned from examining the bodies. He looked meaningfully at me.

Of course! The only thing better than having one undercover spy would be having two! I considered the risk. As far as I had heard on the night Baron and I sprang my father and his men from prison, all the guards had been shouting things like *"get him."* I doubted they even realized it was a girl they had been hunting when I got away under cover of darkness. I could pose as a simple servant girl and pick up information. So long as I kept out of the way with my head down when Baron brought his men to the castle, I could pass undetected.

It was a risky plan, sure. But then again, everything I did was risky, and I loved it. I relished the challenge of facing a formidable enemy. I lived for the thrill of being chased during a close escape. It was the sting of fear during those brushes with death that kept the games interesting for me, making victory so much sweeter. I nodded my head decisively. "I will do it!"

"Wait!" Baron burst out. Father and Little John swiveled to look at him in surprise. "You are sending Laurel off alone without even considering her safety! You don't know what these men are like! It will be dangerous!"

James, the smallest and thinnest of the Merry Men, considered the statement pensively. Alan nodded in agreement. I tossed my head in defiance. So what if it was dangerous?

Father spoke very articulately, as if he didn't want Baron to miss a single syllable. "I would never casually send my own daughter to her death. Laurel goes on these missions because she is good at what she does. Do not think for a second that I haven't weighed the risks. You are not the only person who cares about her."

"Laurel can handle herself," Lincoln insisted. "She has always been able to." I was grateful for his vote of confidence. I could always depend on lean and lanky Lincoln.

"She was captured and held prisoner for months!" Baron shot back. "You call that handling herself?"

I felt heat rising through my body. "I escaped several times," I pointed out defensively.

"And you were dragged back every time!" Baron retorted.

I frowned. "By *you*. But you will be on our side this time. I will be fine."

"Most of those men won't worry about capturing you; they will kill you without a second thought, or else torture you!"

"I'm not afraid!" I snapped.

"Well, you should be!" Baron's hands were balled into fists. He glared around at everyone present. We were all confused at his reaction. It was a brilliant plan, but Baron was acting as though it was the worst idea in the world. It wouldn't work without his cooperation. Why was he so resistant?

"There has to be another way!" he growled.

"Do *you* have any suggestions?" James's unruffled, quiet voice asked.

Baron rounded on him. "*Anything* else!"

James remained composed. "We could try to rally farmers and villagers to our cause and convince them to fight a fully-equipped platoon of armed and trained soldiers."

Baron glowered, and I heard several soft scoffs. Obviously, that wouldn't work. We couldn't subject defenseless civilians to be slaughtered in Richard's name.

"Or we could write and try and convince John to not revolt against his brother," James continued petulantly. "Perhaps he would listen to reason."

Baron rolled his eyes at the suggestion. James spread his arms as if to say *'See what I mean? We have no other alternative.'*

"Do you even know what you are suggesting?" Baron growled, anger still fully kindled. The two prone soldiers began to stir, and I hissed in a low voice to quiet Baron. Alan tended to the men with a well-executed strike to each of their temples, and they grew still once more. Baron stared forcefully around at all of us. "You will die!"

"And that is a risk all of us are willing to take," James quietly responded. "Are you?"

Baron glared around at our resolute faces, then spun on his heel and stormed away.

"What was *that*?" Will Stutely asked quietly.

"Give the kid a break, he probably didn't understand the danger," Little John groaned. "Better that he realize that now than in the middle of a mission."

"He is the son of the Sheriff of Nottingham!" Father spat. "If he didn't understand what would be involved, I will eat my hat! He is being a coward."

I kept quiet. Baron was no coward. I knew he wasn't afraid of the danger. I had a hunch I knew what was wrong, but I needed to talk to Baron to find out for sure.

BARON

I crashed through the forest. They didn't understand. They would never understand. I didn't care where I was headed, I just wanted to get away from their stupid, suicidal idea. What they were planning was preposterous! How the blazes had they stayed alive all these years if they were so determined to take uncalculated risks with no thought for their own safety? I snapped off a low-hanging branch viciously as I tramped on. I wasn't following a trail, just plowing through the underbrush with a vengeance.

Every single one of the Merry Men seemed to take for granted that I would leap at the chance to return to my old camp, announce the Sheriff's death, and place a claim on his position. It wasn't the danger that I was worried about. It was Laurel's safety. Her so-called friends had presented the idea of her working alongside her worst enemy as though it was some ingenious plan. How was she so at ease with it?

None of them had any idea. They didn't know what

John was capable of. I had seen the brutal treatment of his servants. I knew the kind of criminals who were attracted to his dark glamour. And everyone was acting as enthusiastic as if Father Christmas had pulled an extra-large present out of his sack. How could they be so flippant about sending a young woman into enemy territory, let alone a girl they supposedly cared about? It was an outrage! Anything could happen to her!

A wide stream barred my progress forward. I reached down, grabbed a large rock, and threw it into the water with a satisfying splash. Those imbeciles would readily risk Laurel's neck, and to what end? I kicked at the dirt on the path. Loose pebbles flew into the air and ricocheted off the trunks of trees.

The faint sound of a small twig snapping alerted me to someone's presence. When I turned, Laurel was standing there, watching me analytically. I turned my back on her. I didn't want to talk to anyone. I heaved another rock into the stream. The splash was so violent that water splattered back onto me.

"Quite the temper tantrum you had back there," Laurel said sedately. "If you had woken up those two Sleeping Beauties before Alan took care of them, we would have needed to concoct a new plan."

I threw another rock into the water and said nothing. Any plan would be better than sending me to replace my father as Sheriff and sending Laurel right into Prince John's hands. If he found out who she was... the years worth of humiliation my father and Prince John suffered at the hands of the Merry Men would be revisited in kind on Laurel. She would be tortured mercilessly and then killed. I shuddered just thinking about it.

I crossed my arms. "So, do you want to tell me why it is that you are so willing to leap to your death? Do you enjoy putting yourself in danger?"

"That isn't it."

"Then what *is* it? What am I missing? Why are all of you so eager to die?" I clenched my fists again. My anger was bubbling just beneath the surface. Usually, I was able to control my temper, but the prospect Laurel intentionally putting herself in grave danger was unbearable.

I looked to the sky as if searching for my answer there. Was this the life I had signed up for? When I agreed to leave my father's camp with Laurel, I thought I would be *with* her. When I was guarding her as a prisoner, I felt assured that I could protect her from the men who wanted to cause her harm. Now that she was free of the Sheriff's men, I felt less capable of protecting her. Ironic. It was her friends who seemed most ready to sign her death warrant!

Laurel said nothing. It looked like she was waiting for me to calm down before responding. Guiltily, I remembered the previous winter when she said that my rages scared her. I took several deep breaths. I wanted to give in to my temper. I wanted to shout until Laurel realized that this insane scheme was a lost cause. But I was also terrified that if I lost control around Laurel, she would leave me without a second thought – cast me aside just like everyone else in my life had. Just like I had done to countless others.

I couldn't watch Laurel risk her neck over and over. Sooner or later, gambling with her own life would end it. It went beyond *wanting* to keep Laurel safe. I *needed* to keep her safe. I flopped down onto a decaying log. It buckled under my weight with a loud crunch, and I ended up falling backwards into the newly created pile of crushed wood. I stood, cursing, and brushed off the seat of my trousers.

"Smooth," Laurel grinned.

I glared at her.

"I know you aren't scared," she said, stepping closer to me. My heart had been pounding before, but it began to thump with anticipation coupled with my anger. Why, *why* couldn't I keep a level head on my shoulders any time Laurel was near me? She went on, "So what is the problem?"

"I don't want you to die!" I burst out. Losing my mother had nearly broken me as a child. I couldn't handle Laurel dying too. I just couldn't. Without her, my future would loom before me like a desolate wasteland, devoid of any color, light, or happiness.

I closed my eyes and pinched the bridge of my nose, hard. I clenched my teeth and inhaled slowly, forcing oxygen in a steady stream up to my brain to help me calm down. I struggled to fight down my feelings and stay in control. I *could not* lose control around Laurel. We had fought before, but that was prior to us confessing our feelings for each other. I didn't want to fight with her now.

Laurel's arms slipped around my rigid body and she hugged me tightly. After a few long moments, I sensed the tension begin to dissipate and I returned the gesture. Normally, I didn't like being touched by anyone. It felt like a violation of my personal space. But Laurel was different. She always had been. Being around her felt cleansing. I held her close and breathed deeply. The anger drained out of my body as we continued to grip each other.

It never ceased to amaze me that such a small person

could have such a big influence. She had a depth of character that I had never seen in anyone before. She was so vibrant. So alive! She took on every new challenge with enthusiasm and never gave up when things got difficult.

She was my exact opposite in so many ways. She had a naturally kind heart, but covered it up by acting tough, as if afraid people might find out that she really did care about them. But I was a monster, predisposed to be a ruthless killer. I had to fight that instinct every day, forcing myself to be patient, so I wouldn't turn into my father. Even though he now lay dead in a clearing, I still a connection with him, and I hated it.

I had been a traitor all my life. I betrayed one person then another, cause after cause, over and over again. I worked my way up in the ranks, backstabbing anyone in my, never looking out for anyone other than myself. I was scum. I had always despised myself for living that way, but couldn't see any other option. It was all about survival.

Then Laurel had come along – the daughter of my father's sworn enemy. When I first heard Robin Hood's daughter had been captured, I expected to see a sniveling, weak, cowardly girl. But her brazen, defiant attitude and remarkable skill in combat surprised me. I was intrigued. She was the only person I had ever met who didn't seem to be afraid of my father at all. I admired her confidence. I was in awe as she overpowered one guard after another. Her beauty and wit captivated me.

When Father first announced that she would be chained to me, I was terrified. I had seen what she was capable of and fully expected to be the next of her growing list of victims. I had warily watched her every move and awaited my fate. But later, selfishly, I was glad to be tethered to her. It was why I worked so hard to track her down every time she escaped from camp. I wanted to be near her, and I couldn't seem to let her go. She fascinated me in ways no one else ever had.

What started as a healthy professional respect evolved into something deeper as the months went by; something I had never anticipated feeling. I felt the need to prove myself, to be worthy of loving someone like her. For the first time in my life, I felt the desire to protect someone other than myself. I felt needed. She made me want to be better.

Never in a million years would I have dreamed that she would love me back. I was so convinced that she would always despise me for who and what I was that I contented myself to make her captivity as comfortable as possible, knowing that one day she would be gone, and I would go back to hating myself and my life.

All those months, I had been increasingly disgusted with myself as I selfishly forced Laurel to stay imprisoned because I was too cowardly to do the right thing and let her go free. I rationalized it, telling myself that I was doing it for her own good. That she would have died of exposure on her own and would have been poorly treated if she had been chained to anyone else. But it was a lie. She was clever and resourceful and clever and would have been fine. Hadn't she proved that time and again? It was I that would have been tormented by her absence.

It tore me apart, having the woman of my dreams so close and yet still so far out of reach. The slow torture hurt worse than anything my father ever inflicted upon me. I thought I would be driven mad by it. So many times, I nearly reached my breaking point, about to beg her to stay with me, but I always held myself back. A girl like her had no business staying in a camp full of thugs. I was terrified that she would become aware of my feelings and be repulsed by me. If I had professed my love for her and she rejected me, or worse, laughed at me for even thinking there was a chance with her... It was a thought too painful to bear, so I always resisted. I reminded myself continually that it was impossible. We were too different.

When Laurel asked me to run away with her and start a new life, I had hope for the first time. I couldn't refuse and vowed to myself that I would never do anything that would drive her away from me. Here was a way to redeem myself and atone for the sins of my past. I could abandon my post and join her as a member of the Merry Men! A future far greater than being a brutish mercenary-for-hire. A future with Laurel. A future I wouldn't have had the courage to forge on my own without her help. Even a small chance with her was better than no chance at all, and I hadn't hesitated to turn on everyone else I had known. It was what I was best at.

WHEN SHE FINALLY RELEASED ME, SHE SMILED. NOT HER usual cocky smirk, but a warm, understanding smile that seemed to radiate compassion. I couldn't stop thinking about how beautiful she was. "Baron, there will always be risk when we are doing the right thing, but I don't ever go looking for death. If Prince John is really planning a revolt, we need to be on the offensive and stop him before he can build strength. The only thing worse than death would be to live with the guilt of knowing I could have done something more and didn't. Sometimes, there isn't anyone else to step in, and I have to be willing to stand up to fight. If I don't, who will?"

I sighed. The consequences of her eagerness for adventure was what I feared. The odds were too highly stacked against her. Laurel seemed to sense my hesitation and her voice became gentle, but firm. "Baron, I will be going through with this plan, with or without you. I can't sit back and do nothing. I want your help. I feel better knowing that you are on my side, and I think you can do things that none of the rest of us could. But whether you do this or not won't change that I am going through with the plan."

So that was it? She had decided, just like that? Laurel was about to get herself killed for the slim chance to pause a revolution she had no chance of stopping? As courageous as she was, how could one person bring down Prince John's diabolical plan?

I tried to imagine going back to the camp in the tunnels of the Cresswell Crags and taking over. I was the logical choice to replace my father, who had held the position of Sheriff of Nottingham for years. In the past, he had even expressed his desire for me to replace him once he was done. Before I met Laurel, it was my career plan. But now I didn't want to. I wanted to do something worthwhile with my life, not lead a gang of hired mercenaries. But what other choice did I have?

Laurel gently touched my face. "Please help, Baron. I need you."

Blast. How did she always know how to say the exact thing that would make me crumble?

"I'll help," I said grudgingly.

Laurel beamed. "C'mon then! Let's figure out a way to stay alive and cause a little chaos for Prince John." She grabbed my hand and began pulling me along after her. I followed rather reluctantly. I was still convinced that this plan would be doomed to failure. A futile siege. But better to include myself in the plans. I couldn't walk away. Even if it meant risking my own life, I needed to figure out how to protect Laurel from Prince John's army... and from herself.

LAUREL

*W*hen Baron and I got back to the others, they were not pleased. Father looked particularly irritated. I had always been told that my fiery red hair matched my temper, and perhaps it was true for him as well. He was jovial most of the time, but when he got upset, he didn't hold back.

"Answer one question for me," Father growled at Baron. "Why are you here?"

"What do you mean?" Baron asked.

Father threw a glance in my direction before he continued. "Are you here because you *actually* believe in what we are doing, or because you think my daughter wants you to be here?"

"Father..." I began, but he waved his hand to silence me. Baron didn't answer.

"If you just want to try and impress Laurel, I recommend you leave now. There have been plenty of boys who attempted that in vain. You are on probation for this *exact* reason. We need *real* fighters. Brave men and women. Not someone who will crumple at the first sign of trouble and make excuses for failure. Those people are cowards."

"Father!" I reprimanded sharply. "Baron isn't like that! He isn't a coward!"

"It's true, Laurel," Will Scarlet said, in a kinder tone than Father had, but still firm. "If he is only here for you, it could ruin everything. Someone like that will cave the second you are in danger. We can't have that. We can't afford for someone to be emotionally compromised on a mission like this. You have to be singularly focused on the goal and forsake all else. That goes for everyone!" he raised his voice slightly and looked around at the group at large.

I knew Will only added that last part for Baron's sake. I had seen all the men here give up everything for our cause. Fortunes, families, friends. Others even their lives. Would Baron be willing to do the same? I cast a concerned look at Baron. His face was the same as always-stoic and unreadable. I didn't want him to be in danger, but he was even more capable than I was; he would be fine.

I heard Dale groan from the forest floor. He rolled over and I squatted down to pat his back. "Good to have you among the living again, Dale. Sorry about your arm."

Dale eyed me balefully. "You didn't shoot me. Why are you sorry?"

I grinned. "I ripped the arrow out and then used it to shoot the Sheriff."

He peered around and saw Baron's father lying motionless on the ground. "Well, a sore arm is worth it then. Good for you."

Lincoln crouched down next to Dale to catch him up

on everything. As he did so, I raised my eyes to the rest of the group. "Look, we need to make a decision quickly. Anyone else who was just knocked out will be coming around soon."

Father looked steadily at Baron. "Let's have your answer. Whatever flaws our plan has, at least we have one. You haven't suggested any. We need to know if you are one hundred percent committed to this. If you even have a shadow of doubt, it will ruin everything. I have to know *now*."

Baron's face was impossible to read. "I'll do it," he said steadily.

"Very well then, here is the plan!" Father said quickly. "Will Stutely, Alan, and I will go to Vienna and see about breaking Richard out of prison. Unless we steal horses, it will take us at least two weeks to get there on foot. You won't hear from us much. John will need to stay in Sherwood Forest and run things while he recovers. And Scarlet, you and Dale get yourselves recruited into Philip's army and feed us information from the inside."

Everyone nodded in silent agreement. "Baron will take Blackwell's place leading his platoon, and Laurel will pose as a servant at Prince John's castle and gather information." Father stared hard at Baron. "Betray us, and I will kill you."

I glanced over at Baron. He was staring deadpan at Father and didn't show a single twinge of uncertainty. Death threats clearly had no effect on him.

"That leaves Lincoln and James to be messengers. James, you are in charge of Laurel and Baron. Check in on them regularly. Lincoln, you take on Dale and Will Scarlet. Send reports to Little John at least once a week.

Anyone injured or compromised, go back to camp in Sherwood. Everyone clear?"

Heads bobbed up and down.

Father clapped his hands together and rubbed eagerly. "Now for the fun part!"

BARON

*H*ow on earth was this supposed to be fun? I stood in the clearing beside my father's corpse, sword in hand. Several members of the Merry Men, including Laurel, had been tasked with playing dead. The goal was to fool the two members of my previous platoon into thinking that I had killed off several of the Merry Men in a vengeful rage after Laurel murdered the Sheriff. The men in question had been unconscious at the time and would know no different. My biggest fear was what they may do to the bodies of those feigning death.

We smeared blood onto the clothing of Laurel, Will Scarlet, and Lincoln. Dale and Little John had already spilled enough of their own blood and didn't need any extra. I stared around at them all, scattered out on the ground. Lincoln's arms and legs were twisted at odd angles. His body looked broken. Laurel was face down, and the ground around her was stained dark. It looked very convincing to me. Little John and Will Scarlet were in equally believable positions, but Dale's acting was easily the best.

Dale was spread-eagled on the ground, face up, mouth agape. His eyes were open and glassy, and seemed to be devoid of life. I drew close to examine his expression more closely. I had no idea how he could hold so still after everything he had been through recently. He truly looked dead. I waved my hand in front of his face, but he didn't even blink. Reassured, I took several deep breaths, and approached the two men from my previous platoon that were still alive.

I knew both of the men. They joined the military around the same time, about a year before. The smaller of the two was named Sebastian. He was one of the more pleasant men I had worked with. He had a nimble mind, was excellent with a saber, and followed orders well. The other was Dominic, the large brutish thug who had attempted to kidnap Laurel in the first place. He had an extensive criminal history and had spent a good deal of his adult life in and out of prison. I heartily disliked him.

I roughly shook Sebastian's shoulder. "Wake up, soldier!" I barked. He stirred feebly and then lay still. I walked over to Dominic and kicked his boot. "Wake up!" I shouted again. Nothing.

I doused Dominic's face with cold stream water. He let out a roar and snapped awake. I did the same to Sebastian with similar results.

They stared around at the carnage. Sebastian wiped his face and shook water from his sopping wet hair like a dog, then winced and put a hand up to his head. Dominic inspected his arms, where several long gashes were visible, but had been rinsed off in the recent soaking. He had a large lump on the back of his head.

"What happened?" Sebastian groaned. His hands were shaking, and he winced as he felt all over his bruised body.

"What do you remember?"

Sebastian scrunched his eyes shut and thought hard. "We went out looking for you and the girl. You had been gone for weeks."

"Deserter," growled Dominic.

I backhanded him hard across the face. "I will *not* be spoken to like that!" I roared. "I've been working to clean up everyone else's blunders, and you will be grateful for it!"

"Where were you then?" Dominic sneered.

"Looking for the girl, you moron! Everyone knew that she would release Robin Hood the second she got the chance, and now look at the mess she caused! She pulled off a jailbreak and now most of our men are dead because of it!"

"So you failed in tracking her down, then, did you?" Dominic snarled in his gravelly voice. He held his hand up to his cheek, where a red impression of my hand was rapidly rising. But, as ever, the injury had done nothing to encourage Dominic to keep a civil tongue in his head.

"I caught up to her, but she got away again. Is that really surprising to anyone? She got away from everyone else!"

"I caught her!" boasted Dominic proudly. "I caught her the first time I tried!"

"Did you?" I folded my arms and stared down at Dominic. "Or did she jump through a window and you took the credit because you didn't want everyone to know that she slipped through your fingers?"

Dominic's mouth fell open. "How did you know?"

"Because I have a brain and use it, you fool! More than you can say. I was trying to track down all those escaped traitors for Prince John when all of you caught up and assumed the worst."

"Come off it, Baron!" Dominic cried. "We know you set her free."

"Does it look like I set her free?" I yelled and pointed to Laurel's immobile form. "She just murdered my father and I killed her for it!"

Sebastian approached her limp body and cautiously nudged her with his boot. I held my breath. Laurel was a good actress. She didn't react. "You have to admit, Baron-"

"Sheriff," I amended swiftly.

"What?"

"I am the Sheriff now, and you will address me as such."

Sebastian processed my statement then nodded in obedient acceptance. "You have to admit, *Sheriff,* the circumstances were very suspicious. When she escaped from camp, she had been tied up with two guards watching her. Both guards were knocked out, the horses were released, and both of you were gone. It was logical to conclude that you ran off with her."

I rolled my eyes. "Just like everyone concluded that I was pushed off that accursed mountain path by a little girl, right? A lot of geniuses you are."

"Enlighten us, then," huffed Dominic.

I drew a long, calculated breath. Convincing these two was crucial to the success or failure of the mission.

"Let's review the facts, shall we?" I began, "First of all, she was removed from my custody…"

"Because you were kissing her!" Dominic cut in sharply.

25

"She kissed me," I corrected, then added, "She kissed Sneeds too. And I think we all remember how that turned out. If my father hadn't been there to intervene, I am sure I would have had the same fate as Sneeds. I was fortunate that I had backup when I needed it."

"But the Sheriff said you seemed pretty comfortable with the situation."

I shrugged. "Have you seen her? I'm not blind. I'd like to see anyone else do better, if a beautiful girl threw herself all over them. Not that it will ever happen to *you*. Like I said, it was fortunate I had backup before things got out of hand."

Sebastian seemed appeased, but Dominic didn't.

"You should have known better."

"So I was reminded." I said coldly. "And if you recall, I paid dearly for my moment of weakness. I have the scars to prove it. I hope you two learned from my mistake to never trust women, especially the attractive ones."

"She must have had help escaping!" Dominic persisted. "No one could do that themselves. Explain that!"

"See, this is why I was the only one who was able to control her!" I said angrily. "Everyone else was constantly underestimating her! She easily took care of Goric, Flavius, Dorian, and Sneeds, and was tied up all those times too! Everyone seemed to think she was too stupid or weak to escape! Why am I the only one who saw it? I have no idea what she did, but whoever they put to guard her probably turned their back momentarily, and that was all she needed!"

A shadow of doubt flitted across Sebastian's face. "She was tied up though..."

"And she was *chained* when she overpowered Sneeds!

She managed to find a way to break through solid iron chain links!" I roared. "And the dunces used ropes? What fools do I have to work with here? And now, when I go racing off to bring her back for a FOURTH time, everyone blames me for her escape?! Saying that I turned traitor and released her?! This is an insult!"

"Sorry, Sheriff, sorry," Sebastian mumbled. "We just didn't know where you went."

I glared at the two men. "Any fool could have heard the racket that girl made when she released all the horses that night. When I heard it, I knew that she must have let them out to distract us so she could escape *again*, so I set off."

"Without telling anyone?" Dominic growled.

"You are right," I said sarcastically. "Perhaps I should have wandered around until I weighed the risks and benefits, then filled out paperwork requesting the assignment while our prisoner got farther and farther away with every minute. I *assumed* everyone would know that I was fetching her back to try and prevent the jailbreak. That was my JOB! It seems like I am the only one who carries out my duties without direct orders from a superior, which is why I am Sheriff now, instead of fools like you two! I didn't realize you lot were incapable of thinking or I would have left a note. Or can you even read?"

Dominic and Sebastian both hung their heads. I ranted on, "Even my father wouldn't allow her in his tent because he didn't trust her. Everyone else was terrified of being within a stone's throw of her, and yet I was expected to pick up everyone's slack! I was making up for a whole lot of incompetence from you lot! Maybe, instead of blaming your *superior officer*, you should thank me for dispatching that girl and half of the band when they caught you by surprise! You were so focused on falsely accusing me, *an ally,* that you fell right into a trap!"

"That girl had run off and brought along her father and all his men to track US down! Even after everyone else was down, and more of Robin Hood's men showed up, I had to take care of everything!" I waved my hand toward where Laurel, John, Dale, Will, and Lincoln laid. "If I had been on their side, why are they the ones scattered across this meadow, and you are still alive to see it? You should know more about loyalty than that."

"Yeah, I just remembered," Sebastian said to Dominic, "I only saw one of their men go down. It was just the Sheriff against several of Robin Hood's lot. Then Baron showed up. That witch knocked me out at that point. Bar... I mean," he glanced nervously at me. "The *new* Sheriff must have taken care of them all."

Dominic nodded slowly. Now that I had backup to my story, Dominic seemed more inclined to believe it. "Sorry. We made a mistake," he mumbled, avoiding my scowl.

"You better be sorry! It is an insult, and I will not tolerate it ever again! How dare you think I turned traitor? Imbeciles!"

The men apologized over and over. They finally seemed convinced. I let them grovel for several minutes before I finally barked at them to quit embarrassing themselves. I set Sebastian and Dominic the task of digging a large grave. I hefted all the bodies of the men from my father's guard onto one of their supply carts to be returned to their families. The bodies of the Merry Men, all pretending to be dead, I placed into large burlap sacks to be buried.

"I hope you can breathe down there," I whispered to Laurel as I pulled a bag over her. Dominic and Sebastian were grunting and sweating over the pit at the other end of the clearing. They wouldn't hear.

Laurel peeked one eye open and flashed her cocky smile once, then went limp again. This girl and her games would be the death of me. I tied the last burlap sack closed and went to inspect the grave.

"Bit shallow for five bodies, isn't it?" I pointed out.

"I don't even see the need to bury them," growled Dominic mutinously. "Let the wolves have them."

"We are better than that!" Sebastian said. "I daresay if it had been us in their place, Robin Hood would have left us for the vultures, but we can show that *we* are honorable men, not outlaws!"

"Well said, soldier!" I said, then grinned at Dominic. "But if the wolves dig a bit, all the worse for this lot, right, Dominic?" I jerked my head to where the five bags lay. Dominic gave a throaty chuckle. "Besides, it's more important to get our own men back to their families. Leave the graves unmarked. Common criminals do not deserve any recognition, even in death."

I went over and began lifting the Merry Men one by one and laying them in the grave. Except for Little John, of course. I could only fit his head, torso, and down to his thighs in a bag. His legs and feet I left exposed, and I had to drag his body to the grave. I felt for him as I saw his body thud into the pit; he was already injured. I gently placed Laurel in last, then assisted in shoveling dirt on top of all of them as quickly as I could. Whatever Robin Hood said, this did not feel like a game. I was burying Laurel alive.

LAUREL

I marveled at how easily Baron could lie. He seemed so honest and forthright all the time I had known him. Did I really know him as well as I thought? I was suddenly aware that he could be just as manipulative and deceitful as me when the situation warranted it. The entire time he berated the two soldiers, I felt an insect crawl slowly up my arm and forced myself to not so much as flinch. I didn't know if anyone was watching me or not. But if everyone else could pretend to be dead, so could I. The most terrifying part was when one of the men approached me and poked me with his boot. I was worried he would kick at my body and I wouldn't be able to avoid reacting. I was honestly shocked they hadn't done more, given how difficult a prisoner I had been for them.

Baron slipped all of us into bags, then placed us in a hollow in the ground. With each shovelful of earth that fell on my bag, a few particles of dirt would powder down into the bag with me. It took all my self-restraint not to sneeze or cough as the fragments tickled my nose. Finally, all noise was cut off from the outside. I held my hands up in front of my face, pressing the bag outward slightly, to create an air pocket against the press of cool earth. The dirt was heavier than I had expected, and it was difficult to move. Not that I would have fidgeted, anyway. I knew better than that. My air was limited, and I needed to save every bit of it. It was fortunate that the graves were shallow; I would have been crushed by any more dirt.

It was pitch black, and I felt claustrophobia setting in. I closed my eyes and pictured myself back in Sherwood Forest, bundled up in thick blankets during the winter. I held onto that image for a long time and refused to allow myself to think about the pressing mounds of dirt piled up on top of me. I drew air in slow, measured breaths. It was just a waiting game, that was all. Just a waiting game. I could wait.

I counted slowly to two thousand, then back down again. Baron and his two companions must be gone by now, along with the cart of the other bodies. I drew a deep breath, struggled to pull a knife from my boot, and slit open my bag. Dirt poured in on me, and I clawed my way up to the surface. Finally, my hand punched through the last layer of dirt and I crawled out of my grave.

The others must have felt my movements because they were also beginning to emerge from the earth. I brushed the dirt from my face and saw Father swinging down from his lookout position, with the rest of the Merry Men sliding down trees behind him.

"Good timing!" he informed us. "They are all gone. I was just about to come dig you up myself."

"We will need to remember this idea for when we have someone we need to scare!" Will Scarlet laughed merrily. "I rather like the notion of dressing up in rags and creeping out of graves in the dead of night! It would give anyone the collywobbles!"

"It gave me the creeps to watch it in the daylight!" Will Stutely said fervently.

"What an actor that Baron is, though!" Dale said. "Did you hear him?"

"Even I almost believed him!" Alan said.

"Yes," agreed Father dryly, and he glanced at me. "He was a little too believable. You had better be right about him, Laurel. We are taking an awful risk here, and you will be the one in the most danger if he turns on us."

"He would never betray me."

"I hope you are right." Father hugged me. "Be safe. I love you."

I gripped him back. "I love you too. Write soon."

FATHER, ALAN, AND WILL STUTELY STARTED OFF AT ONCE. They had a long journey ahead of them. Dale bound up his arm and left with Will Scarlet. Little John was weak. Lincoln and James volunteered to get him back to Sherwood Forest before they began their task of carrying messages. I watched them begin to help Little John limp away, then turned my sights back toward Prince John's castle.

I couldn't show up in my Merry Men uniform. I pulled off my cloth belt, turned my tunic inside-out, so the brown peasant cloth showed, then reknotted the belt. I cut a swath of burlap from one of the bags in the grave and fastened it around my hair, and then fashioned myself a skirt in a similar fashion to hide my un-ladylike leggings. Lincoln was the tailor of our group and he always ensured that we would be able to disguise ourselves effectively when needed. The double-sided uniforms were a pain for him to create, but I was grateful for his foresight. Within a few minutes, I had transformed myself into a simple farm girl. No need to smudge my face with dirt, I was already filthy.

~

BY LATE AFTERNOON, I ARRIVED AT THE CASTLE. I approached the massive drawbridge and hesitated. A bored guard looked at me and took in my bedraggled appearance. "Let me guess, you are looking for a job?"

I nodded humbly. "Yes, sir, I am."

"Go in and ask for Agnes. She will take care of you. They always need new maids." He waved me through. "And you may want to wash up before you see her. She won't take kindly to someone arriving in that state."

That was it? I expected to be interrogated. Prince John must be a bigger fool than I thought, to allow anyone in the gates like that. I walked in.

I felt like I walked every inch of the castle at least three times during my search for Agnes. One person after another claimed to have seen her, and when I walked in the specified direction and asked someone else, I would be sent to a completely different wing. Even with my good memory, I got turned around several times as I navigated the twisting and turning passageways. It took me until after nightfall before I finally tracked her down.

"Good evening, would you be Agnes?" I asked politely.

She took in my appearance and curled her lip in distaste. Evidently, I hadn't washed well enough for her standards. "I would. Who is asking?"

"Isabella, mum."

Agnes was a plump, middle-aged woman with iron gray hair pulled into a tight bun. She had an air of no-nonsense about her. "Very well, Isabella. I'm looking for help with cleaning the barracks. Pay is one silver coin a week. You get one day off in ten, as well as festival week. Is that agreeable?"

"Yes, mum." Good grief, did people actually work for so little? I took bags filled with gold from nobles constantly; did they really expect peasants to live on a mere silver coin each week?

She briskly led me to a storage room, pulled a bundle of clothes from a shelf, and shoved them at me. "Wear these then give them to the laundress when they are dirty. She will replace them as needed." She piled on a different bundle. "For sleeping."

I accepted the shifts and Agnes lifted my skirts to look at my footwear. My knee-high boots didn't seem to pass muster, because she grabbed simple flat shoes and added them to my pile. I fumbled to balance everything. Agnes brushed past me and I nearly dropped my load. I hurried after her. She continued to speak in a brisk, scripted way, as though she gave this same lecture several times a day and had done so for years.

"Get up at the first bell of the morning. If you sleep in once, it is a warning. Second time, you are dismissed. You will be trained for one week, and then get assigned your own duties. A supervisor will oversee your work. First time it is inadequate is a warning, second time you are dismissed. Understand?"

I nodded, then realized she may not be able to see my head from behind the mountain of fabric hiding me. "Yes, mum."

"Go on then. Ask for Walter. He will assign you sleeping quarters. He is the one who is always wearing gloves. Scat!" She shooed me away.

So off I trotted again, arms full, this time looking for a man with gloves. It felt like an hour before I finally found the right person. Several of the courtiers wore gloves, which was confusing, as I didn't know what occupation Walter had. I assumed something to do with servant management, but I knew so little of castle protocol that I was ignorant as to how high of a station that was. The courtiers I did stop to ask cringed away from me as though I was vermin. Most didn't even deign to respond, clearly affronted that a lowly peasant dared to speak to them and disturb their oh-so-noble thoughts.

When I finally did locate the correct person, Walter assigned me a sleeping area down in the cellar with the other servants. All the other servants were fast asleep by the time I crawled onto my musty smelling straw tick. It was nearly midnight and I only had a few hours to sleep before the bell would sound. But I had been accepted into the castle. My work had begun.

BARON

*T*he Cresswell Crags loomed ahead of me. I was back. Back to a place where I swore I would never return. Back to the life I vowed I would abandon forever. Sebastian, Dominic, and I all began hiking up the narrow path that led to the base camp.

"Hey, Sheriff!" Sebastian called companionably. "Remember when you and that girl fell up here?"

"Vividly," I responded dully. I still hated Dorian for making an attempt on Laurel's life. I hoped he was still with the platoon. I looked forward to making his life miserable. "And I remember everyone leaving us, too."

Sebastian fell silent, embarrassed. Dominic, however, spoke up. "We didn't know you would survive. Dorian just wanted to be rid of her. But if she survived that fall, anyone could."

"I could push you off now to test that theory," I suggested coldly.

Dominic grumbled an inaudible, sullen response.

I glared at him. "As far as I am concerned, what has happened in the past is irrelevant! What matters now is that we prepare for the future. And that begins with getting to camp all in one piece, so pay attention to where your giant feet are, you lummox." We continued to trek up the mountain, but the climb seemed much farther without Laurel with me.

When we finally reached the top, Sebastian called out immediately to some of his friends. They cheerfully answered, then fell silent as they saw me beside him.

"Baron?" one man said hesitantly. "We thought you left."

I ignored him and addressed the group at large. News had spread quickly; everyone came pouring out of the mouth of the canyon. "The Sheriff was murdered!" I said loudly. "Robin Hood's daughter did it, and I killed her for it. She was more trouble than she was worth. The *former* Sheriff couldn't see that until it was too late."

A ripple of shock ran through the crowd. "Good!" one man called. "It was about time!"

Mutinous muttering began to grow louder and louder. "What about the others?" several people shouted.

"We were the only survivors," Sebastian said sadly.

"Against one girl?" someone asked.

"Her father and all his men joined her!" Sebastian said defensively. "It wasn't a fair fight." I noticed that Dominic didn't speak up in my defense, and stood near the rear of the group, arms crossed and a scowl plastered on his brutish face.

"What about Baron?" a wheezy voice called out. A pimply face stood out from the crowd. It was Sneeds. "Didn't he run off with that girl?"

"He was the one that saved us!" Sebastian said. "We would have all been killed, and they would have all gotten away, but Baron showed up! He was the one that killed

Robin Hood's daughter and several of Hood's fellow outlaws! I was there!"

He hastily repeated everything I had told him after he woke up. Coming from a second source, the story suddenly seemed much more believable to the men. Sebastian was well-liked enough that most people were quick to believe him.

"We buried their outlaws and brought the bodies of our comrades to the nearest village to return to their families," finished Sebastian.

A stunned silence met his words. As well liked as Sebastian was, I could sense that many of the men assembled still did not believe the story he told of my glorious redemption.

"And did any of you think," I said, venom in my voice, "that if I was truly a traitor, I would be so foolish as to return? Anyone with half a brain would know to stay away."

"So, what now?" piped up Sneeds. "The Sheriff is gone."

"Now, I am the Sheriff," I announced authoritatively. "I was a senior officer before, and I was his son. That position belongs to me."

"I challenge that!" Dominic spat. I wasn't surprised. I suspected he would be slower to believe me than trusting, congenial Sebastian was. "Whatever story you fed us, the fact remains that you deserted us for weeks! We can't trust you. *I* place a claim on the position!"

A murmur of assent rippled through the crowd until it became a roar. "Challenge by arms!" the men shouted. They were eager to see a fight. The long, isolated winter had made them bloodthirsty.

"Challenge accepted," I said calmly, shrugged off my shoulder pack, and drew my sword.

The rest of the men rapidly shuffled away, leaving a clear circle for the duel. One of Dominic's friends ran forward to hand him a weapon and take his pack. Dominic swung the sword experimentally and performed several impressive-looking spins and practice jabs with accompanying yells and war cries. It was a performance, that was all. The other men watched and nodded approval. I stood perfectly still, sword tip pointed at the ground on my side of the circle. I observed Dominic's wild gestures with mild indifference. Such wasted movement. I waited patiently until Dominic had finished his childish whooping and waving his sword around. I never moved a muscle.

At long last, Dominic rushed across the circle towards me. All the men cheered wildly. I waited until the very last second, then raised my sword. In one swift movement, I deflected his blow and threw a single, solid punch with my free left hand. My knuckles landed squarely between his eyes, and he instantly crumpled to the ground, out cold.

I watched him fall at my feet, then raised my eyes to the surrounding crowd. "Anyone else?"

For several long moments, the soldiers said nothing. Then Sneeds' thin voice rang out, "All hail the new Sheriff!"

"Hail!" the men chorused.

I stepped over Dominic's immobile body. It took some time for me to sift through the soldiers to select officers. It was imperative that I choose men who would support me wholly. A few disgruntled soldiers, I could handle. I wasn't concerned about complaints and resentment about me taking over. When I had been appointed as a captain early in my career, I had heard similar gripes. What was more disturbing was the thought of the other officers becoming mutinous and overturning my position. Now that I was committed to this plan, I was going to do everything in my power to make it a success.

The four men I chose were all hardened criminals, but were all loyal to me for one reason or another, or at least as loyal as a mercenary for hire could be. Trevors was a burly man in his fifties with broken front teeth whom I had worked alongside for years. I judged him to be a reliable man who could be counted on to get a job done, but also was one of the few in camp who didn't lust after power. Humphrey was one of my father's previous officers. He had been one of Richard's knights before defecting to join Prince John's army. During a boar hunt years ago, I pulled him out of harm's way, and he had never forgotten it.

Rufus and Bart were both young, perhaps in their early twenties. They were fit and capable warriors, but lacked leadership abilities. I knew no one would follow them if they ever had the notion to turn on me. Their enthusiasm and eagerness to please would make them easy to bend to my will. I had always found it easy to determine which people would be easy for me to manipulate.

"Follow me," I snapped, and lead my officers through the winding, gloomy tunnels of the Crags.

The Cresswell Crags was a limestone gorge with expansive caves pockmarked throughout it. During the years when Prince John and my father were in good standing with King Richard, our army had no need of camping in caves, and would winter in the Nottingham

Castle barracks. But in the last few years, Richard's soldiers had been more proactive about searching out and arresting those who followed the Sheriff of Nottingham.

But now that Richard's army was in the Holy Land, and Richard had been captured- of course Prince John would seize the opportunity to finally take the throne. Many soldiers poked their heads out of the tents they had pitched inside the caves. Even with my back turned, I could tell that Rufus and Bart were holding their heads high with self-importance.

I came to the largest cave. My father's tent was gone, no doubt taken down when he went off to search for me and Laurel. But several of his belongings remained, piled neatly into a corner. I had Bart start a fire near the mouth of the cave. I waited until the smoke began winding its way up through the gorge's interior before I pulled out the scroll Prince John sent to my father and spoke in a low voice. "I was able to intercept this message before Robin Hood and his men found it," I waved the scroll.

Once their attention was completely focused on the scroll I continued, "Richard has been captured. Prince John is ready to take his place on the throne. He already has support from King Philip of France. The time of King Richard's reign is over and it is time for war."

The four men all grinned brutishly. Trevors growled, "We are ready! When do we move?"

"Yeah!" Rufus nodded eagerly. "The men are ready now! We can do it!"

"I will take two of you with me to meet Prince John and make arrangements, then we will bring the soldiers back. No sense in moving everyone just yet. Once Richard is released, as I'm sure he eventually will be, we will be ready for him. And his army."

LAUREL

J had been slightly apprehensive about sleeping through the first bell. I expected a gentle chiming that could be easily ignored, or else unconsciously worked into a dream. But the deafening clangs that rang out in the morning jolted me instantly awake. I flew two feet straight up into the air and grabbed for my knives, then realized they weren't there.

I stood, breathing heavily with my heart thudding madly and saw Agnes walking down the sleeping hall toward me. Each straw tick that lined the corridor held a girl, each of whom was groaning and trying to pull blankets over her ears.

I snapped to attention as Agnes drew level with me. Agnes gave an approving nod to me. "Glad to see *someone* is a morning person!" She marched off down to the other end of the hall, clanging the bell all the way.

I stared in bewilderment at all the other girls trying to stay asleep. How they could possibly sleep through that earsplitting racket was beyond me. The girl whose bed was next to mine stirred and rubbed her eyes sleepily.

"Morning already?" she yawned. She stretched her arms wide and emitted a drawn out, high-pitched yawn.

Agnes came marching back down the hall, now with a long wooden spoon in hand. If any girl was still left in bed, Agnes would hit the wooden spoon sharply on an exposed part of her body. When the girl next to me heard the whistling cracks coming up the hallway, she rolled out of bed and straightened her blankets. She looked over and noticed me still standing beside my unmade bed.

"Make your bed, quick!" she hissed at me.

I straightened the solitary blanket and plumped the sack of chaff I used for a pillow. Agnes passed by without comment and hit the exposed head of a girl two beds down. She yelped in pain and jumped out of bed.

The girl who told me to make my bed nudged me and whispered, "You are supposed to get dressed before she comes back!"

I looked around the room. All the other serving girls were pulling off their nightgowns and donning their servant's uniforms. I hastened to copy them. The dresses assigned to me were bulky and itchy, and about as comfortable as burlap made from poison ivy. I was never fond of dresses in general, but this one made me vow to never wear one again after the mission ended. I fastened the strings of the long white apron behind my back and smoothed the wrinkles out of my clothes.

The flat black shoes I had been issued were floppy and slightly too big, so I pulled on two extra pairs of woolen stockings to compensate. I saw Agnes headed back down the hallway and stood, but before she reached me, I felt someone poke me again. "Your hair! Cover your hair!"

One quick glance around the room showed me that all the girls were knotting headscarves loosely around their hair. Some of the older women bundled up knots of braids and fastened their scarves neatly to hide every strand. So many layers! I tugged the long white linen strip from the pile Agnes had given me the night before and imitated the other girls. At least with all these layers and bulky coverings, there was little chance I would be distinguishable from any other servant girl. The less attention I drew to myself, the better. By the time Agnes was level with me, I looked the same as everyone else. She passed by without comment.

"Thanks," I told the girl who had helped me. She was thin, with dirty blonde hair that cascaded down to her waist. She had it pulled over her shoulder and plaited it quickly. Her nimble fingers flew down the braid before tossing her hair back. Her most noticeable feature was how wide her mouth was.

She smiled brightly, and I could see everyone one of her teeth. "That is alright! I wished someone had told me what to do my first few days. I am Aalis, by the way."

"I am Isabella," I told her. A completely fictitious person would be safest to impersonate.

Aalis pulled me over to where a meager breakfast was laid out for the servants. She chattered away merrily as we spooned soupy grey porridge into our bowls. Aalis was a chipper, bubbly kind of girl. The kind of girl that I never knew how to talk to because we shared so few common interests. Fortunately, Aalis did enough talking that I didn't have to struggle to make conversation. I made a valiant effort to get along with her. I needed to be accepted. I asked her about herself once, then endured nearly an hour of her life's story. She had a high-pitched, girly voice, yet managed to talk at a remarkably fast pace. I was mesmerized by how she could fit so many words into a single breath of air. But then again, her abnormally large mouth must have helped. Aalis, however, took my focus to mean that I was fascinated with what she was saying.

"And so, of course, Mum told me that I needed to find work since I wasn't married yet, and who should be hiring but Prince John's housekeeper! Who wouldn't want to work for royalty? You know what I mean, don't you Izzy? Anyway, I was hired about a year ago and have been working here ever since. I like it, you know. The festivals are fun and I never would have been able to attend them otherwise. You will love it; there are so many gowns they let us wear that day and we look just like ladies of the court! And a whole silver coin a week! I've never felt so rich in my whole entire life!"

The words seemed to flow endlessly out of Aalis's mouth. I could hardly understand what she was saying because her sentences flowed together in a torrent of words. She kept calling me "Izzy" and introducing me to every person that walked by. I kept trying to determine if I appreciated this or not. On the one hand, I did need to get to know everyone and wanted to be accepted. But I also couldn't tell yet if Aalis was a popular girl or the obnoxious kind that everyone merely put up with.

"Isabella!" Agnes bustled up. "You are on barracks duty. Follow me." Several girls nearby let out sympathetic groans. Aalis gave me a comforting pat on the arm as I rose.

I fell in after Agnes's footsteps. She spoke in the same brisk manner she had the night before. Even though I knew she had been up just as late as I was, she didn't seem the least bit tired. I kept up with her quick pace as she led me out of the castle and across the training fields to long rows of dingy buildings where the men-at-arms and soldiers lived. The buildings seemed structurally sound but gave me the immediate impression that no matter how many maids cleaned, or how long the walls were scrubbed, they would always feel dirty.

From the first step into the barracks, my suspicions were confirmed. The stench of unwashed men hung so heavily in the air that it was surprising anyone could breathe. It was no wonder that Agnes was always looking for maids. This place reeked! No one would stay long in this hovel. Black grime lay thick upon the walls, the straw on the floor had turned a dark grey color, and a brownish film clung to all the windows.

Focus, Laurel, I reminded myself. *Remember why you are here.*

Agnes turned sharply to look at me and gauge my reaction. "Start in this room," she said crisply. "And I will come check on you around mid-day. Cleaning supplies are here," she gestured to a storeroom across the corridor. "Any questions?"

That was the extent of the training they gave new maids? "Yes, mum. When I finish here, what do I do next?"

"You won't finish today," Agnes sniffed. "But once you are done here, you move on to the next room."

I nodded. Without another word, Agnes bustled out of the room.

I had to remove the dirty straw from the floor before I could even start scrubbing. I took two trips outside with my arms full of the straw before I got smarter and opened the window. The welcome breeze helped a little to waft the heavy stench from the room, and then I began to shove all the disgusting straw out the window. I could move it later. For now, I just needed it out.

Once I had removed all the straw, I grabbed a scrub

brush and pail of soapy water and began scouring the floor. It was disgusting, smelly work, and I loathed every moment. The black filth seemed to permeate every crevice of the stone floor, and I had to scrub vigorously to make any difference. I slowly began to see some of the grey stone underneath and sighed in relief. At least it was possible to remove a little of the grime.

By the time I was halfway done with the floor, my back ached horribly. I stood and began to wipe the windows and walls. It was at that point that I had a horrible realization. The soapy water that I scrubbed the wall with mingled with the dark dirt and trickled down to the scrubbed floor. A layer of residue was left as the water trickled to the low points in the floor. It would have to be washed again. I groaned in frustration. This was going to take a lot longer than I thought.

It took most of the morning to wash a single wall. I felt somewhat vindicated as I looked at the clean wall. I was halfway done with a second wall when Agnes showed up again. She inspected the room closely. "You are a good worker, Isabella. Most girls don't have the strength to scrub off this much. You must have been raised on a farm, am I right?"

"Yes, mum," I answered, and inwardly thanked my father for drilling me so often with the bow. My back and shoulder muscles were hardened and tough from all the intense exercises I was required to do.

She nodded approvingly. "Well done. Keep up the good work!"

I didn't know if I was supposed to stop for meals or not, so worked through the entire day. I quickly figured out that I needed to work from the top down, so I would start as high up as I could reach and let the soap and water cascade down the wall as I worked. That way, by the time I reached where the wall met the floor, the grime wiped off with relative ease. I had to throw out my bucket of blackened water at regular intervals, and then draw new water from the well. The floor was easier to scrub at the end of the day, after it had been soaked for hours. But it still took a lot of work to uncover the stone.

In addition to the scrubbing, there were chamber pots to empty, the fireplace to clean, and then I had to bring in clean, fresh straw for the floor and restuff the mattresses with. I wondered if the mucking out the nearby stables would have been easier.

Night fell, and still Agnes didn't come back. A steady stream of soldiers passed by throughout the day. Most ignored me, and I them. A few made crass comments, which I also ignored. The torches were lit by the time I was finished with the room, and I had just thrown down the last armload of straw when soft tapping at the door alerted me to someone standing there.

"Miss?" It was Walter, the manservant who had shown me to my sleeping quarters the night before.

I wiped my brow with my sleeve. "Yes?"

Walter entered the room and looked around in amazement. "You did all this today?"

"That is my job, isn't it?"

"Agnes is going to expect the same level of work every time." He meticulously studied the room. He wasn't old by any stretch – younger than my father, but older than Baron. Walter gave the impression of a fit man who had recently let himself go. His stomach protruded slightly to the front, just enough to show that he enjoyed his ale, but didn't overindulge constantly. He had a large, bushy mustache that made me imagine that a very fuzzy, fat, brown caterpillar had crawled across his face and settled there.

"No good, it will need to be done again," Walter said flatly.

I began to object, but then saw his mustache twitch ever so slightly. "You are awful!" I told him.

"A maid who appreciates jokes!" Walter beamed. "How refreshing!"

I liked him immediately. His eyes had a permanent twinkle in them, as if life was one grand joke, and he couldn't wait to see how everything played out. "And a manservant who isn't condescending! I am impressed!" I told him.

He waved one of his gloved hands. "I am the one who is impressed. Agnes may not believe that you did this alone. I can help you take credit."

I poked him in the chest. "Over my dead body! You didn't scrub those filthy walls. I did!"

He grinned mischievously. "Alright, alright, you win, but just this once!" He held open the door for me. I put away the cleaning supplies and followed Walter back to the main hall. He was chatty and told me all about his past, which I was grateful for; I was too tired to talk. He said that he was raised in London, joined Prince John's army for ten years, then became a manservant at Nottingham Castle when he was done with the military life. He liked fishing and playing dice, and his dearest ambition was to be the Prince's personal steward.

He reminded me strongly of Will Scarlet. He was quick-witted, fatherly, and ambitious. He seemed like the kind of person who would be easy to befriend. When he found out I hadn't eaten anything since early that morning, he nearly had a fit. "You are too skinny to miss any meals, Isabella! Now, don't you dare do that again. You will blow away! Promise me!"

I promised him that I would do better the next day. When we walked by Agnes, he made sure to stop her and describe in detail the wonderful job I had done. He spoke in a loud enough voice that several other servants took notice too. Agnes didn't seem impressed. She merely acknowledged what Walter said and told me she would assign me another room the next day.

BARON

 $\mathcal{M}$ y horse's hooves clattered as I crossed the drawbridge, flanked by the two officers I had selected to accompany me- Rufus and Bart. I told the two other more experienced officers back at camp to keep things running smoothly. If Laurel had managed to go undetected and get herself hired, there was a chance we would run into her. What if she was one of the serving girls at mealtimes? That was a risk I hadn't been willing to take. But as Rufus and Bart had never met Laurel when she was a prisoner, the danger was minimal. Besides, they believed the story that Robin Hood's daughter was dead.

I tried to force my eyes to look straight ahead as we entered the courtyard, but I couldn't help myself. Any time I saw a hint of red hair, my gaze was irresistibly drawn. But, despite my surreptitious searching, I didn't find a single serving girl with red hair. All the women were dressed the same here, so it would have been nearly impossible to pick Laurel out of the crowd, anyway. Servants scurried out of the way, parting before us as we rode on. My officers and I reined in our mounts in the center of the courtyard. Several gardeners were busy chopping down a dead, burned tree, and I saw that there was a young, healthy tree waiting to replace it. I smiled wistfully. Laurel had burned down the old tree the night we sprung her father and the Merry Men from jail. She was so quick-witted in situations like that. Normally her impulsivity worried me, but her rash actions probably saved all of us that day.

The captain of the guard greeted us. Once I introduced myself, he snapped to attention and led us immediately to a receiving room. One of the male servants scurried off to inform Prince John of our arrival. We were offered food and drink, which my officers eagerly accepted, but I refused.

It felt like a long time before one of the servants announced that Prince John was available to see us. We were led down one corridor after another, then up several winding staircases until we came to the royal quarters. Two guards stood sentry at the doorway, but they opened the heavy wooden door for us as we approached.

Prince John stood when I entered. "Come in, come in!" He gestured to a simple wooden chair in front of his desk, and settled himself into an ornately carved throne covered in red velvet cushions.

"No, thank you, Your Majesty. I prefer to stand," I said crisply.

Prince John studied me. He was much shorter than I remembered. His feet barely reached the floor. He had a round, barrel chest and a pale, pasty complexion, but he also looked friendly. I knew enough about him to know that he was often considered to be polite and kind, but then would flip without a moment's notice and lash out in violent, unpredictable outbursts.

"What happened to Blackwell? You are his son, are you not? Baron, if I recall correctly."

I inclined my head. "Robin Hood's daughter killed him, sire. I was there."

"But she didn't kill you?"

"That is right."

"What happened?"

"I killed and buried her myself, as well as several of Hood's men. We held funeral services for my men in the village."

Prince John smiled smugly. "Well done. Those outlaws have done too much harm for too long. I am glad to hear that some of them are gone for good." He sighed. "I am sorry to hear about your father. He was a great man and will be sorely missed. I look forward to working with you in his stead."

"Father always spoke very highly of you, Your Majesty," I said. "I will never be the man he was, but I will strive to do my best."

"Taking care of those annoying bandits was no small feat. You are to be commended for your service!"

"Thank you, Your Majesty, but I did not come for compliments or to exchange pleasantries. Rufus, close the door. No one else needs to hear what we have to say." Rufus pulled the door shut with a resounding *thud*.

"Just as efficient as your father, I see. No need to clutter our time with small talk."

"Indeed," I barked. "I will be brief. Robin Hood is still at-large. If you have any extra men, I want a task force out looking for him. I found the message you sent to my father. I currently have my platoon stationed in the Crags, but they are available to join us as soon as two weeks from now. When will Philip's army be here?"

"Two months hence, I presume."

I nodded curtly. "I will have my men here and ready in two weeks and we can drill until Philip arrives. I trust they will be accommodated?"

Prince John seemed pleased with my haste. "There is room in the barracks. We will be ready whenever Richard's army arrives. But there is no rush. Richard won't be back soon. We have time." John went on to detail my duties, most of which I had already known from watching my father for so many years. I would be primarily tasked with collecting taxes, and enforcing the law. I had the authority to arrest and imprison anyone I wanted, save Prince John himself. It was no surprise to me why my father had loved this position. The power associated with it was palpable.

"Is Richard is still being held by the Austrians?"

John shook his head. "No, they don't have him anymore. Leopold sent him off somewhere else but neglected to tell me where. Blasted shame, that is."

"What do you propose?" I asked.

John smiled and held a glass up to toast me. "I propose a tournament held in your honor. It will be an opportunity to introduce you to everyone. The nobility always like to know the sheriff. We can even invite Duke Leopold and his son and encourage them to disclose the information of where my brother is now."

"An excellent idea!" Rufus piped up enthusiastically. "What cunning! What foresight! Well done, Your Majesty! Such an honor to be in your presence! With you as our lead-"

I raised my eyebrows at him. Rufus stopped talking

and blushed. I turned my attention back to John. "As you wish, Your Majesty. Though truth be told, it doesn't matter who has him presently, so long as we are prepared for when he returns."

John grinned. "I like the way you think, Baron."

LAUREL

"*R*eady, Izzy?" Aalis wriggled with eager anticipation. "It is *finally* time!"

Of course. The stupid tournament. From what I had heard, it would be nothing like Father's annual tournaments back in Sherwood Forest. If I was allowed to participate, it would be a different story. But from what Aalis had described during the many nights she lay awake, chattering endlessly from the bedroll next to mine, girls would lace themselves up in ridiculously tight corsets, hoping to be noticed by the contenders. I had no intention whatsoever of displaying myself like livestock at an auction. My time would be much better spent playing sleuth and working to find out information on where King Richard was being held. I had also heard rumors of secret tunnels and passageways leading out of the castle. I could use the time during the tournament to investigate, or to sneak into Prince John's empty quarters while everyone else was distracted...

"Aalis," I groaned, "I really don't want to go. Aren't there chores we need to do?"

"How can you even think of work right now? There will be *boys!* Maybe even *without shirts on!* We *have* to go!"

Honestly. It sickened me that girls' thoughts could be so shallow. Why anyone would want to giggle and ogle boys instead of doing something productive was beyond me. "I... have someone back home I am interested in," I lied.

"Oh, *please!!!* There will be lots of people there! Prince John invited everyone! There will be royalty from all over! There is a new Sheriff of Nottingham, and he will be there too! I heard he is very handsome! We can see if the rumors are true!"

Wonderful. Just what I wanted, other girls swooning all over Baron in front of me.

"No."

"But Isabella! You are my best friend! You *have* to come with me! I can't go alone!" Aalis protested and tugged on my arm. I still couldn't understand why she had decided I was her friend at all, let alone her best friend. "Prince John is attending, and the Duke of Austria, and his son, and..."

"Wait, who was that last one?"

"What?"

"You said the Duke of Austria?" According to the letter we found, that was the man who had captured Richard. Could it be...?

"Oh, yes! Leopold the Fifth! I heard Gwendolyn say that he will be there. Him and his son, Leopold the Sixth! I don't know anything about them though."

This was the exact opportunity I was waiting for! Why try to rummage through John's papers for an old letter when I could go straight to the source?

"Okay, you convinced me. I'll go," I told Aalis.

She squealed and clapped her hands. "Oh, Izzy! This will be so much fun! Agnes has trunks of dresses that she saved from rich ladies of court. We can help each other get ready and do our hair and everything!"

"I don't know how to do any of that stuff."

Aalis gasped. "What? Well, of course, you are so pretty you don't ever have to dress up! You could wear a potato sack and you would look glorious! Let's get ready!"

I SURVEYED MYSELF IN THE SOLE MIRROR IN THE SERVANTS' quarters. I felt ridiculous. I already felt ridiculous every day here with no weapons on me except for a small dagger strapped to my inner thigh. But now even more so. Aalis had laced me into a corset so tight that I was worried I would snap in half if I bent at all, and my waist had been reduced so far that I could nearly circle it with my hands. My skirts were long and flowed out behind me. It was a completely impractical outfit. What use were long skirts?

My bodice was uncomfortably tight and my bosom threatened to explode out of the top. My sleeves were tight and I couldn't even lift my arms above my head. My tight shoes had a pointed toe and squeezed my feet. There was a new-fangled fashion in which girls placed a peg-like heel on their shoe, which Aalis had done for me. I would be worthless in a fight, or if I had to run. There was no way I would be able to reach my dagger without splitting every seam on this gown.

But even beyond the clothing, Aalis had worked all the snarls and knots out of my hair, dabbed rouge onto my lips and cheeks, and darkened my eyes. It would be impossible to surreptitiously slip through a crowd, though

I wondered if anyone would even recognize me. I looked so unlike my normal self.

Aalis had her hands up to her mouth. "Oh, Izzy, you are *beautiful!!!*"

"I can't breathe."

"Who cares? You look stunning! Everyone will want to dance with you tonight!"

Stunning was one word for it. Torture also came to mind. I groaned, "We have to go to a dance too?"

Aalis fixed me with a stern look. "No, *Isabella*. We *get* to go to a dance!" she sighed and held her hands to her heart. "I hope Conrad asks me to go with him!"

"Conrad?"

"Conrad, the one with rippling muscles and eyes like a storm! Conrad, who is in love with me but too shy to say! Conrad-"

"The stable boy?"

"Yes, that one!" A sappy look came over Aalis's face. "Handsome, isn't he?"

"Um, sure."

She suddenly narrowed her eyes at me, and her smile faded quickly. "Don't you go making a move on him now, Izzy! I didn't get you all fixed up so you can steal him away from me! You can have any other boy there, but not Conrad!"

"You don't have to worry, Aalis! He isn't my type," I told her with deep sincerity.

"Who is your type?" She hitched her overly-bright smile back onto her face with lightning speed.

I thought of Leopold. "Rich and titled."

Aalis giggled girlishly. "Well, with your face and figure, I'm sure you can get any man you want! Let's go!"

~

THE MORNING WAS WARM AND BRIGHT. AALIS LINKED HER arm with mine and led me out to where the tournament was set up. Areas were roped off for spectators. Horses pawed at the ground, and the armor on the knights reflected the sunshine. Heads turned as Aalis and I passed. I hated feeling like everyone was watching me. Any cover I had could be blown at any time if I wasn't careful.

"Smile, Izzy!" Aalis nudged my side. "You look like you want to kill someone! Remember, the goal today is to be asked to accompany someone to the dance!"

"Maybe *your* goal is," I grumbled under my breath. Aalis didn't pay any attention to what I said. She waved merrily at everyone who looked in our direction and beamed.

Well, if this was my undercover role, I may as well play the part. I forced a smile onto my face and held my head high.

"That's better!" Aalis said, then clutched at me. "Here he comes!"

The stable boy loped into sight. He had a rangy gait that reminded me of the wildlife I hunted with Father growing up. He had sandy blonde hair, was tall, though not nearly as tall as Baron, and had a very freckled face. He spotted Aalis and shuffled over to us.

"Hello, Conrad," Aalis said sweetly. "Beautiful day!"

"It is," agreed Conrad. He and Aalis both studied their shoes. I looked from one to the other with interest. For supposedly being madly in love with in each other, they certainly weren't showing it.

"Are you going to the dance tonight, Conrad?" I asked

loudly. He jumped and looked puzzled, as though he couldn't figure out if I had spoken, or Aalis.

"Erm, yes. Yes, I am." Conrad's voice was a little raspy. "You?"

"Aalis wants to," I said. Both Aalis's and Conrad's faces grew red. Aalis cleared her throat.

"Oh, Conrad! This is my friend Isabella," Aalis introduced us. "Isabella, I think you know Conrad?"

I shook his hand. His handshake felt like a limp fish. Why Aalis was head over heels in love with this boy, I couldn't tell. "Not really. But it is nice to meet you." I smiled at him, but he avoided my gaze. Maybe he wanted to speak to Aalis alone. I turned to her. "Aalis, I need to go see Agnes. It will only take a minute. Wait for me, will you?"

Aalis knew exactly what I was doing. She smiled her appreciation and turned back to Conrad.

I meandered off. Twenty minutes or so should be long enough for them to figure out how to talk to each other. Heads continued to turn as I walked through the crowd. I wished I had a cloak to cover up this lurid outfit and conspicuous makeup. I didn't want to be noticed. I wanted to blend in, and this outfit was about as far from helpful as it could be.

I saw Agnes filling drinks at a table. "May I help you?" I asked politely.

She glanced up and tilted her head. "Isabella, is that you? Why, I barely recognized you!"

"I barely recognize myself. Aalis helped me get ready."

"Well, you look lovely dearie! Pass these out, would you? Just grab a few and find anyone that looks important and hand them out."

That was easy enough. I grabbed several mugs and set

off. Chairs were set up in the spectator area for royalty and their guests, and they were beginning to fill up. I headed that direction. I handed out mug after mug. Most nobility accepted drinks without even glancing up to see who their serving girl was. Several men stared until the woman they were sitting with cleared her throat or placed her hand over his as a gentle reminder that they had brought someone to be with.

An older gentleman was sitting with his bored son, who looked to be about Baron's age. "Drinks, good sirs?" I asked, after dropping into a curtsy.

"Thank you, my dear," the older man said, and nudged his son. The son did a double-take when he saw me.

"Yes, thank you!" he said, and accepted the mug. I curtsied again and swept away.

"See, Leo? This won't be all that bad! Look at all the girls you have to choose from!" I heard the older man say as I left.

Leo. He could have meant Leopold. I made a mental note of what the son looked like, but it was unnecessary. Shortly after, an announcer stood to introduce all the nobility, and my suspicions were confirmed when the gentleman and his son were introduced as Leopold the Fifth, Duke of Austria, and his son, Leopold the Sixth.

I returned with drinks to that group several more times before Agnes told me to go enjoy the party. I had hoped to see Baron. All the servants had been abuzz that the new sheriff would be present. I had assumed he would sit with the nobles now that he had such a highly esteemed position. Naturally, we wouldn't be able to give any indication that we knew each other, but I wanted to see him. I had only been here a couple of weeks, and I already missed him. But he was nowhere in sight.

I began to get slightly worried. The last I had seen Baron, he had been leaving with two known enemies. Had they not believed his story? Had they betrayed him? Perhaps he wasn't the new sheriff after all. After I finished passing out drinks, I returned to where I had left Aalis.

She was still there, but Conrad had disappeared. "Oh, *there* you are, Izzy! I wondered where you had got to!" she linked arms with me again.

"I was helping Agnes with drinks," I told her.

Aalis looked shocked. "I thought you were only saying that so you would leave me alone with Conrad! Which, *thank you* for doing, by the way! He asked me to accompany him to the dance!" She let out a gusty breath of air. "You will need to find someone to go with, and we can all get a table together and dance the night away!"

"Wouldn't that be fun," I said dully. Aalis missed my sarcasm.

Trumpets blared and she squealed, "Oooh! It's about to start!" Her voice was so high-pitched that it rang in my ears. "Let's find a good spot to watch!"

She dragged me over to the rope barrier. It was beyond me how Aalis could run in these strappy high-heeled shoes, but she managed it. I, on the other hand, twisted my ankle.

Jousting was first. Knights on horses thundered across the field toward each other, and aimed their lances at each other, trying to knock the other from their seat. For all my initial hesitation to attend, I had to admit- it was thrilling to watch. I had never attended a royal tournament before. I was glad I came, just to see the incredible feats of strength, skill, and stamina that were being displayed. Knight after knight matched their skills to the others, until only one knight remained. He was given a rose, which he promptly presented to a woman in the crowd. She tucked it into her hair and handed the knight a handkerchief, and the crowd cheered wildly.

"What is all that about?" I asked Aalis.

"Oh, of course, you haven't been to a tournament before! When a champion is crowned, he is given a flower to award to the woman of his choice! She accepts it and gives him back a token of her affection, like a handkerchief. Then they will go to the dance together tonight."

"What if she doesn't accept it?"

Aalis goggled at me. "Why would someone *not* accept a rose from a champion?"

"Maybe she doesn't like him. Maybe he's a pretentious pig. Maybe he's ugly."

"...but he would be a champion knight," Aalis said, confused. She couldn't comprehend a situation in which someone would not want to accept a rose. I let the matter drop.

ARCHERY FOLLOWED JOUSTING. I WATCHED KEENLY AS MAN after man stepped up and shot at the target. There were certainly skilled archers, but none came close compared to Father.

"Do women compete?" I asked Aalis interestedly. I wasn't up to Father's skill, but I could shoot just as well as any of these competitors. I wouldn't, of course. A skilled archer with red hair was too much of a giveaway. I wished I was back in Sherwood Forest, where I would be able to compete in the tournaments.

Aalis wrinkled her nose. "I suppose they could. But why would they want to?"

"Maybe she wants to prove that she is the best at that sport. Or maybe she wants to give a rose to the man of her choice."

Aalis laughed. "You are so funny, Isabella! Imagine, a girl giving a boy a rose..." she trailed off into a fit of giggles.

Conrad sidled up to Aalis, and she turned to talk to him. I wandered off. I saw the older gentleman's son, Leopold the Sixth, leaned up against one of the posts that held up the rope barrier, watching the archery event intently. He was a lean man, with a thin face and trim mustache. His nose was incredibly straight and pointed, and his hair was parted more neatly than anyone else's I had ever seen. His impeccable clothing gave the impression of great wealth and power.

"His arrow is going to veer right," I said aloud from behind him. "He isn't compensating for the breeze."

He jumped slightly and looked around, then looked back at the target. The archer's arrow sank into the right side of the bullseye. The man turned back to me. His grey eyes gave me an immediate impression of a spoiled brat who got everything he wanted. Yes, this was the one I needed to get information out of.

"Beautiful *and* intelligent! May I ask your name, my lady?" His voice was oily and arrogant.

"Just Isabella, sir. No title. I'm a servant." I began to curtsy, but he took my hand and bowed, pressing my fingers to his lips instead.

"Isabella, then. It is a pleasure to meet you. Allow me to introduce myself. I am Leopold the Sixth, son of Leopold the Fifth, Duke of Austria."

I swept him a grand curtsy, inwardly cursing the

corsets that made every breath and movement a struggle. "Your Grace."

Leopold invited me to stand beside him, and I did so.

"What brings you so far from home, Your Grace?" I asked with a dazzling smile.

"Just business to attend to. Although I must say, I am enjoying the sights immensely," he smiled at me, and his eyes slowly took in my entire outfit. Ugh, what a creep. The things I had to endure for my missions! I knew this type of man only too well. He was the sort who knew the things to do and say to make women fall at his feet, and young girls fawn all over him. He knew it too. His self-satisfied smile told me that he was confident he would get whatever, and whomever, he wanted, and that he thoroughly liked what he saw.

I turned my attention back to the tournament. Leopold edged closer to me. "So, tell me young lady, how do you know so much about archery?"

"Oh, I watch the men-at-arms practice sometimes," I said innocently.

"If you have the time, I would be more than happy to demonstrate my own prowess at arms," Leopold offered.

"Your Grace is too kind, but I have already taken up too much of your time today. A servant cannot occupy the time of someone as important as yourself," I said politely, spun on my heel, and left.

The look on his face nearly made me laugh out loud. He seemed so shocked that any girl would walk away from him. *'Always leave with the audience wanting more!'* Dale had instructed our troupe over and over when he gave us lessons on performance. This was certainly a performance I was putting on. I absently tugged at my tight corset. A performance that required an uncomfortably tight costume. I held my anxiety about Baron at bay. Whatever my personal feelings were, I couldn't let them get in the way of my mission.

I walked back over to Aalis and made sure my figure was clearly visible to Leopold, but didn't look back at him. I could sense his frustration and reveled in it.

Trumpets blared again. The archery portion of the tournament was over and the champion was handed a rose. He walked over to give it to a simpering girl in the crowd. Again, the girl squealed and handed him a handkerchief in return. She was all of a dither, pressing the rose to her heart and fanning herself with her hand.

Then came javelin throwing, wrestling, and footraces. Aalis was preoccupied with Conrad, and I didn't want to impose on their time together. I wandered around the grounds, watching the events while still keeping my eyes open for Baron. Where *was* he?

The sun blazed overhead. I stopped my search for Baron to curiously watch what was proclaimed a "melee", where two teams of horsemen crashed into each other. Both teams attempted to stay in formation and force the other back. It was fascinating. I had never fought as part of a cohesive team; the Merry Men were very individualized when it came to fighting style and methods. It mesmerized me to watch the group tactics each team used to press back the other's offense.

Minstrels strolled through the crowd. If one passed a couple, the minstrel would strum a love song. When entertaining large crowds, the ballads were jaunty and comical. The next time the trumpets blared, the announcer boomed out, "Next up, our contestants for swordplay!"

The next line of contestants marched onto the field. I

glanced at them, then felt my jaw drop. Baron was among the contestants. He was dressed in solid black leather from head to toe. His mouth was set in an unfriendly grimace, and the shadows along his jaw showed that he hadn't shaved in a few days. With his facial expression, dark hair, and massive build, he looked intimidating. He truly did look like someone who would be the Sheriff of Nottingham, which I reminded myself, he now was. All the other contestants were eyeing him nervously. Baron looked around and saw me standing at the edge. I couldn't help it. I flashed a quick wink that went unnoticed by everyone else but him. He didn't alter his facial expression at all and stared forward again. I grinned. He was a good actor.

The tournament director gathered all the contestants and explained the rules of the bouts about to take place. No fatal blows, no permanent damage, the order would be lowest to highest ranked for the first round, then mixed afterward, that sort of thing. I had eyes only for Baron. I watched him for the entirety of the opening speech.

Once the director was done speaking, the first match began. Baron wasn't a part of it, but he stared intently at both men. I knew he was analyzing every movement, watching for telltale giveaways. Little John taught me about this. Some people would inhale deeply a second before attacking or shift their weight slightly before a feint. If you were familiar with your opponent's style and habits, it gave you an advantage during the duel.

The men who were in the arena first were two squires, and their swordplay was mediocre at best. They whacked at each other for a few minutes, and one was declared the victor, and was allowed to sit down while the next pair entered the sparring area. I watched each match with vivid interest. I had always found it mesmer-izing to study the different styles and techniques people used.

"So, Isabella, you enjoy watching this sort of event?" a voice said behind me. I glanced over my shoulder and saw that it was Leopold. I had wondered how long he would stay away. Men like him could never bear the thought of a woman who wasn't madly in love with them. My best tactic right now would be to show how disinterested I was. It would drive him mad.

"Yes, Your Grace. And yourself?"

"Sometimes. I prefer to participate more than watch."

I made an uninterested noise and turned back to watch the duels. Leopold snapped his fingers for a servant and asked for chairs to be brought. The servant was Walter, the one who was known for always wearing gloves, and he hurried back with two seats. I waved cheer-fully at him, and Leopold frowned slightly. He snatched the chairs and shooed Walter away. As Walter walked away and Leopold turned his back, I saw Walter roll his eyes. I grinned.

"A seat, my lady?" Leopold gestured grandly for me to sit.

"Thank you, Your Grace. You are too kind."

Leopold sat down next to me. We watched as two more men, who both showed a good deal of skill and tech-nique, clashed sword against sword.

"I prefer the javelin, myself," announced Leopold.

"Do you?"

"Oh yes. I probably would have competed profession-ally if I wasn't so busy managing the treasury. It is a big job. Our family is *immensely* wealthy!" He paused, as if expecting me to fall all over him because he had money. I smiled to myself. If only he knew how many people I had robbed in my lifetime.

"I have found that it isn't how *much* money someone has that matters so much as what they do with their wealth," I commented lightly, still avoiding his gaze.

"We build a lot of churches," Leopold hastened to say. "And we distribute supplies to the needy."

"Those are noble causes," I remarked, but didn't sound excited about it. I could tell Leopold was beginning to get frustrated with my lack of enthusiasm. He needed a nudge in the right direction.

"Are you friends with King John?" I asked, careful to emphasize the title.

"Yes."

I finally turned to face him. "Well, I am glad to hear of someone who supports him! Everyone seems to be on his brother Richard's side. They just don't understand, do they?"

Leopold leapt on that eagerly. "Yes! Yes, I fully support John! He is a much better choice between the two of them, isn't he?"

"Absolutely! You must be very intelligent to see the truth past all the lies people spread," I agreed, bestowed a dazzling smile on Leopold, then turned my attention back to the tournament.

Baron was about to take his first turn. After his match, each winner from the first rounds would pair off with another in a random order, and the second rounds would begin again. Baron stepped into the ring and swung his massive sword around in easy circles. There was a great deal of murmuring from the crowd around us. I heard the word *Sheriff* used over and over. Several girls were oohing and aahing over Baron's chiseled physique.

"Impressive man, that one," I observed keenly, nodding toward Baron.

Leopold frowned again. "He looks mean."

"He probably is," I responded. "He *is* the Sheriff of Nottingham, after all. I wouldn't ever want to make him angry!"

"I can't imagine anyone would ever be angry with you. You are too pretty," Leopold said smoothly.

"Oh, I wish that were true! But unfortunately, servants tend to be blamed for everything," I said with a gusty sigh. "The head housekeeper is very strict with us."

On the field, Baron raised his sword in a salute to his opponent, a stocky knight with a broad chest. They began their duel, weaving back and forth, darting in and out, and holding up their shields when needed. The knight's shield was a typical round buckler. Baron's was a large black kite shield with the Nottingham coat of arms painted on the front. The knight was a good fighter, but I could tell Baron was better. Baron blocked every one of the knight's advances with ease, and then began his own assault with crushing power. I couldn't help a smile spreading slowly over my face. Baron was the epitome of manliness.

"You probably could do with a night off from all that work, couldn't you?" Leopold hinted.

"I do get one night in ten off," I said. Baron was beating the knight back with a barrage of attacks.

"Do you have tonight off?" Leopold asked.

"All day today and tonight!" I answered cheerily. "The older servants said they wanted the youth to enjoy themselves. Some of my friends and I are going to go to the dance together."

"You aren't accompanying anyone in particular?"

I didn't answer. I watched the knight drop his sword and fall to his knees. Baron raised his arms in triumph, and I applauded wildly along with everyone else. Baron glanced once toward me before taking his place at the winner's bench.

The tournament director paired Baron as part of the first set of opponents for the second round, which I felt was unfair. The crowd surrounding me seemed to agree, and there was some mutinous muttering. Everyone else had ample time to recover, but Baron was going straight from one match to the next.

I watched the entirety of Baron's second duel. He was coupled with the winning squire from the very first duel. I needn't have worried. The entire bout lasted about ten seconds. The squire tried a half-hearted thrust, and Baron's sword smashed against his opponent's blade with such devastating force that the squire's sword was knocked clean from his hand. The squire yelped and retreated, and the audience laughed. Baron raised his fist triumphantly into the air.

"Quite an arrogant showman, isn't he?" Leopold said nastily.

"He did just win back-to-back rounds. He has reason to be proud!" I said and clapped along with everyone else.

"He had an easy opponent."

"Would you be a more difficult opponent?" I asked sweetly. I could tell just by looking at Leopold that he would not pose any threat to Baron.

"I would!" Leopold said staunchly.

"Of course you would be. I suppose you could always challenge him later to see who is better," I suggested, and smiled innocently. "I would very much like to watch that."

Leopold's eyes flicked over to Baron. Baron was

standing with his enormous arms folded across his broad chest. Even from a distance, his colossal size was obvious. He looked more like a huge bear than a man. "I don't need to prove anything. I know that I would win. Especially in a javelin contest."

I smiled sweetly and didn't say anything. I watched as two knights parried and swiped at each other. Apart from Baron's most recent duel, all the matches were getting longer and fiercer. The opponents were tiring from their repeated battles, and the men were puffing for breath between each attack, which increased in intensity. Despite their exhaustion, the rush of competitive adrenaline kept the contenders on edge. I knew that rush only too well and missed it immensely. What I wouldn't give for a good fight right about now. Scrubbing floors and tending fireplaces wasn't particularly thrilling.

Finally, the competition was whittled down to just Baron and his last opponent. The knight Baron was fighting was flushed bright red, and his movements grew slower and clumsier. But Baron looked like he was just getting warmed up, and he won the match easily. I applauded long and loud.

"So, Isabella, you said you are going to the dance tonight, but didn't answer if you are going with anyone."

"No, I'm not accompanying anyone, Your Grace."

"No need for ceremony. You may call me Leopold," he flashed a toothy, dashing smile that was full of arrogance and pomp.

"Ah, begging your pardon, Your Grace, but I don't think that would be proper. I am just a servant. I wouldn't feel right calling someone of your stature by his first name," I informed Leopold.

The tournament director approached Baron with a

rose and handed it to him. They exchanged a few words, but I couldn't hear over the roar of the crowd.

I saw Baron glance up and then make a beeline in my direction. He couldn't possibly be thinking... What was he planning to do? People would suspect! Baron was only ten feet away. Girls behind me squealed and called out silly things like, "Yoo-hoo, Sheriff!" and "Hi there, Handsome!"

"And what if I were to ask you to accompany me to the dance tonight?" Leopold asked quickly, also glancing at Baron's approach. "Would you feel more comfortable then?"

"Um..."

Baron stood in front of me. "Would you accept this rose and accompany me to the dance tonight?" he asked solemnly.

"I asked her first!" Leopold snarled.

Baron raised his eyebrows mildly. "I wasn't asking *her,*" he said with a head jerk toward me. "No offense, milady." He raised his eyes to a person standing behind me.

I turned. There was a girl there. She was pretty, with a trim figure, long brown hair, and was smiling radiantly. She looked more than excited to accept the offered rose. "Yes!" she handed Baron a handkerchief, and he tucked it into his pocket and bowed. Even though I knew that Baron couldn't act like he knew me, and wouldn't want him to, it still caused me a ripple of irritation to see this girl hanging all over Baron.

Two could play this game. I turned to Leopold and slid my hand into the crook of his elbow. "Yes, I would love to go with you to the dance, Your Grace."

BARON

J had never been so deeply amused as I was that
day. I watched from afar as Leopold tried to
impress Laurel all afternoon. She was very coy in her
approach- she acted indifferent enough that Leopold had
to work hard to keep her attention, but then she would
show just enough interest that Leopold didn't get discour-
aged. She would occasionally catch my eye and flash a
wink when Leopold wasn't watching.

I should have given my own date more notice, but she
didn't seem to mind my inattentiveness. I didn't even
remember her name. She latched herself onto my arm
and was waving merrily at anyone and everyone who
looked in our direction. She sometimes asked me questions, but rarely waited for an answer, and would chatter
away nonstop.

During the feast, I was only a few seats away from
Laurel and Leopold, but it was impossible to eavesdrop on
any of their conversation. A running stream of men came
up to me with questions and concerns about laws, taxes,
and recent arrests. I answered each one at length, mostly

so I wouldn't have to listen to the girl at my side, who still tried to fill every spare moment with foolish gossiping. I was never serious about any girl before Laurel, and now I was reminded why. Most girls would go out of their way to giggle endlessly and talk in high-pitched voices about the most empty-headed of topics; my date was the same. I don't think I said more than ten words to her during the meal.

Any time I needed to leave the table briefly, my date would trill something like, "Hurry back soon, Handsome!" Each time Laurel heard, she smirked at me.

A great number of courses were laid out, one after the other. Every one was good, but because of all the attention I received, I was prevented from eating as much as I would have liked. My date seemed uninterested with my conversations and played with her food. I made no attempt to alleviate her boredom.

After the final course was cleared away, servants came and directed everyone into a large ballroom. Right, the dance. I watched with a hint of jealousy as Leopold swept Laurel through the dance floor. They were both graceful dancers, and heads turned everywhere to look at them; mostly the heads of men, whether they had their own dates or not. I had never seen Laurel look so beautiful. She had always been unusually attractive, and would have been striking in whatever she wore, even if it was her old green tunic and leggings, with hastily combed hair. Even as a prisoner in camp, heads had constantly turned to stare at her.

But tonight, she was stunning. The dress she wore was low-cut and form fitting, her long hair flowed down her back, and her face was done up to accentuate all of her best features. I could barely tear my eyes from her, just like every other man on the dance floor. Several men tried to cut in, but Leopold rebuffed them every time, and refused to let Laurel dance with anyone else. It was no surprise that she kept Leopold so intensely interested.

I was no expert when it came to what women found attractive, and I didn't understand why women were fawning all over Leopold. All I could tell was that he was tall and thin and gave an immediate impression of someone who was comfortable with power and would not hesitate to use his position to get whatever he wanted. Girls seemed to notice him, so he must be considered handsome. Laurel was certainly giving him plenty of attention. I kept reminding myself that it was all an act on her part, but I couldn't prevent myself wishing that it was me she was looking at that way.

I led my partner through the dance moves the best I could, but I was far from accomplished in the area of social graces. The most I could hope for was to avoid stepping on my date's feet as I stiffly went through the dance steps. I saw Prince John dance with his wife, and several of the knights I had competed against earlier cheerfully swapped dance partners with each other every time a song ended.

My date's previous boredom from dinner had evaporated, and she clung to me during the dancing, waving at all her friends that she saw. I tried to avoid watching Laurel and Leopold, but it was impossible. Laurel's red hair seemed to pop out at me everywhere I looked. She seemed entirely too comfortable with Leopold, and I didn't like the greedy look in his eye at all.

During one spirited song, they danced close by. As Leopold twirled Laurel past me, I felt brief tug on my left side trousers pocket. Laurel raised her eyebrows meaningfully at me over Leopold's shoulder as he swept her off again.

I left my date at a small table so I could get us drinks. She seemed pleased that I was showing her some attention at last. I walked slowly to the table where tiny glasses were lined up and slipped my hand into my pocket. At first, I only felt my coin purse. But I dug around and my fingertips touched a tiny fragment of parchment. I withdrew it, made sure no one was watching, then read Laurel's handwriting.

Richard in Trifels Castle. To be tried by his Holy Emperor, Henry the Sixth. Destroy message immediately.

I arrived at the drinks table. I inconspicuously folded the message into my palm and picked up two glasses, then returned to the table. My date was there, as well as Laurel and Leopold. Laurel was fanning herself with a napkin and chatting merrily with my date. They were both laughing gaily at some remark Leopold made. I offered a drink to the girl I was with, which she happily accepted, and I sat in the empty chair between her and Laurel. Leopold clicked his fingers annoyingly at a servant and had a dish of cheeses and fruits brought over. He offered it to Laurel with as much pride as if he had harvested the fruit and made the cheese himself.

"Thank you, Your Grace," she trilled, and accepted the plate. She set it down on the table, then glanced over and noticed the folded paper tucked between my thumb and palm. There was no change in her facial expression, but her eyes caught mine, and I understood immediately. The message needed to be destroyed, and quickly, before it was discovered.

But how on earth was I supposed to do that? I couldn't place the paper into the flame set in the middle of all of us. If I dropped it, or even ripped it, someone would be able to piece it back together. I debated how successful it would be to allow my glass to spill and soak the parchment, but that seemed transparently obvious.

"So, you are the new Sheriff of Nottingham, are you?" Leopold asked me. "Tell me, what exactly does that position entail?"

"His job today was to make all the girls swoon!" giggled my date. I ignored her, and heard Laurel hastily turn a mocking laugh into a hacking cough. Leopold reached over and rubbed her back, and I forced myself to look away. What a smarmy bloke. The girl continued, "And you never said what you want me to call you- Baron? Ooh, or maybe Bear-Bear?"

"Sheriff will suffice," I told her shortly, then redirected my attention to answering Leopold's question. "I am in charge of taxes and criminal arrests, as well as their punishments, and I lead King John's first platoon of soldiers."

"Do you practice with the javelin?" Leopold asked swiftly.

"Rarely."

"I do!" Leopold said self-importantly as he puffed out his thin chest. "I excel at it! If you ever need tips, I am the one to consult! It isn't about brawn, either. It is about skill! A fine art, as I tell my *many* servants. It is all in the shoulder and wrist."

My date seemed impressed by his grandiose statement and leaned forward to ask more.

Leopold continued to monologue, and Laurel placed a hand gently on his arm. He smiled at her in a way that made me want to punch him. "Why, Your Grace, this food is divine!" Laurel gushed, and fed him a few grapes. He curled his arm around her and pulled her closer. I had an immediate desire to break Leopold's arm.

"Sheriff?" Laurel turned her attention from Leopold to me and offered the small plate of cheese cubes and grapes. "Why don't you try some? Here, *eat it.*" She smiled mischievously, glanced once at the paper still concealed in my hand, and raised an eyebrow meaningfully.

What other choice did I have? I picked up a few tidbits then tossed everything from my palm into my mouth and swallowed.

I tasted ink all night.

LAUREL

*A*alis gave me an enthusiastic thumbs-up as she left with Conrad, impressed that I had such a high-profile man as a dance partner. Baron and his date sat at the same table for nearly an hour before they finally decided to end their evening. I could still hear the girl's high, silly laugh ringing inside my head. It had annoyed me immensely- her constant giggling. I knew Baron wasn't that funny! Skilled, yes. Handsome, yes. Intelligent, yes. Worthy of being laughed at like he was a court jester, no.

Leopold led me through several more dances. It was getting late, and my feet were in agony in the tiny, pointed shoes that Aalis had insisted I wear. Couples were beginning to disappear from the dance floor, either to find a secluded bench in the gardens, or else to end their evenings and go their separate ways.

I was eager for the latter. I had all the information from Leopold that I needed. The only reason I was continuing to entertain him was to keep up my cover. Leopold, however, had consumed far too many drinks. He kept dropping comments about how lowly my station was, and how I should be honored to have the privilege of being there with him, and should show my gratitude accordingly. I expected nothing less from an entitled, chauvinistic pig like him. He was also beginning to get overly handsy on the dance floor. I was glad Baron and his date had already left. If Baron saw where Leopold kept trying to put his hands, he would have ripped his arms off.

After the third time of redirecting Leopold's hands, I insisted that I needed to sit down to rest my feet. I plopped down in a chair and watched the few couples still left on the dance floor. Leopold pulled his chair close to mine and draped an arm around my shoulders and leaned in. I could smell the alcohol on his breath and wrinkled my nose.

"Done dancing, are you, Isabella?" he asked, his face barely three inches away from mine.

"Yes, Your Grace. I am exhausted."

"My room is close. You should join me." He nuzzled his nose into my neck.

Ugh. Did he actually think any girl with any amount of self-respect would accept such a revolting invitation? I held my breath so I didn't have to inhale his strong odor, and shrugged his face away from my neck. "No, thank you, Your Grace"

"You sure? My bed is very comfortable. Far better than whatever they give you in the servants' quarters."

"I am absolutely sure. You will need your bed all to yourself tonight so you can sleep off everything you drank. Besides, I need to get up early to work tomorrow."

I could see Leopold's eyes trying to focus on me, and his speech was slurred. He placed his hand on my knee and fumbled clumsily on the fabric of my dress as he tried to slide his hand up my leg. "Isabella, I am seducing you. You know that, right?"

I glared at him. There were few things farther from seduction. "I will give you three seconds to get your hand off my thigh, or I will break all of your fingers," I told Leopold through clenched teeth. He grinned like I had made the funniest joke in the world.

"Don't be like that, now. Don't you want to have some fun? This is my first visit to England, after all. You should make sure I enjoy my stay."

"You will enjoy your stay a lot more, if you don't have to leave in a coffin," I said icily.

"Oh, come on now," he wheedled. "I know how to show a girl a good time."

I stood. "Show a different girl. I am leaving!" I walked out of the room to the empty corridor beyond.

Leopold followed me, staggering a little as he weaved drunkenly down the hall. "Want to find a more private area for us, do you? I get it, I get it! I'd like that too."

I pivoted and stepped in close to Leopold, ignoring the strain I was putting on my gown and corset, both of which felt ready to tear as it was. "You aren't getting the message! Leave me alone, or you are going to regret it!" Any pretense of flirting or sweetness I may have had was now gone.

"I could have you arrested, you know. You are just a servant. I am the best you will ever get." His words were slurred, but his irritation was quite plain. He lumbered toward me and grabbed at my waist.

Well, I had given him fair warning. I slammed the heel of my hand underneath the point of his chin. His head snapped back and his body followed along the same trajectory. I grabbed the shoulders of his shirt and pulled him forward, so he lurched back down again. I brought my knee up sharply, first into his stomach, then onto his nose. I felt it instantly break and blood began to pour from his nostrils. I heard my dress rip loudly, but I didn't care. All I wanted was to teach Leopold a lesson.

The poor fool offered no resistance, he was either too drunk or too stunned to react, or else a combination of the two. While he was still bent forward, I cracked my elbow down onto the back of his neck. He collapsed onto the floor with a hefty *oof*. I gave a swift kick to his ribs with my ridiculous pointed shoes, then daintily picked up my skirt and stepped over his body and directly onto his fingers. He let out a high pitched yelp of pain, then lay moaning and groaning on the floor.

"Have a good evening, Your Grace."

BARON

*L*ong past midnight, I was still wide awake, reading through reports and trying hard not to think about Laurel and what she and Leopold might be doing. I forced away the mental images my brain was conjuring at lightning speed – of Laurel flirting with Leopold to get information from him, and Leopold enjoying every second. I had left the dance early because I couldn't bear watching them any longer and Laurel had seemingly made a point of testing my limits, knowing I had to pretend she meant nothing to me. My own date seemed disappointed in the evening, but I didn't care. She could tell her friends that a tournament champion had given her a rose. Wasn't that what all the girls wanted? There was a knock at my door. "Come in," I boomed.

The Duke of Austria and his disgusting weevil of a son entered. "We need to report an attack!" the Duke said. I eyed Leopold with interest. He was a mess.

I leaned back in my chair and placed my hands behind my head. I had a good idea what happened and was very much looking forward to hearing the story directly from Leopold. All my concerns about Laurel seducing information out of Leopold vanished. "Tell me about it."

The Duke gestured his son forward. Leopold limped to the opposite side of my desk. Blood streamed down his face from both nostrils, and his entire front was splattered with the residue. Two black eyes were swelling spectacularly, and his speech was slurred, either because of the broken nose or due to the fact that he was heavily intoxicated. "You know dat gurl I wad next to when you cabe over to give de wose, and I thought it wad for her? Idabella?"

"Yes, the tiny little redheaded servant girl," I said with relish, emphasizing the *tiny*. "She sat beside you when I brought drinks over. I remember."

Leopold glared. "She attagged be."

I leaned forward, a look of great concern on my face. "She attacked *you*? Well, we will have to deal with that immediately! You are an honored guest here. We can't have that. Tell me exactly what she did!"

Leopold had the grace to look embarrassed. "Id doesn't batter."

"Oh no, it does!" I said emphatically and pulled out parchment and a quill. "I need to write up a report and discipline her. I only wish I hadn't left the dance earlier. I would have been able to deal with her promptly, if I had stayed! I am so sorry I left you alone with her; I had no idea she was so dangerous. She didn't look powerful enough to overpower anyone! So tell me, how did she attack you?"

Leopold's father gave him a little push forward to encourage him to speak. The gesture made me think of a mother pushing a small child forward to say hello to a stranger.

"Well, she hit be."

"I can see that," I said, and scribbled down, *Offender: Isabella, servant.* "Go on, go on!" I urged. "Did you strike her back?"

"Well, no. I didn't have timb. But she hit me about a hundwed timbs. And... and bwoke my dose!"

"How did such a small girl do all this to you?" I asked, still with the expression of immense concern on my face. "Did she do it alone, or did she have accomplices? Weapons? She must have had!"

Leopold nodded vigorously. "Yes! She had a... a cwub!"

I added under *Offender* another line and listed *Weapon: Club.* I tsked sympathetically. "My deepest condolences, your excellence. Any accomplices?"

"Um..." Leopold's eyes slid in and out of focus. I watched him carefully. His nose would never be straight again. I resisted the desire to smile. "Yes! They hit me too! And... Idabella stepped on by hand! I allbost *died*!" he finished dramatically, then pulled off a glove to reveal his fingers. They were turning every shade imaginable of blue and purple, then lifted his shirt to show another bruise blossoming into existence. I scribbled notes about his injuries, my eyebrows furrowed seriously.

"Well, you are fortunate to be alive!" I said, very seriously. "Anything else?"

"She diwespected be."

"By hitting and kicking you, you mean? With the club, of course. And having her accomplices attack you?"

"Dose tings too. But all I did wad invite her to spend timb wif me, and she wefused. I ab the futoor Duke of Austwia! I deserb more wespect than dat!" Bits of slobber

87

flecked out of his mouth as he spoke, and I calmly wiped the droplets from my parchment.

"I will tend to it immediately," I told him. "Thank you for bringing this to my attention. Please know that she will be dealt with swiftly and severely."

"Good!" Leopold said. "You were wucky to hab had a nice girl! Mine wud cwazy!"

LAUREL

So much for my dress. During the scuffle with Leopold, I had ripped the overly tight gown in several places. The seams on the shoulders, back, and down the sides under my arms had all burst, and my corset was visible all along the sides where the dress had torn. I sighed. I would have to find a way to repair or replace it, which was more than a month's wages. I was just about to undress and start removing all the makeup Aalis had caked onto my face when Baron stormed into the servant quarters. "Isabella!" he barked.

Several girls were named Isabella, most of whom had been sleeping. All of them squeaked in fright and scrambled forward, staring at the floor.

"Not you," Baron said, cupping one girl's chin up then shoving her away. "Or you... or you..." he was cycling through all the girls. "A plague on you all! Where is the Isabella with red hair?"

I stepped into the main walkway between the mattresses. "I am here."

"Come with me!" Baron ordered. "You are needed for

questioning." He really did look aggressive and mean. He was still clad in all-black leather, his hair and the scruff on his face were black, and his arms and chest bulged with muscle. His hand was on the hilt of his sword, and all the servants I saw behind him looked beyond petrified of this intimidating, hulking man.

Baron reached forward, clenched his fingers firmly around my upper arm, and marched me out of the servants' quarters. As I passed, I saw that Aalis had her mouth open in a silent O. The servant girls probably wouldn't have been surprised if I never returned. Forget being detained for questioning- Baron was making this look like an execution! I fought to keep from laughing as I was hauled off by Baron and arranged my expression into one of terrified obedience. He wrenched open the door to the corridor beyond, flung me through the doorway, and stomped off down the hallway. "Follow me!" he barked, earning him several more nervous glances from the soldiers posted at intervals along our path. One young guard gave me a sympathetic look as I passed.

We trooped down corridor after corridor without a word, me doing my best to look meek and humble to the interested maids and guards who stared at us. Finally, we arrived at one of the doors in the barracks. Baron opened the door and waved me in. I stepped into the chamber and he pulled the heavy door shut behind us.

Once alone, he rounded on me, a slight smile on his lips. "You love making my job difficult, don't you?"

I beamed. "Who, me?"

"Yes, you! Leopold just filed a report."

I pretended to gasp in amazement. "Leopold filed a report? Whatever for?"

Baron rolled his eyes and chuckled. "Like you don't know."

"Jealous?" I asked.

Baron's eyebrows contracted slightly. "If you saw a girl acting the way Leopold did around you, would you be jealous?"

I laughed. "Not at all. I would tell her to be prepared for your thunderous snores and prodigious appetite."

Baron chuckled. "Right. I knew this was coming. I was watching you two all evening."

I moved over to Baron and leaned against him. "Why, Sheriff, why would you care about watching a lowly servant girl and her date?"

Baron couldn't suppress a smile and wrapped his arms around me. "Maybe that servant girl needs to be looked after so she doesn't go around attacking nobility, and the Sheriff knows it, so he has to pay extra attention to her."

"She sounds like a handful," I said.

"She is."

"And, speaking of which," I pushed back from Baron and walked my fingers up his chest, "I need some money; I tore this dress and have to replace it. Luckily for me, I know the Sheriff personally and he is becoming very wealthy, what with his new, higher wages. Do you think he would be able to help a poor servant girl?"

Baron grinned. "I dunno, isn't Leopold rich? Maybe you should ask him. It seemed like he was more than happy to help you out today."

"I don't think he would be so keen on that, even though it *was* his fault the dress was torn in the first place! I couldn't move in this stupid thing when it was together!"

Baron raised his eyebrows. "Well, sounds like you have a conundrum then. As the Sheriff, I can't just go giving out money to every criminal who breaks the law, no matter how pretty she is. It would be bad for my reputation. Fortunately for you, Leopold wants to keep your little incident hushed up so that no one knows a girl got the best of him. Want to fill me in on the details of what happened?"

I told him my version. He scowled when I described what Leopold had tried to pull. "But really," I finished, "he was so drunk by the end of the evening that a six-year-old would have gotten the best of him in a fight. I doubt he will remember anything tomorrow."

"You certainly left quite a few impressions on him that he will not soon forget," Baron responded. "I've said it before, and I will say it again. You're a terrifying woman!"

I laughed and pushed playfully against Baron's chest. "I've got nothing on you! When you walked out onto the field today, you looked so scary! Everyone was talking about that intimidating new Sheriff!"

"And what do you think?" he asked as he cupped my face in his hands and kissed me.

"I think you aren't scary at all. You're a big puppy dog. Are you going to arrest me now for embarrassing the future Duke of Austria?" I kissed Baron back. It had been too long since we had any time alone together.

"I am supposed to. Or else reprimand you severely. Maybe I will yell at you where a lot of people can hear."

"No, let's have you publicly humiliate me by putting me in stocks while the Duke leaves. That would be brilliant! And besides, I've always wanted to try that!" I snickered. It was hysterical to be undercover here with Baron; my favorite assignment yet. No one else was aware we knew each other. It all felt like a giant joke he and I were playing on everyone else in the castle. I loved imagining all the gossip that must be flying around the servants' quarters right now, about why I was being hauled off for questioning by the scary Sheriff of Nottingham.

"You really do look beautiful today," Baron said, and tucked a strand of hair behind my ear. "I understand why Leopold was trying so hard."

I shrugged away the compliment. "It was all Aalis's work, not mine. This isn't even my dress, if you can call it a dress anymore. It is more like shredded rags now." I kissed Baron one last time, then let go of him and moved toward the door. "I need to go; I am due to meet James tonight. Tomorrow, I will tell all the servants that you threatened me to within an inch of my life and that they are right to be terrified of you! In the morning, put me in the stocks. That will send Mr. Handsy off with a good impression of your ability to crack down on hardened criminals."

"Wait, didn't you need money?" Baron reached into his pocket, then frowned and checked his other pocket.

"Not anymore!" I said chipperly. I held up his coin purse and jingled the contents slightly. "You may want to stop getting distracted when beautiful girls kiss you." I winked and left.

BARON

I locked Laurel into the pillory outside the castle gates the next morning, just as the Austrians were due to leave. Laurel had suggested the public stocks in the village, where she would have had things thrown at her and been mocked. But I put my foot down. No one was going to treat Laurel like that, not if I could help it. Instead, there was a one-man pillory off to the side of the castle's entrance. Discreet enough that most people would never know she had been there, but also right along the path the Duke and his son would take as they left.

When the Leopold came to the end of the drawbridge, I stopped him and his entourage. He looked dreadful. He had cleaned the blood off his face, but both his eyes were swollen, puffy, and bruised purple and black. He had a fat lip and his nose, which had previously been so straight, was now slightly crooked. He would never be quite so handsome again.

I issued Leopold a formal apology and showed him how his offender was being punished. Leopold smiled smugly, dismounted, and walked toward us. It gave me immense satisfaction to see him limp with every other step. Laurel's head and hands protruded through the holes on the near side of the frame and hung down in shame.

Leopold pulled Laurel's hair back to get a good look at her face. Laurel kept her eyes downcast. He glanced back at his father, as though seeking confirmation that this was indeed the girl he had spent the entire previous day with. His father gave a small nod, and Leopold cuffed her sharply across the head. Laurel cried out piteously. Even though I knew it was an act, the sound went through me like physical pain. It took all my self-control to master the impulse to finish what Laurel had started with Leopold.

"She will be whipped?" Leopold asked, the relish evident in every syllable.

"Naturally," I answered. Leopold's leering grin widened, and he returned his focus to Laurel. He hit her again, even harder this time. Once more, Laurel cried out in pain. I had to clench my fists to stop my hands from shaking.

"Remember Leo, you are a gentleman," his father said mildly from behind me. "Whatever this *woman*-" he said the word as though it was the greatest insult in the world, "did to you, we are above it. You need not sink to *her* level. The Sheriff will attend to her punishment."

Leopold looked reluctant to leave now that Laurel was confined and at his mercy. I saw his fingers twitch, as though they were just itching to strike her again. I stepped forward. "Please know, your highness, that this matter is a top priority. And once again, I plead with you to accept our utmost apologies for the actions of one servant girl. I assure you that she will be severely punished, and her position here has already been terminated."

"Good, good," Leopold said nastily. "When will the whipping be?" It could not have been plainer that he was willing, even eager, to wait to watch it happen.

"In two days," I said.

Leopold's shoulders sagged. "*Two days?*" he asked incredulously. "So long!"

"I like to starve the offenders before whipping them," I said casually. I spoke with the same vicious spite I had heard in my father's voice hundreds of times. "I want this girl to spend the next two days and nights waiting. Every time she feels the pangs of hunger, she will know that it is nothing compared to what is coming."

Leopold nodded thoughtfully.

"Remember- the best punishment is one of the mind," I sneered. Then I lowered my voice conspiratorially. Leopold leaned closer to listen. "Injuries heal. But fear lasts for a lifetime."

I bowed. Leopold returned the action and finally, he was gone. The instant he was out of earshot, I said in a low voice, "Are you okay?"

Laurel snorted derisively. "For all his bragging about his prowess with a javelin, he has no strength whatsoever."

After Leopold's company rounded the bend in the road, I moved over to examine Laurel. Blood dripped from her mouth. "You are hurt!"

"It is nothing!" Laurel said casually. "Don't be a mother hen. This is part of the job."

I made to unshackle her from the pillory, but Laurel resisted. "He may come back! Give it a few more hours."

At her request, I waited until mid-day before I finally released her. Since it would look too suspicious to stay right by her side while I waited, I went about my regular duties. By the time I got back to release Laurel, the back of her neck was sunburned. "Sorry," I said quietly as I lifted the upper part of the frame.

Laurel pulled her head and hands backward and flashed her arrogant grin. "I was the one who told you to put me there! Don't apologize! Now, I need to hurry and clean before Agnes makes you put me back in the stocks! Unless you were serious about terminating my position, that is. I take it that was just for Leopold's benefit?"

I nodded and she glanced up at the towering wall behind me. "There are guards over there. You better start shouting at me now." She bowed her head in perfect imitation of a servant with a broken spirit.

I yelled for the better part of five minutes, then sent her back inside with orders to double her workload. Laurel let tears trickle down her face as I shouted. Dale had taught her well. She left the tear streaks on her cheeks as she returned to the servants' quarters.

I tried not to think about what might have happened. If Leopold had gone straight to Prince John instead of me... If Leopold had insisted that I whip Laurel in front of him... If she had been unable to defend herself the night before... If someone had discovered that Laurel was not really Isabella... It was all too precarious. I didn't like it.

But seeing Laurel in her element- with her on our side, it almost made me feel like we had a chance to win.

LAUREL

*T*he moment I re-entered the castle, Walter ran up to me. He was panting heavily and gasped, "Are you alright? I heard what happened! I was scared that... that..."

He looked so wildly panicked that for a moment, I felt something must be wrong. "I am fine now!" I assured him. "What did you hear?" I wanted to know what rumors were being spread.

"They said the Sheriff took you! I thought..." he looked me all over and sighed in relief. "I just know that the new Sheriff is brutal. I was worried about you."

"Thank you, Walter, you are so sweet!" I said and patted his arm. "It was pretty terrifying. He interrogated me for hours about what happened to the Duke's son. I couldn't think straight by the end."

"Was he the one you were with yesterday?" Walter said. His breathing was returning to normal. "He looked like trouble. What happened?"

I fabricated a story that Leopold was so drunk that he fell down the stairs. "Anyway," I finished, "the Duke claimed that I pushed him, so they put me in the stocks."

"A little girl like you attack someone?" Walter said incredulously.

I shrugged my shoulders innocently. "That is what they said. I didn't push him down the stairs, I promise! But that Sheriff won't believe a servant girl when a Duke said something else. Just my rotten luck. I never want to go back to the pillory. I was so scared!" I gave a hearty sniff.

"Don't you fret," Walter told me. "You just stay away from the Sheriff and you will be alright. He is a dangerous man."

I nodded my head solemnly. "He seems cruel."

"He is," Walter assured me. "I know. He is the kind of person who enjoys hurting others."

My curiosity was piqued. How was Walter so certain of Baron's character? "What do you mean?"

"Never you mind," Walter said. "A nice girl like you doesn't need to know."

I wanted to ask more, but at that point, Aalis and her friend Gwendolyn sprinted over. Whatever rumors were going around the servant's quarters must be horrific. Both girls looked positively terrified. "Izzy!" gasped Aalis. "Are you alright?"

"No, I died," I said. "Can't you tell?" Walter sniggered, but Aalis placed her hands on her hips.

"It is no joking matter! The Sheriff took you last night and put you in the stocks this morning! What did you *do?*"

"Nothing!" I said. "The Duke fell down the stairs last night when he was drunk and I was the only one who saw. But we can't have visiting nobility get injured with no punishment. So the Sheriff put me in the stocks while the Austrians left. That was it."

"What was he like?" Aalis asked anxiously.

I shuddered. "Horrible! He is so big and I was scared he would hurt me."

Gwendolyn, a plump, cheery girl with curly blonde hair, smiled encouragingly at me. "You were so brave! When we heard about what happened, we all chipped in and did your work for today."

I hadn't expected that and was taken aback. "Th... Thank you!" I stammered.

The girls smiled. "We servants need to stick together."

"I told Agnes I sent you for water when she came looking for you," Walter said.

"And Aalis and I worked on your assigned barracks room. You can rest today," Gwendolyn offered.

"I don't know what to say! Thank you, everyone! You are all good friends!"

"You were a good friend to help me with Conrad yesterday!" giggled Aalis. "It is the least I can do!"

After the three of them went back to their duties, I deliberated about what I wanted to do with all the rest of my day. There was no way I would be able to sneak into Prince John's quarters. Though now that I thought about it, I should have offered to help Gwendolyn with her work. If I remembered correctly, she was the maid in charge of cleaning Prince John's personal apartments. I certainly didn't want to hang around the servants' living quarters.

The coin purse I lifted off Baron weighed heavily around my neck where I had tied it. I perked up. I could take the dress into the village too get repaired or replaced. I ducked out of sight when Agnes came around the corner, and set off toward the village.

Being free from the musty castle where all the air felt

stale was a blissful relief. I inhaled deeply. The warm spring breeze blew across my face as I walked toward the village. A pointed, thatched roof came into view. I smiled at the memory of Sam and Tildy nursing my father and the rest of the Merry Men back to health as I passed their cottage. However fond of memories as I might have had there, I had no desire to talk to Sam. Or rather, listen to Sam prattle on for hours. Besides, it was safer if the few people who knew my real identity were kept in the dark.

The village center was a bustling, busy place. Shops lined the main street, and shopkeepers called out eagerly, keen to draw in business. Most of the items held no interest for me. I had no use for silly things like tapestries or jewelry. What an utter waste.

There was a rather impressive display of knives that caught my eye. I wandered over and inspected them closely. Whereas the other shop owners had been trying to attract customers, the man whose stall I was at was unimpressed with me being there. It could not have been plainer that he didn't think I had the money to purchase nor skillset to handle his merchandise.

"These are real weapons, miss, not toys," he said grumpily. I picked up one of the blades and spun it around in my fingers. "Careful!" he barked. "You could hurt yourself!"

I raised an eyebrow. "The balance is off, anyway." I set down the knife. The shopkeeper rolled his eyes at me. I felt annoyed. Who was he to decide who should or should not have weapons?

"You had your fun. Now move along there, miss," he said, and made little shooing motions at me, as if he was driving off a stray cat. Anger rippled through me. If he had any idea who I was...

"I will move along when I feel like it," I said coldly. "Customers have a right to inspect merchandise before purchasing, do they not?"

The shopkeeper huffed and glared daggers at me. "Go on and inspect then, but don't blame me if you get hurt!"

I frowned. "You really think you are something, don't you?" After Leopold yesterday, I'd had it with arrogant men. "Can you even throw one of these things?"

"Naturally," the man said smugly. "Want a demonstration?"

"I would love one," I answered.

The man walked to the side and whipped the cover off a large circular board, larger than a man. It was set upright and as the cover was pulled off, it spun with a faint whirring sound. The wooden disc was divided into six differently colored sections, and leather straps hung limply down from where a person would be strapped to the board. Dale had one of these with his minstrel equipment, and Will Scarlet and I loved it. Several people stopped their shopping to watch.

The shopkeeper picked up several knives and backed up several paces from the board. He waited until the board had stopped spinning. "Red!" he called, and threw a knife. It thudded into the red section. The small crowd applauded, and more people joined the throng around us.

"Blue!" he hollered next, and threw again. *Thud.* The blade sank into the blue section.

"See?" he smirked at me.

"I see," I told him. "Can you do it while it is spinning?"

"Yeah, Nero!" someone called out. "Can you?"

"I was just giving this girl a lesson. She seems to think she can throw." He made a mocking bow and offered me the handles of two knives. "Want to try?" The crowd laughed. It was obvious that they expected me to slink away, embarrassed.

"Gladly," I responded. I walked toward him as if I was about to take one of the offered weapons. Then with blinding speed, I drew my concealed knife and yelled, "Yellow!" I spun and threw the knife. *Thud.* It hit the center of the yellow section.

The crowd instantly fell silent. Then a loud "Oooh!" rose up. The shopkeeper, Nero, turned bright red. I walked forward and wrenched the knives out of the board. I flipped the blades and offered him the handles of his wares.

"Spin it," I challenged. "Let's see how good you really are."

His shocked expression cleared. "Well, well, well. I underestimated you."

"Most people do," I said, and gave the wheel a spin. "Throw."

Nero concentrated hard. As the wheel began to slow down, he called "Red!" again and threw. *Thud.* The wheel stopped, and Nero's knife was embedded just above line between red and yellow. It was still in the red section, and the crowd applauded with even more enthusiasm.

"My turn." I said. I nodded to a girl standing nearby. She looked at Nero for permission, who nodded as well. She reached up and with a small grunt, set the wheel to spinning again. I analyzed the pattern rapidly. "Green!" I called. *Thud.* When the wheel stopped, my knife was firmly stuck into the green section.

The crowd cheered wildly. "You've met your match, Nero!" someone called. "I think she is better than you are!"

"No, she isn't!" Nero said, clearly affronted. "She

wouldn't have the guts to do it with someone strapped in there."

"Hop on up and we will test that theory," I goaded. I loved these sorts of competitions. Nero blushed and didn't move.

I reached into Baron's coin purse and pulled out a fat gold coin. "A gold coin to anyone who will strap themselves in!" The crowd went deathly silent. Each townsperson glanced eagerly around. Everyone wanted to see someone spin on the wheel, but no one wanted to take the risk. Several teenage boys nudged each other, but none stepped forward.

"I will!" someone finally volunteered. James walked up from the back of the crowd. I was slightly surprised to see him, but shouldn't have been. I knew he was remained in the area between my and Baron's debriefings with him. Of course he would need a place to stay in the village.

I grinned and flipped the coin to James. "Thank you, my good sir."

The crowd watched with bated breath as I helped to strap James into the contraption. "Don't you dare miss," James said in a low voice to me.

I pulled sharply to tighten one of the leather straps. "Do I ever?" I asked smugly.

I backed up. "Spin him." The girl, who now looked terrified, reached up and set the wheel in motion again. The wheel spun more slowly with James's weight on it, but still quickly enough that it would be a difficult throw.

I watched the wheel begin to decrease in speed. "Blue!" I yelled, and flung my knife. The *thud* of the knife was cut short as James let out a long, loud, piercing scream. In a panic, I rushed forward to stop the wheel. What had I done? How had I been so irresponsible and arrogant? My hands were trembling as I fumbled to remove the straps from James's wrists. His body twitched horribly.

I wrenched one of the straps off of James and heard laughter behind me. What inhumane heathens would laugh at a stabbed man? The knife... Where was it? While I unfastened the other wrist strap, I scanned all over James's shaking body to locate the handle. I didn't see it anywhere. I glanced up at James's face, and saw that his body was shaking not from the pain of being stabbed, but from laughing. The knife was embedded directly where I had aimed it- in the blue wooden section between James's left arm and leg. In my frantic haste to untie James, I hadn't even noticed where the knife had landed. My breath was still coming in choking, ragged gasps.

"I hate you," I told James, and punched his shoulder. Nero was breathless and doubled over, laughing fit to burst.

"You were getting too conceited," James told me.

I frowned and turned the wheel so James was dangling upside down from his bound ankles. Blood rushed up to his head. "Hey!" he protested, and the crowd howled with more laughter. Every time James tried to crunch his body upward to untie his ankles, I swatted his hands away.

"I give up!" James finally cried, arms dangling down to the ground. His face had turned purple from being inverted too long.

I figured he had been punished long enough. I rotated the wooden disc and released his ankles. He stumbled and grabbed at my arm to steady himself. "James, you are truly one of the most sadistic people I have ever had the misfortune to meet," I told him.

He grinned. "I don't get an opportunity like that every day. I had to take advantage of it!"

It had been a long time since I had seen him so playful. Nero was wiping tears of mirth from his eyes as he approached us. "Thank you both for the entertainment! Here," he offered me two knives. "For the lady. Even if they are off balance."

I accepted the knives. "Good throwing today."

"Likewise." All his previous haughtiness was gone. "It was a pleasure to meet you, miss. You are welcome here any time." He hurried off to tend to several customers that lined up at his stall. Our performance had brought him a good amount of business.

After the crowd around the wooden wheel had dispersed, James and I went for a meal at the local tavern. We got several congratulatory comments and slaps on the back.

"You need to be more careful," James said in a low voice. Now that the thrill of the moment was over, his calm and steady manner was back. "It isn't wise to show off like that when you are supposed to be undercover. Why aren't you at the castle, anyway?"

I told him all about my friends who stepped in to help me out. When I described Walter's apprehension of Baron, James frowned. "Did he say why?"

I shook my head. "He said it wasn't for a lady's ears. So who knows? Probably all rumors. Baron has only been Sheriff for a couple weeks."

"Hmmmm..." James said, deep in thought. "Maybe."

I decided to change the subject. I pulled the leather pouch of coins from my bag and tipped the contents into James's hands. "Here."

"What is this?" James asked, then with an anxious

glance around the pub, said softly, "You haven't robbed Prince John, have you?"

"Not yet!" I said with a twinkle in my eye. "No, this is from the honorable Sheriff of Nottingham!"

"Willingly?" James asked.

I shrugged. "More or less. Some will have to go toward replacing this," and I held up the dress I had worn the previous day.

"What about the rest?" James asked.

I grinned. "Give it to the poor. The Sheriff can afford it."

BARON

I plodded down the hall. It felt like that day would never end. I fretted so much about the consequences of having Laurel in the stocks that morning that every time anyone approached me, my insides would clench horribly, prepared to hear that Laurel's identity had been compromised. I drilled my platoon for hours, and carried out two whippings on men at arms who were disrespectful. Before meeting Laurel, I hadn't been bothered by punishing insubordinate soldiers. But now, it disgusted me. Soldiers constantly came to me with minor squabbles, and my captains and officers seemed wholly incompetent and unable to deal with such things. The servants ran away anytime I entered a room. Whatever Laurel had told them had clearly frightened them all.

Being disliked and feared by so many people didn't bother me, because the feelings were mostly mutual. Besides, I had Laurel and the Merry Men. I didn't need anyone else. I pulled out the rusty key to my quarters, inserted it into the keyhole, and turned. The heavy door creaked open. At least half of the candles had gone out, so the light in my rooms was dim and flickering. I closed the door and locked it again, then moved down the short hallway into the main room.

Laurel was there, sitting at my desk. The chair was leaned back onto two legs and her bare feet were propped up on a tall pile of papers. She was perusing some of the reports handed in by my captains and glanced up over the tops as I entered.

"How did you get in here?" I demanded.

"There is no lock that can't be picked," Laurel said slyly.

"I shouldn't be surprised by anything you tell me anymore," I told her, a smile creeping onto my face. I couldn't ever be around Laurel and not smile. "Pickpocket, thief, spy, burglar..."

"It's only burglary if you take something. In this case, I was putting something back." She tossed my money pouch back at me. I caught it. It was significantly lighter than it had been when she had stolen it from me.

"What did you get? This is empty!"

She shrugged, completely unabashed. "New dress, a few knives, a couple favors. Just the essentials for a simple girl like me." She flashed me that cocky grin of hers that I loved so much. I couldn't ever stay mad at her.

"Huh. So, I am giving up all my wages, my time, my sleep, my previous life, and I am constantly in danger of being discovered and betrayed... Remind me what I am getting in return?"

"Me," Laurel said simply. "So, it sounds like you are getting a good deal." She tossed the reports back onto my desk, linked her fingers together behind her head, and gazed around my room, taking in the drab stone walls and floor. "You could do with a window or two in here. This is gloomy."

"Sheriff's privilege. They assigned me a top security room. Or, it *was* a top security room until you came along with your lock-picking skills."

She waved this away. "Oh, don't worry. That lock took me *at least* fifteen seconds. You are safe and sound."

"Well, to what do I owe the pleasure of a pickpocket's company?"

Laurel swung her feet off the table, plunked the chair's other two legs onto the floor, and stood. She fixed me with an intense, burning stare that made my heart pound wildly. Every step Laurel took toward me made more and more of my concerns about the day trickle away. She leaned against me and tilted her face upward. My previous tiredness and frustration with my soldiers evaporated on the spot. I moved in to kiss her, but she pulled a piece of parchment out of her sleeve and slapped it across my mouth.

"What, you think I broke into your room for *that*? Think again, Sheriff!" she laughed. "I don't know what kind of girl you think I am, because I came here strictly on business!"

"You are cruel," I said.

She curtsied. "Why thank you. I try my best."

I unfolded the crumpled and smelly parchment she had swatted across my face. "Where did you get this?"

"Amazing what John will throw away, knowing that his current maid can't read. I offered to help her this evening because she helped me out this morning. I snuck that treasure out of the garbage. Pretty productive day, don't you think?" Laurel smirked and flopped onto my bed.

"This bed is awful! I don't know how you can sleep at night!"

"With all the work I have to do, I don't," I grunted in reply, lost in trying to decipher the scribbled letters. "I can't read this!"

"Of course you can't, silly, it is in French! So, unless you learned somewhere..."

"Then why did you even fish this out of the trash? You can't read it either, can you?"

"Oh no, I have no idea what it says. I was always too busy to sit down and learn another language." She stared at me, as if the message's meaning was obvious.

"So..." I said, and looked down at the paper again. What use was a letter I couldn't read?

Laurel rolled her eyes, got off the bed, and snatched the parchment out of my hands. "You CAN read who it is addressed to, right?"

"To Prince John," I answered. Any fool could tell that.

She flourished the letter in front of me. "And who do you know that would write to Prince John who speaks French?"

The implication dawned on me; I was embarrassed it took me so long to understand. "Oh." I glanced down to the bottom of the page. A very artistic and loopy signature was at the bottom. The first letter- P- stood out clearly. Of course. King Philip.

Laurel rolled up the paper and swatted it lightly across my head. "I knew you would get there. Now all we have to do is hand this off to James. Friar Tuck speaks French, and James can get it to him to be translated!"

I held out my hand to take it. Laurel nearly placed it in my hand, then snatched it back. "If you give it to James, you have to give me credit! I was the one that rummaged around in muck to find it!"

I rolled my eyes. "Sure."

"I'm only letting you hand it in because it is your turn to meet him. If I had it earlier today, I would have given it to him."

"Not everything is a competition," I said.

Laurel grinned. "If it was, I would win."

"Yes, I remember you doing so well when it was you versus me those times you ran away from camp. How many of our fights did you win? None, last I recall."

Laurel poked me in the chest. "You got lucky those times. Want to go another round to be sure?"

I grabbed her hands and kissed her. "Nope. I already won."

THE NEXT DAY, I MET WITH PRINCE JOHN IN HIS PRIVATE quarters. He was in an unusually agitated mood all morning. He tore several documents in frustration and yelled at anyone who approached the door. I didn't comment on his anger even once. I knew from past experience with my father that it was best to let tempers simmer down with time.

Prince John cast several aggravated glances at me, as if he was annoyed that I didn't want to argue, but I calmly ignored them. I had heard enough of his volatile moods to know I didn't want to aggravate him any more than he was already. I patiently wrote out list after list of supplies that were needed for my men before they would be battle-ready. Prince John huffed.

There was a knock at the door, and a woman called out, "Maid service!"

"Come in!" snapped John irritably. A girl entered the room. She had curly blonde hair and a round, pleasant face. Her clothing was the exact same as all the other serving girls, except that she had added little pink bows to the corners of her apron pocket. She curtsied and began to sweep a feather duster over everything.

"You wrote down '*wooden beams*' twice," John growled, and jabbed a finger at my parchment.

"So I did," I said, and added additional notes to each entry. "The first set of wooden beams is to build barricades and fortify our stronghold. The second set was to create catapults."

Prince John grunted, which turned quickly into a yell of frustration. The maid had passed behind him, brushing a cloth along a bookcase as she did so. While doing so, she had inadvertently swept dust from the shelves that descended upon Prince John himself.

He leapt up in a rage and backhanded her forcefully across the face. She screamed and scrambled backward, apologizing profusely as she went, but it was too late. Prince John advanced on her, striking anywhere he could reach and shouting foul names mingled with a string of oaths. I rose, intending to shield the maid from further abuse, but John had stopped before I reached her. "Out! Get out!" he yelled. The maid held her arms up to her face, where a red impression of John's hand was now visible and rising rapidly. She fled the room.

"Never come back!" he bellowed after her.

After a few more angry huffs, John brushed off the dust that had settled onto his hair and shoulders. I remained silent and unmoving for several minutes while John took deep breaths. Eventually, he looked at me. There was no remorse or guilt in his expression. Instead, there was an unspoken challenge. I immediately realized his intention. He wanted to see how I would react. He wanted to see if I enjoyed violence as much as my father had.

I smirked. "Serves her right. No one should ever treat you with anything less than the dignity you deserve. Anyone who does otherwise should be beaten and dismissed immediately."

John's face twisted into a cruel smile. "I am glad to see we agree, Sheriff. Now see to it."

LAUREL

$\mathcal{T}$he morning bell rang, and I jerked upright immediately. After years of sleeping lightly – ready for a fight at a moment's notice – I couldn't get used to that infernal bell. Each clang vibrated in my head, and I stared around at the other girls, all of whom were either still dead asleep or else covered their exposed ear and burrowed deeper into their blankets.

I leapt out of bed, pulled the blankets tight, and dressed quickly. Agnes was walking the aisles, whipping blankets off girls, cracking her wooden spoon on them, and barking at everyone to wake up. She cast an approving nod at my tidy sleeping area. "Well done, Isabella. Glad I can depend on *someone* to do things right!"

She began to move on, but I forestalled her. "Beg your pardon, Agnes, but I heard a rumor that Gwendolyn left yesterday?"

"Word travels too fast around here," she said, clearly annoyed that I was taking up her time with gossip.

"I would be happy to help with her duties until you can find a permanent replacement!" I volunteered.

Already, I was bored of the typical servant routine. There wasn't enough danger! Working so close to Prince John would be risky. But the greater the risk, the greater the triumph. Besides, I was Robin Hood's daughter! No challenge was too great for me.

Agnes looked distrustfully at me. "Why? No one ever wants more work."

I shrugged modestly and inspected my shoes. "I am worried I may oversleep one day and want to be in your good graces, if that ever happens. I really appreciate having this job, you know. I don't want to lose it. My family needs the money I send back home."

Agnes's prior suspicion melted, and she smiled understandingly. "You are a good girl, Isabella, and yes, it would be very helpful if you took over Gwendolyn's work. Tidy up in the dining hall after meals and then clean out the royal apartments in-between. Just don't annoy his highness, he has some volatile moods."

I bobbed a curtsy. "I will!"

Agnes sighed. For the first time, she looked tired. "I really appreciate your willingness to help, Isabella. It is rare to find someone as hardworking as you. I want you to know- I notice when you are the first up in the mornings and offer to do extra. I won't forget it! Keep this up, and in a few years, maybe *you* will be the housekeeper!" She spoke as though this was the greatest aspiration anyone could ever dream of, then bustled off, all signs of tiredness gone once again.

I grinned at her retreating back, inwardly praising my acting skills. One step closer to success.

I LET GO OF THE LINEN CART AND KNOCKED ON THE HEAVY wooden door with my free right hand. My left was laden down with the heavy wooden bucket filled with soapy suds. I rapped once loudly to announce my presence, then twice softly, as if to apologize for my intrusion, the standard protocol for a servant.

"Maid service!" I called out humbly.

"Come in," a bored voice intoned.

I pushed the door open and awkwardly wheeled the clunky wooden cart piled with linens inside. The door closed behind me, and there was Prince John. His desk faced the door through which I had entered, and he didn't even glance up from his many scrolls spread out across his desk. Even though he was seated, I could tell he was a short man, my height or possibly even shorter, with a barrel chest and dark red hair. What surprised me was the immediate memory of my mother that sprung to mind. Her hair had been brown, but her nose and dimples were exactly the same as John's, and I could tell that, when he stood, he would have been her same height. I had been so focused on getting information out of Leopold at the tournament that I hadn't paid any attention to John.

'*This is my uncle,*' I suddenly realized. Well, not actually my uncle. I think he counted as my first cousin once removed, but I wasn't positive. Any time Friar Tuck had tried to diagram my family history, I had lost interest and tried to sneak out of his lectures.

I quickly hid my surprise at our family resemblance. I was glad that my hair was covered. As far as I knew, John had never been aware that my mother, his cousin, had been married and had a child. He shouldn't know about me at all. Mother had been determined to sever all ties to the throne. I swept a grand curtsy. "Your Majesty."

John still didn't look at me and waved a hand, indicating for me to get on with my duties. *Royalty*, I thought scathingly. *They think they are so much better than everyone else.* Peasants believed the royal line was hand-picked by God to rule. What utter nonsense. Anyone could govern better than the man in front of me.

I quickly entered the side bed chamber and stripped the rumpled bed sheets, switching them for clean linens. I tucked crisp corners, fluffed pillows, and even placed a small dish of spiced pastries I snuck out of the kitchen on the bedside table. I then set to work scrubbing the floor, moving quickly and efficiently. I made sure to wipe down all the surfaces and walls and dusted the shelves of books that were stored along the walls. Gwendolyn must have been rushed or else was inattentive; there was a significant amount of dust that could not have collected since his room had been tended to last.

Once the bed chamber was done, I moved into the washroom. I pinched my nose as I flung the contents of the chamber pot into the moat far below. I grimaced at the memory of when I had to swim across those rancid depths to escape after freeing my father from the dungeons. Ugh. Who would have guessed I would pose as a servant at the very place I attempted to burn down?

After scrubbing the wash basin and refilling the water pitcher, I moved into the chamber I was most excited to study in-depth – the office. This was the antechamber through which I had entered, where Prince John still sat, poring over his scrolls.

I gathered up the rumpled bits of parchment that had been flung to the floor and placed them carefully on the top of the rubbish bin in my cart to examine later. It was far more convenient than rummaging through the trash pile. I then busied myself with beating rugs and tapestries out of the window, wiping down the stone walls, and polishing the brass handles of the doors.

"Beg your pardon, your Majesty, but is there anything else you need?" I asked after I could find nothing else to clean. "May I bring you anything? A meal or drink?"

"Glass of red wine," Prince John requested as he dipped his quill into a nearly dry ink pot, then muttered a curse as the quill refused to write properly.

I dipped a curtsy, which went unnoticed, and hurried from the room. I all but flew down to the kitchen to collect the drink, and then paused twice more. Once, to wrench a dainty vase full of honeysuckle and foxglove flowers from the middle of a table arrangement, and the second time at a storage closet for a fresh ink pot.

Less than five minutes later, I sprinted up the winding staircase, taking it two steps at a time in a most unladylike fashion, all while never spilling a drop. I steadied my breathing as I turned the corner, curtsied to the two guards outside the door, then knocked the same way as when I first entered. A single loud knock followed by the two quieter, more apologetic knocks.

"Come in," John's voice said again.

I entered, bobbed yet another curtsy. "Your Majesty," I handed over his glass of wine.

For the first time, he looked up at me. His eyebrows briefly furrowed, as if in vague recognition.

"Begging your pardon, Your Majesty, but I thought you might need some ink." I offered the fresh inkpot.

His confused expression cleared as he smiled and accepted the ink. "It is nice to see a servant anticipating needs for a change!"

"Your Majesty is too kind." I swept into another curtsy.

My knees would likely give out soon from all this confounded curtsying! It was no wonder women barely thirty years old were complaining of sore backs and weak knees. I walked across the room to place the flowers in the washroom.

"Where are you going?" John sounded suspicious. "Didn't you already clean?"

I dipped into yet another infernal curtsy and held up the vase. "Begging your pardon, Your Majesty, but I thought some flowers would freshen up your washroom. I wouldn't wish any foul odors on our King."

At the mention of *'King'*, John seemed to straighten and hold his head higher. What a pompous peacock he was! First in line for the throne, if something were to happen to his brother, and he still needed his ego stroked by servants. Such arrogance.

"Very well," he said, and waved me on to continue in my task.

I placed the flowers and began to leave. But just as I was about to exit-

"One minute, maiden!"

Down I went again for what felt like my hundredth curtsy that day. "Your Majesty?"

"What is your name?"

"Isabella, your highness."

"And your surname?"

"I haven't one, Your Majesty. I don't know who my parents were. I was raised an orphan."

He nodded, content with my story. "Isabella, then." His attention snapped back down to the leaflets fanned out on his desk. "Easy enough to remember. That is my wife's name. Thank you for the ink and wine, Isabella."

"My pleasure, Your Majesty."

~

LATER THAT DAY, AGNES FOUND ME. "YOU ARE ON permanent duty taking care of His Majesty's chambers, Isabella."

I smiled, satisfied with my success. I now had easy access to John's apartments that would be unquestioned.

"Thank you, Agnes!" I smiled back. "Does this mean I don't have to clean the barracks anymore?"

"Ah, so that was your plan, was it?" Agnes asked shrewdly. "Do an extra good job for his Majesty and you get off of barracks duty?"

I shrugged. "Can you blame me for trying? I get heckled every day down there, and it stinks of sweat."

Agnes laughed. "No, I am actually impressed! Most girls just up and quit. But you figured out a way. Just be careful, you may find you prefer barracks duty. The king can be pleasant at times, but he also has an unpredictable temper."

I nodded vigorously. "I heard about what happened to Gwendolyn. I will be careful!"

Agnes pointed a fat finger in my direction. "See that you remember!"

BARON

*I*t never failed to amaze me how good Laurel was at what she did. For the next month, it seemed like she could do no wrong. No one suspected her. Everyone seemed to like her; she became popular among the servants for her quick wit and confidence. Agnes and Walter sang her praises constantly, saying that they had never had such a dedicated worker. Even Prince John, after one of our meetings during which Laurel came in to clean, said, "That maid is the best one I've ever had. She seems to know what I need even before I do. You know she brought me buttered crumpets this morning? Without me even asking!"

During those weeks, Laurel brought a light and energy into my life that I had never believed possible. Any time I began to feel bogged down by all the heavy responsibilities I had, Laurel's face would shine through my gloom, giving me the motivation to push ahead. She was the reason I wouldn't give up. She seemed to believe anything was possible, and never hesitated to go after what she wanted. Her enthusiasm and optimism were infectious.

She would frequently leave little notes for me, some serious, some flirtatious. She always tucked them discreetly into places only I would look- tucked between reports, in my coin purse, or even in my trouser pockets. I marveled at her stealth in being able to put them there; I never saw her do so. It brought a smile to my face every time I found a new note.

Even with how busy we both were, we would still find stolen moments to be together. On rare occasion, we were able to coordinate so that James met with both of us at the same time late at night in the forest to debrief us. After he left, we would take the scenic way back to the castle. Those were the best times of all- being alone together without the anxiety of being seen. We held hands as we strolled and talked about everything, from our day-to-day doings to our hopes and dreams for the future. We discussed our beliefs and debated our differences of opinions. Every time I saw Laurel, I fell more deeply in love with her.

Despite the fact that I was getting less sleep than I ever had, with double the amount of work, had no family, and felt like I had no friends besides James and Laurel, I was the happiest I had ever been in my entire life. As difficult and dangerous as my undercover work was, I knew I was making a difference. I was finally the hero in the story, not the villain.

LAUREL

*M*y days fell into a familiar pattern. Each morning, I would wake up early, choke down the disgusting slop the other servants called breakfast, and go about my daily duties. I cleaned the great hall after the courtiers and royalty dined, and tried to minimize the damage to the mess hall where the lower ranked servants and soldiers ate. I always tried to avoid the soldiers when I could. Now that Baron's platoon had moved into the barracks, there was the chance I could be recognized. I did my best to remain unobtrusive.

I had to continually remind myself of my role. Baron and I were here to collect information so we could help prevent a war, not to do anything else. Prince John had become comfortable to the point of ~~arrogance~~ complacence during his brother's extended absence, and I longed to humble him. But James continually reminded me that my duty was to maintain my cover and gather any tidbits of information I could until Father returned with King Richard. But despite his reassurances, I longed for more action in my routine.

I could tell that Agnes and Walter genuinely did their best to make life enjoyable for the servants. Agnes would give out little prizes and rewards for the staff that worked hardest each week. On every tenth day, for our day off, Walter would bring in a minstrel or acrobat to perform for the servants as entertainment. The minstrels and acrobats he hired were usually ones that were either just starting out or down on their luck. Their clothing was patched and shabby, but their eagerness for employment, no matter how temporary, showed in the earnestness of their performances.

On one such night, I hurried down from Prince John's apartments. My investigation had yielded no results that day. The only papers I saw were dull and useless. Documents that enumerated trade prices with various countries, and a list that Prince John's wife had written of all her many complaints about the staff. Things had been so quiet that I was beginning to wonder if Father would ever come back.

I saw Walter turning a corner up ahead and broke into a jog to catch up to him. He heard my footsteps quicken behind him, then grinned and began to run as well. We were nearly back to the servant's quarters before I finally caught up.

"Will you hold still for two seconds, you lout?" I teased Walter and grabbed at his gloved hand to pull him to a stop. My grip closed around strangely empty fingers of the left glove, and it slid smoothly off Walter's hand. The glove I had gripped in my hand had wads of cloth stuffed into the areas where Walter's fingers should have been.

I stopped running and froze. I couldn't help myself. I stared long and hard at Walter's exposed hand. I shouldn't have done so; I knew it was rude, and I did my best to avert my eyes. But his missing fingers simultaneously repulsed and fascinated me, and my gaze was constantly drawn back to the grisly sight. The thumb was completely missing, and the other stubby digits only had one joint. I had heard of mutilation as a form of punishment, but this was my first time seeing it up close.

"Quite a piece of work, isn't it?" Walter watched my gape at his stub of a hand and held it up for me to see better. "It's what I got for mouthing off to the captain in my last platoon. Charming man, that one was."

"I'm... I'm sorry, I didn't mean to stare," I stammered.

Walter shrugged. "I know it makes people uncomfortable. It's why I usually wear the gloves." He looked meaningfully at the glove I was still holding. I awkwardly handed it back to him, looking anywhere but at his disfigured hand, and he pulled it back on.

Seeing injuries shouldn't bother me. There was a girl back in Sherwood Forest, Dale's youngest daughter, who was born with one leg oddly short and twisted so that her toes pointed out to the side. Teresa always limped around with a crutch, but had inherited Dale's light-heartedness, and was one of the few girls I could tolerate being around without wanting to rip my hair out. But that disability seemed different from the calculated cruelty of maiming Walter's hand!

Trying valiantly to appear blasé, I commented, "Well, that must have been quite the mouth-off to deserve something like that!"

"Ah, little lady, be glad you will never serve in the military." Walter used his other gloved hand to pat my shoulder. I could tell by his touch that this hand was whole and undamaged. "Places like that aren't for an innocent girl like you. You wouldn't last ten minutes with those brutes."

I solemnly nodded my head up and down to show my absolute acceptance of his statement. "Which platoon were you in?" I asked.

"John's First Battalion."

First Battalion. That was the group that had held me captive. A horrible, creeping sensation came into my gut. "How long ago?"

I wasn't sure if Walter was opposed to talking about it or not, but he didn't seem to mind. "It was about four years ago. I should have known better than to give lip to someone who feels like he has something to prove."

"What do you mean?" The creeping sensation grew more ominous and pressing.

Walter shrugged. "The captain was barely in his twenties and needed to make an example out of someone. His father was the Sheriff of Nottingham, so most of us felt he hadn't done anything to deserve the promotion over older and better qualified candidates. He is the Sheriff now. That is why I was so worried about you when I heard he brought you in for questioning. I make sure to steer well clear of him whenever I can."

It felt like I was learning about Baron's parentage all over again. In the back of my mind, I could hear Walter talking on and on, but time seemed to slow down, and Walter's words garbled together in a haze of sickened disbelief. Buzzing thoughts flooded through my brain, blocking out everything else.

Baron did this? The image of Walter's mutilated hand swarmed into my mind. Then that mental picture was immediately replaced by one of Baron raising his sword high over his head, an ugly look overtaking his face... I forced the image out. It made me physically ill to think about it.

It couldn't be true! Baron was kind and compassionate. He was the one who made sure I had been fed and kept warm during my captivity. He cared about me. He was the one who risked everything to set me free. Baron was the one who was working ceaselessly to help the Merry Men, who wanted to be inducted as a fully-fledged member. Baron couldn't have done such horrific things... could he?

Walter's words faded in and out, but I couldn't concentrate on them. Memories of the Sheriff shouting that I had no idea what things Baron had done, that I would never love him if I knew what he was really like... Had he been right? Baron was his son, after all. The Sheriff had undoubtedly known him better than I did.

No! No, I couldn't think like that. I knew Baron. I trusted him! Baron was working undercover for us. Baron was calm and generous and patient. I just couldn't see him as a foul-tempered, power-hungry, heartless tyrant. But was he? Could all I knew about Baron be a façade? Was it all an elaborate act he put on whenever he was around me? Could someone pretend that well for months and months? Isn't that what I was doing right now, staying undercover? What if, all this time that I thought Baron had been on our side, he was just infiltrating our ranks, and was passing the information back?

I wanted to scream with frustration. I couldn't tell what was real and what was not! All that time I had been held prisoner; he had never mistreated me. Ever since I had escaped, he was on my side. He loved me. All this time we had been at the castle together, he had never betrayed me.

He couldn't be the man Walter was describing, he just couldn't! But even if it was him, Baron had changed, right?

He had forsaken his previous life to be with me. To join the Merry Men. Then again, could anyone really change that much? Could Baron really switch his personality and inclinations to be the complete opposite of what he was raised to be? I tried to imagine myself in his position, choosing to alter myself completely like that. I doubted it would ever last. How long would it be until Baron relapsed into his old ways?

Walter continued to talk, but I was only vaguely aware of nodding my head and agreeing with whatever nonsense he was spouting out. The entirety of my mind was encompassed with the repulsive image of Baron's face twisting into a demented, cruel smile just like the one his father had. Could I ever stay with someone who had intentionally and brutally tortured people?

I recalled how frightened I was of Baron after we returned from being pushed off the cliff. How he was about to whip the man who pushed us, but at the last minute decided not to, claiming that doing so would have killed him, and he wanted him to stay alive to suffer. How could I have been so blind? That wasn't kindness, that was cruelty! The words Baron had muttered months ago resurfaced in my mind, "*I am a monster.*" He was right.

"Izzy? Isabella?" Walter reached out and shook my shoulder. "Are you alright?"

"Oh, sorry, I am just tired. Cleaning all day, you know." I faked a fatigued smile.

"Best get some rest, then. That morning bell comes early! But just think- it isn't long until Festival Week. You can have some fun and catch up on sleep then." Walter clapped his undamaged hand on my shoulder, gave me a tiny, reassuring squeeze, and left.

I slowly walked back to the servants' quarters, but I couldn't sleep. I had to know the truth.

BARON

I sighed. I had spent all day reviewing the troop's drills, and they were far from adequate. There had been more than a dozen quarrels amongst the soldiers, I still had to meet with all the captains that night, attend to the lengthy reports handed in that day, write up a summary of all those reports to give to Prince John, *and* I was supposed to meet James in the forest at midnight.

I ran my hand through my hair and blew out a long exhale. I had never admired my father before, but knowing that he had managed to handle this immense workload was impressive. Subtracting out the double-agent work, of course, but still...

Soldiers saluted as I passed them in the hallways. "Sheriff!" they called respectfully. I kept my eyes straight forward, and didn't acknowledge anyone. That was what Father had always done, and what I intended to do as well. Father had ignored more of the men-at-arms because he considered himself to be several classes above them. But I had ulterior motives. There was only a short amount of time before I betrayed them all. The less I knew about them, the easier it would be.

I had no reservations about stabbing someone like Dominic in the back. But some of the other men like Sebastian would prove to be more difficult. There were some good soldiers, genuinely good people, but they were just on the wrong side of the battle. I couldn't go to them and ask them to join me in bringing down their leader. My position was already precarious enough as it was.

I opened the door to my private room, then locked it once I was through. I pressed my face against the door and momentarily closed my eyes. With a few hours until the captain's meeting, I may have enough time to get caught up on the infernal reports that had begun to over-flow from my desk.

A soft noise from the corner alerted me to someone else's presence in the room. I whirled around. A cloaked figure threw back their hood. It was Laurel.

"You shouldn't be here! Anyone could recognize you!" I told her. She didn't often visit me in my quarters, but I was always glad to see her. I went over to hug her, but she backed away and held up her hand to stop my advance. She had a hardened, angry look in her eyes. I was baffled. What was she mad at me for?

"What?" I asked.

"Did you do it?" Laurel said in a choked voice.

"Do what?"

"My friend Walter! His hand is missing his fingers. Did you do that?"

I swallowed. I had to be honest. "Yes."

Laurel closed her eyes. "Was that the only time? Or were there others?"

I hesitated. I wanted to lie. I wanted to claim that it

was an accident. I knew Laurel would hate hearing details from my former life. But I also knew I had to tell her the truth, and while she hadn't intentionally maimed people that I knew of, her past wasn't all roses either. "He wasn't the only one."

Laurel shook her head at me. "How could you?" she looked disgusted.

"You have to understand, that was before!"

"Before what? You decided that a life of torturing people wasn't for you? You had a blissful epiphany and saw the light?" The venom in her voice took me aback.

"You aren't being objective," I said calmly. If Laurel would look at this logically, she would realize that she had no room to criticize. "You've injured people during your missions too. You don't hear me berating you for that, do you?"

"Self-defense is different from intentional mutilation!" she nearly shouted. I shushed her, anxious about the guards outside hearing her voice. Laurel was so impatient! She was quick to action without thinking things through carefully first. It would be her downfall.

"Should I tell that to the families of the men you killed when we were springing *your* father from prison? It seems like you shot first and asked questions *never* in their cases. A few fingers look pretty good in comparison to that, don't you think? You don't understand what it is like! Not all of us can flip our hair and bat our eyes when we want someone to do what we want."

"I didn't hear you complain when it was *your* neck I was saving! Sometimes, I have to take a life, but I never torture people just for the fun of it!" Laurel shot back.

"I *don't* torture people just for the fun of it! Didn't you say that you would forgive me my past if I would forgive you of yours? Were you lying when you said that?"

Laurel angrily shoved me aside and stormed toward the door. Her hypocrisy astounded me. How was it that Laurel felt like I was the one in the wrong here? Yes, I had carried out some heinous atrocities in my life, but I had repented of them! I had changed. But here Laurel was, condemning me for actions I perpetrated long ago while taking none of the credit for her own! Was I supposed to stand by and take that abuse?

But just as her hand reached for the latch, a knock sounded on the other side. "Sheriff?" a soldier's voice floated in. "Are you alright in there?"

"I am fine!" I responded quickly, and waved Laurel away from the door. She crossed her arms, huffed, and didn't move an inch.

There was a pause. "We heard a voice."

"That is me talking, you morons!"

Another pause. "It was a woman's voice."

I glared at Laurel. Yet another consequence of her hasty, impulsive actions that I had to cover up. "Yes, I have a woman in here, you imbecile! And we want to be alone! Now get lost!"

"Oh!" the soldier began stumbling over his words. "I see, I see. Well, in that case, perhaps I should…"

"Get lost!" I roared through the door.

His footsteps shuffled down the hallway, and I heard him wheeze, "The Sheriff doesn't want to be disturbed right now, he is entertaining a lady friend." His remark was met by several hearty guffaws.

I waited until the sound of his retreat had diminished, then eased open the small sliding panel in the door so I could see who the soldier had been talking to. Several soldiers from my platoon were milling around in the hall. Some sat rolling dice. A few stood leaning against the stone walls under a torch bracket, talking in low voices. Several would know Laurel from her time as a prisoner. Any one of them could recognize her if she walked out. She had been too conspicuous and memorable of a hostage for them to have forgotten, even if they did all believe her dead.

I closed the thin wooden panel and ran my fingers through my hair, thinking. I had a meeting soon. I had to get Laurel out safely by then. How long were the soldiers going to be there? Or were they all waiting to talk to me about more stupid rows they had amongst themselves?

I heaved a sigh. Laurel had pulled back from the door and was sitting on my bed, arms folded and glowering for all she was worth.

I resisted the urge to say something like, '*Now see what you did!*' to her. I didn't want to fan the flames any more than I had already done. If I left Laurel alone long enough, her anger would fizzle out.

I crossed to my desk and began rifling through the sheafs of parchment stacked on it. The hourglass dripped slowly as I painstakingly reviewed report after report, all the time feeling Laurel's heated gaze trying to burn a hole through my head.

"Pretty normal for you to have women in your room, is it?" she asked snippily after a long time. "They didn't seem too surprised by your story. After the dance that night, did you bring your date back here then brag to everyone about it after?"

"You are going to be mad at me no matter what I say, so I am not answering that," I responded delicately. Of course I hadn't had other girls here; she should know that!

It seemed like Laurel *wanted* to have a fight. Someone between us had to be rational.

Every half hour, I would get up and pull back the sliding pane on the door to check if the coast was clear yet. But still the men remained. I cursed them under my breath. It would look too suspicious if I ordered them to leave. Or I could leave the room and command them to follow me... I ran through the possibilities, but none of the options I thought of seemed good enough to keep Laurel safe from detection.

After one such trip, Laurel spoke up. "I can go out, I'm not afraid of them."

I refrained from rolling my eyes. "Even if you aren't afraid, they could blow your cover. I won't let you go out."

She stood, face nearly as red as her hair. "Excuse me! *You won't let me?* You, Baron Blackwellson, do not own me! I am not property! You don't control what I can or can't do!"

Ugh! Why did she always take everything I said out of context? Why were relationships so incredibly difficult? I didn't know how to handle this! "I know that! What I mean is... you just need to think!"

"Oh, you are saying I don't think? You are saying I'm stupid, aren't you?" With every few words, Laurel stepped closer to me, until she was right beside me.

Argh! It seemed like she was purposely misinterpreting my words and twisting everything I said. I inhaled slowly and deeply. "No, you know I don't think you are stupid. But you *are* impulsive! You act without thinking of the consequences of your actions."

She grabbed my water skin from my bedside table and splashed some of the water over my head. "Oh look, there is me being impulsive! I just can't control myself!"

Women! I coolly wiped the water off my face. "Was that really necessary?"

Laurel got up and backed toward the door. "Ooh, look, here is me being impulsive, walking to the door! Maybe I will get caught and blow the entire mission! Wouldn't that be fun?"

"Laurel!" I hissed. "Stop it! Just calm down and think, would you?"

She crossed the room in a few swift strides and poked me hard in the chest. "That is the problem with you, Baron! You are always thinking and never *doing!* You analyze everything to death, and it is really annoying!"

"Anything would annoy you right now; you have a temper," I informed her.

Her cheeks flushed angrily. "Oh, but you don't, huh? How about that little temper tantrum that you threw when we first came up with this whole undercover idea? Then it was *you* acting like a two-year-old and yelling at everyone."

I was determined not to take her bait. I had only done what I had to try and protect her, and I wasn't going to apologize for it. "I had to show everyone how serious of a situation they would be getting themselves into! None of you were thinking ahead! Someone can get hurt or die and no one seemed to care!"

"No one cared about what? Your individual safety? Poor baby, you're worried that your own personal comfort is more important than our country's future?"

"I joined your little band, didn't I?" I shot back. I wasn't going to let her bully me. "Didn't I just agree to run around in the woods wearing tights for the rest of my life and then you all sent me away right after! It is like you don't even want me around!"

Laurel stared hard at me for a long time. I refused to break eye contact. I wasn't going to be someone's punching bag. Especially when that someone was being completely irrational.

"Why do you even want to join?" Laurel finally asked.

The question caught me off-guard. "What do you mean?"

"Are you joining us because you actually believe in what we are doing, or because you thought I wouldn't want to be with you, if you didn't join?"

I hesitated to answer. This interrogation was absurd! I resisted the impulse to get angry. The truth was, I never would have left my father's camp at all if Laurel hadn't asked me to come with her. I certainly never would have sought out Robin Hood to follow in his footsteps. And, if I had refused to consider joining, Laurel *would* have left me, simple as that. But now that I had lived among the Merry Men, I did believe in their cause. I wanted to stay.

"That is irrelevant. I am here now, and I am working on the same mission you are. I thought we were a team."

The fury was slowly fading from Laurel's eyes, replaced with a different emotion I couldn't quite place. "I thought we were too," she said sadly. "But I was wrong. We are too different. This isn't going to work out between us."

It suddenly felt like there was no air in my lungs. There was no air in the entire room. I was falling, falling into nothingness. She couldn't mean...

"Wait, wait, wait. Let's sit down and think about this!" I began.

"No!" Laurel's anger flared up again. "I am done thinking about it! I thought we could figure this out, us being together, but we clearly can't. Didn't you want me to think ahead? Well, congratulations, now I am! Are you happy now?"

I opened my mouth to speak, but no words came out. A whine of panic began in my brain and overwhelmed the rest of my senses. She was leaving me. I was going to be alone. "No..." I croaked. I wanted to beg and plead for her to stay. I knew I shouldn't have to apologize for being right, but I was willing to if it meant I could keep Laurel.

"Goodbye, Baron."

She kissed me briefly on the cheek and moved toward the door.

"They will see you!" I had to stop her. I had to explain. One fight wasn't the end of the world. It was just one argument! If she would just stay, we would make up. I would apologize. I could fix it! She had to stay.

"But I am impulsive, remember?" Laurel snapped. She pulled her cloak hood down over her head, flung open the door dramatically and screamed, "What is *that?*" and pointed down the hall. Every head swiveled to look in the direction she had indicated, and by the time they looked around, she had darted down a side corridor.

She was gone, taking many of my hopes and dreams with her.

LAUREL

*T*hat arrogant, condescending blockhead! How had I been so deluded as to think I ever loved him? He was controlling and critical and never showed an ounce of emotion! I stomped back to the servant's sleeping quarters. No one followed me. '*See, Baron,*' I thought, '*I know what I'm doing. No one caught me.*'

Impulsive, indeed. I would show him. I would figure out a way to get all the information we needed without his help. I didn't need him. I didn't need anyone.

I didn't even bother to undress and put on one of the ludicrous nightgowns the servant girls always wore. I flung myself down onto my straw tick. I was angry at the world.

BARON

*I*t was nearly midnight. I hadn't focused on anything my officers said at our meeting. Everything felt foggy. Laurel left me. She was gone. My father's dire prediction floated back to me, *"She will hate you and abandon you and then you will be alone with nowhere to go."*

I wondered if this situation meant I was automatically disqualified from ever joining the Merry Men. They had become like family to me – the only friends I had in the entire world. Without them... what was I supposed to do? Would James even show up to our midnight meeting? Maybe Laurel had already told him about what happened and they would forsake me now. Maybe they would pretend to include me out of fear that I might expose them, then drop me when I was no longer useful.

I sat at my desk and read the same line of a report over and over. I didn't understand a single word. The things I said to Laurel kept echoing in my mind. I shouldn't have said them, but they were true! Laurel needed to be aware that when she behaved erratically, she was endangering herself and the rest of us as well. I knew she would never willingly divulge information, but if she didn't think about her actions and was captured...

I thought back to some of the terrible deeds I had done in my past, and the things I had witnessed others do to pry information out of reluctant sources. I knew Prince John's officers far better than the Merry Men ever would. These officers would not hesitate to torture her. Their methods would break anyone. I couldn't let that happen. I needed to protect her. Even if she hated me and there was no chance of reconciliation, I had to keep her safe.

I heaved myself upright and grimaced as my feet took on my full body weight. I was exhausted. Physically, mentally, and emotionally exhausted. Every day was spent drilling troops, then I still had to stay up past midnight each night to play double-agent without showing my hand to Prince John. And now, on top of that, I had to deal with picking up the pieces from a broken relationship and find a way to protect someone who now hated me. Laurel had been the one bright spot in my life, but now that light was gone. My future seemed gloomy, dismal, dark, and empty.

I pulled open the door and set off down the barrack hallways. I needed to meet James, assuming he would show up. I stomped across the corridor. A few maids were polishing a suit of armor in a nearby alcove I passed.

"He is a petulant one, that one is," I overhead one of the maids say to a new trainee in an undertone. "One can never tell what he is thinking. Don't you get on his wrong side! He can turn very nasty, I've heard."

I acted as though I hadn't heard them. Was that what people thought about me? That I was a dark, brooding character to avoid? Everyone treated me like I was dangerous. Laurel was the only one who had never been afraid of me. Everyone else told me what they thought I wanted to hear because they didn't want to get on my bad side. Laurel always told me exactly what she thought.

I missed her. I missed her independence. I missed her fiery spirit and quick wit. It had only been a few hours since we split up, but already, I wanted her back. I had no idea why people thought I was terrifying. I was a sap. If anyone ever found out how much control I had let a girl have over me, I would be laughed at.

I trudged on. One of the guards at the gate heard my boots approaching and turned. I straightened my back to my fullest height and forced my face into an ugly sneer.

"Out for another late-night stroll, Sheriff?" he asked after saluting.

"Can't sleep," I barked. "Too many people asking nosy questions. Now lower the drawbridge at once!"

The guard who spoke clamped his mouth shut and saluted again. He stepped back smartly and allowed me to pass, and his companion gestured for the drawbridge to be lowered.

I marched off, over the moat, and out into the forest beyond. I made no attempt to quiet my footsteps. It felt satisfying to crash through the underbrush. Every time a thick branch snapped under my feet, I felt slightly better. I wanted to vent the frustration I felt into something, and nature didn't talk back to me. Nature didn't interrogate me about past misdeeds. It just allowed me to crunch and kick everything I could.

James was waiting for me in the clearing. In the dim light from the moon, it was difficult to see him. It wasn't until he waved me over to where he was sitting that I was able to pick out his thin profile. Even if he had already talked to Laurel and was only pretending to still be on my side, it was good to see a friendly face.

"It is a wonder you are a tracker. I could hear you coming a mile away," James teased when he saw me. "Thought you were a bear for a bit there."

I grunted and sat down heavily on the other end of the log James was seated upon.

"Bad day?" James asked after a few moments of silence.

I didn't want to talk. I feared if I opened my mouth, I would say something else that would drive away one of the few remaining friends I had. If he really was still my friend.

"I will just give you a quick update, and then you can get back for some sleep." James suggested. "I won't keep you long. I know you have a lot to deal with."

Did he know? James started to babble about how our information helped Robin Hood find where King Richard had been kept, but Richard had already been moved, so they are looking for him again, and blah blah blah. There was something about Philip's army coming closer and the report Dale and Will Scarlet sent in, but I couldn't focus.

"Stop," I finally said. I hadn't comprehended anything he was saying, and it would be useless for him to keep talking when he would have to repeat it all again anyway. I closed my eyes and pinched the bridge of my nose.

James fell silent. We sat for a few minutes. I could hear insects chirping, an owl hooting, and a snake slithering somewhere nearby.

"Did you talk to Laurel today?" I asked eventually.

"No, I haven't seen her in the past three days," James responded. "We are supposed to meet tomorrow."

So he didn't know yet.

"Is anything wrong?" he asked.

I swallowed hard. He would find out eventually. Better sooner than later. And better from me than from Laurel.

"We aren't together anymore," I said. I was glad to hear there was no shake in my voice. I stayed calm and collected. I didn't want people to think I had dissolved into a blubbering mess because some girl decided she and I weren't meant to be.

"I see."

We sat for a long time without speaking. That was one thing I liked about James. I could sit in silence and not be expected to fill every moment with talking or joking or laughing. James understood what many of the others did not- sometimes the best thing you can say is nothing at all. It wasn't ever awkward to sit in silence with James.

It was I who spoke first. "It was her idea."

"I figured," was James's simple reply.

"What is that supposed to mean?" I demanded. Did everyone think I was so desperate that I wouldn't ever suggest Laurel and I go our separate ways? That I was a hopeless romantic who couldn't imagine life without some girl? Did they think Laurel was indifferent to me and it was only a matter of time before she left me?

"Just that Laurel can be flighty. She acts first and thinks later. She is..."

"Impulsive?" I supplied dully.

"Exactly."

We sat in silence again. It was good to know that it wasn't just me that saw those things about Laurel. I still felt a little miffed that he hadn't thought for a minute that I could have been the one to call it off, but also vindicated that James thought she was impulsive and flighty too.

"Do you want to talk about it?" James asked.

It was so dark I doubted he saw me shrug. "I don't know."

"How about I tell you what I think," James suggested, "and you can take it as just my opinion and ignore it if you want to, okay?"

"Okay."

"Laurel needs you more than she realizes, and much more than she would ever admit. Laurel feels like she has something to prove. She is Robin Hood's daughter, so she believes that she has to live up to his name, *and* she is the first woman in our group. Those are big shoes to fill. Because of that, she feels like she has to be tougher than anyone else. She thinks she has to show that she doesn't need anyone's help. Everyone expects so much of her; she has a longer way to fall if she fails at anything, so she does everything in her power to avoid appearing weak."

I listened. I hadn't ever thought about it like that before, but it was true. What James was saying made sense. He continued.

"When we first saw her with you, everyone was a bit shocked. Honestly, we all thought she was stringing you along just so you would help her escape and break us out of prison. But then I realized how different she is when you are around. She doesn't have to be strong around you. She can relax and have someone to lean on when she needs it. She really loves you; you know."

"Not anymore," I countered.

"Why do you think that?"

"I said... stuff... today. She got really mad at me."

"She will get over it. Just give her time."

"I dunno."

"What did you say to her?"

I hesitated. I didn't want to repeat what had been so

offensive, but James did seem to be genuinely concerned for me. He understood Laurel. "That she doesn't think ahead and is impulsive."

James laughed.

"It isn't funny!" I said angrily.

He stopped laughing. "I am sorry. You are right, it isn't funny to you."

"But it is to you, huh?"

James chuckled under his breath. "I laugh because I think each and every one of the Merry Men has told her that she is impulsive and arrogant at least twice. Her father usually told her daily. She always reacted the same. Once she threw soup all over Little John. Dumped it right over his head."

"She threw water on me today."

James laughed again, though quietly. "At least it wasn't hot pea soup."

I could just imagine a younger Laurel, furious that someone had suggested a flaw in her character, react by dumping a pot of soup on them. I smiled wistfully. She was so dramatic sometimes. It had usually been entertaining, but it wasn't today.

"She needs you," James said. "You ground her in a way no one else does. I know that can't be easy for you. She can be stubborn and headstrong."

"Yeah, she can be," I agreed.

"But she is also courageous and determined and clever..."

"And beautiful," I added morosely. The most beautiful girl I had ever known. Laurel was the most enchanting girl I had ever met. Witty, resourceful, confident, deadly if you crossed her path... There was no one else like her.

James nodded. "She has a lot of qualities, some good

and some bad. We all do. You have to decide if you like her good qualities enough to put up with the bad ones. And I am not saying that it is all on you. Relationships go both ways. I'm sure she thinks you have good and bad qualities as well."

"More bad than good," I muttered dejectedly.

"My wife used to always say that when we fought," James said quietly. "But only when we fought. People say things they don't mean when they argue."

I forgot that James had been married. He was almost fifty, and his wife passed away ten years before. They hadn't ever had children. Robin Hood told me that James used to be more energetic and fun-loving, but he had changed after his wife's death. He rarely spoke about her.

"I think she meant what she said," I sighed glumly.

"Oh, there is always some truth to what they say. That is why it hurts so much. And that is the danger of relationships. But if you only focus on one flaw, which is what happens during a fight, then it seems like a bigger deal than when you look at the whole person when you are calm."

I knew James was trying to help. But this didn't help me at all. I wouldn't be able to salvage my relationship with Laurel. It was already over. She had called it off. And if we weren't together, how could we both be members of the Merry Men, if I was accepted? It would always be awkward and uncomfortable.

"Do you still care about her?" James asked.

"It doesn't matter if I do or not, does it?" I said coldly. "She doesn't want me."

"She will once she calms down. I've known Laurel her whole life. She will be too proud to admit it, but once she realizes what she lost, she will regret her hasty decision."

Again, this didn't help me at all. Even if she did decide that she wanted to get back together, I didn't want to be at her beck and call all the time. I wouldn't grovel. I wouldn't let her feel like I was easily disposed of whenever she couldn't be bothered with me. I was done being ignored. Maybe I would go on and find someone else who wouldn't cast me off so easily! Maybe it would be someone who was even better than Laurel!

I sighed. I was kidding myself. I hadn't met another girl who was even a tenth as captivating as Laurel. Of course I still cared about her. Of course I still loved her. I couldn't just shrug off those feelings. I hated feeling like I was a slave to my emotions. But I would have to get over it. I couldn't be with someone who didn't want me back. Although... James seemed to think there was still a glimmer of hope. But then again, I debated, he might just have said that to make me feel better.

"Do you really think there is a chance?" I asked. The second I said it, I felt pathetic. I felt like a desperate child, eager to latch onto any shred of hope, no matter how unrealistic their plan. I wanted to retract my question, but it was too late.

James nodded solemnly. "Like I said, none of us ever saw Laurel behave the way she does with you. She may try and fight it because she doesn't want to feel like she needs anyone. But she does need you. She will realize that. Laurel is young and doesn't know how good she had it with you. She wasn't just looking for anybody to be with. And it wasn't for a lack of options. There were plenty of boys back in Sherwood Forest who made plays for her. Little John has a son who was rather aggressive about it. Still is, actually. But she never paid them any attention. She never paid anyone attention until she met you."

James didn't know about my past crimes. I didn't know how to bring it up, and even if I did have the words, I didn't want to confess my previous actions to anyone. That was precisely why I had neglected to divulge everything to Laurel in the first place. I was terrified that James would desert me as well. I couldn't lose one of the only friends I had left, so I decided not to say anything about it. Instead, I went on, "She thinks I only asked to join for her."

"So, what if you did?" James asked flippantly.

So, what if I did? Wasn't that what people had warned me about over and over? The Merry Men said constantly that they only wanted someone invested in the mission around, not someone who was trailing after a girl like a puppy dog.

"What do you mean?"

"Dale never would have joined if Robin hadn't helped him when he needed it. Alan only joined because Dale is his brother. I wouldn't have considered it, and then ended up chasing down Lincoln after he picked my pocket and we ended up in Sherwood Forest. Most of us never went looking to join. It just... happened. And once it did, we chose to stay."

I felt relief sweep through my body. Maybe I wasn't as much of an outcast as I thought I had been. Not everyone else had actively sought out Robin Hood and asked to become a member, as I had thought. Of course, none of the rest had been in a relationship with the leader of the band's daughter. James seemed to read my thoughts.

"We aren't going to throw you out, you know," he said lightly. "Your probation will end, and you will be just as valuable a member as Laurel or Will or anyone. You already are! None of the rest of us could do what you are doing. We plan on keeping you around, whatever happens between you and Laurel."

I inwardly heaved a huge sigh of relief. I may have lost Laurel, but I hadn't lost my friends. I had never had this experience before- being able to talk to a father figure about my concerns. It felt like an immense load had been taken from me, even though my problems hadn't been.

James slapped his knees and stood up. "I have to get going, and I am sure you need sleep too. If you want Laurel back, my advice is to show her you are still invested in this mission, whether or not you are together. Show Laurel this isn't about her. I won't say anything to her, okay?"

I rose to my feet as well. "Thanks, James. You are a good friend."

He slapped my shoulder and walked back into the cover of the forest.

LAUREL

I resolved to never think about Baron again and focus all my attention on my mission. I didn't need him. And I would prove it!

Over the next month, I squirreled away everything I could from Prince John's living quarters and gathered a good amount of information from the scraps of parchment. I did my best to befriend all the servants, particularly the guards who stood sentry outside John's rooms. I steered well clear of the barracks and of Baron's men. Even though I did my best to keep my hair covered and face averted, and was believed to be dead, I didn't want to risk my identity being compromised. I wasn't so much afraid of what they might do to me personally, but I didn't want to let the Merry Men down; they were counting on me. And I certainly didn't want Baron to have any reason to think he was right!

I worked ceaselessly, every day from well before sunup to long past sundown. Agnes marveled at having such a dedicated worker, and Prince John was always pleased. James commended the work I was doing, and how I had been able to furtively work my way into everyone's good graces.

But as the weeks of silence dragged by with no word from Father, I began to grow anxious. Had they been captured as well? Surely, if they had released King Richard, I would have been sent word? Or else one of the letters I fished out of the trash would have had some mention of it. But no- weeks followed without a single update. I felt completely isolated.

"Not every mission is a quick one," James reminded me after another glum day with no news from Father. "Sometimes, it is just a lot of work."

"I know that," I said irritably. "And I won't quit. But I just want *something* to happen!"

"Something that works in our favor, preferably," James corrected.

I didn't respond. I wanted to talk to someone, but the only person I had was James, and I didn't have any more information to give him. Aalis was friendly, but I rarely got a word in. She wanted someone to talk *at,* not talk *to.* Besides, it wasn't like I could confide anything in her. Each day became more and more difficult to resist the urge to seek out Baron. He was always a good listener- so patient and tolerant. Then I had to re-commit myself for about the millionth time to not think about him anymore. I was determined to stay mad at Baron. But it was difficult when I thought of all we had been through together. Every day, I had to continually remind my brain to focus on his flaws, otherwise my heart would take over. I couldn't stop feeling in love with him, and it frustrated me to no end.

Maybe I was just frustrated with my life in general. All the other Merry Men were busy or off on daring missions while I was stuck here, emptying chamber pots and scrubbing tables. I wanted to be done here. I was done with the tedium of a servant's life.

My hands itched to throw my knives again. I needed to practice with my bow. I wanted to do *something* other than patiently wait for more information to fall into my lap. I was finished being patient! I wanted to rally the guards to our side and stage an uprising! I wanted to storm into Prince John's workroom in the dead of night and steal everything he had!

"John finally recovered," James said.

"Recovered?" I asked, confused. Prince John was in perfect health. "From what?"

James looked puzzled. "Being slashed across the chest. You were there, were you not?"

"Oh!" Of course, Little John! I felt slightly guilty- I hadn't given him much thought lately. I had been so preoccupied with trying to scrounge up any information that I hadn't inquired after Little John's health at all. "Yes, I know what you are talking about now. Isn't Peter a healer now?" Last I had heard, Peter Little, John's son, was studying to be a healer.

"Apprentice." James amended. "Sybil took him on. They did a lot for John."

"Good," I said, but I didn't have any heart in my voice. Of course I wanted John to recover. I wanted all of the Merry Men back and safe. I wanted to be back in Sherwood Forest.

"Baron has been-" James began, but I cut him off instantly, as I always did when he brought up Baron.

"Don't you need to get going soon?" I asked loudly.

"No."

I pursed my lips. "Well, the others will wonder where I am if I am gone too long."

James stood up. "I can walk part ways back with you."

I began to stride off. James and I always met in the forest just beyond the moat. There was a small clearing that I liked. It was beautiful on nights where the full moon shone brightly.

"Baron has been making progress with getting Prince John to confide in him," James said.

"Hmm."

"He says Prince John won't make a move for at least another couple weeks. Not until Phillip's army gets here."

I ignored James. I didn't care about anything Baron had to contribute. We had done fine without Baron before he came along, and we could do just as well without him. "I'm surprised he hasn't sold us all out yet," I commented snippily. "I assumed he would have betrayed us by now."

"You know he wouldn't do that, Laurel," James said quietly. "He cares about all of us. You knew that before anyone else."

I snorted. At my core, I knew it was true. Baron really had changed. But there was no way I would go running back to apologize. I would never beg for anything, especially from him.

James didn't elaborate. I wished he would. It felt good slandering Baron. I wanted to vilify him. I wanted to hear someone agree with my accusations. I wanted to find reasons that proved he was an enemy. It would help keep the pain of breaking up with him at bay.

"He probably found someone else already," I said.

James didn't answer. In my mind, I knew I should stop talking about Baron, but it was as if someone else was slowly taking control of my body and forced words out of my mouth. "Only a coward would torture someone. I would never love a coward."

James still didn't say anything. I ground my teeth in frustration. I wanted James to validate me. Or deny the accusations I was making about Baron. Or something! I wanted to argue. But James wouldn't engage at all.

"See you next week, Laurel," he said when we reached the edge of the thicket, then he left.

My shoulders sagged. This mission had started off so entertaining. I had loved having Baron close by and had loved feeling like he and I were pulling the wool over everyone's eyes together. Now, it felt like I was utterly alone. I had no one at the castle to confide in. I missed the camaraderie of the Merry Men when we were all together. I missed Sherwood Forest. I missed the danger and excitement of previous missions. I missed Baron. But my pride would not allow me to admit it.

I shook off my self-pity. *'Snap out of it, Laurel,'* I told myself firmly. *'Whining and complaining won't help. Just get the job done.'*

I hoped Father would be back soon. If he was captured or killed, there was nothing I could do about it from here. Besides, Prince John would not keep news like that secret. If Father had been killed, word would be spread far and wide.

But that wouldn't happen! Father was too clever and canny to be caught. He would be back. And I wanted to be ready with good news and a job well done when he did return. I certainly didn't want him to come home and realize I had accomplished nothing.

I walked back across the servants' footbridge and entered through the small side door. Walter and Otis, one of the guards, were laughing at some joke when I came in.

"Where were you off to at this hour?" Walter asked, still grinning at whatever joke Otis had told him.

"Moon flowers," I said simply, and lifted the small basket I was carrying. "I think they're pretty."

Walter and Otis waved me on and returned to their conversation. As I walked back to the servant's wing, I squared my shoulders. Three weeks. I would give myself three more weeks, and then I would have something to show for all my time here.

BARON

I was resolved to follow James's advice. I gave Laurel a wide berth and redoubled my efforts to prove that I would stay loyal to the mission. My duties often took me away from the castle, for which I was grateful. Whether I was drilling my troops for battle, training captains, or assessing the taxes, I maintained an image identical to that of my father- ruthless, hardened, and devoid of all pity.

Such a façade was easily managed when the only ones who saw were the soldiers. The most difficult times were when we visited the small towns to "assess the tax situation," as Prince John called it. A better phrase would have been "raiding and pillaging the poor." I had never been intricately involved in such dealings before, when my father was Sheriff of Nottingham. As a tracker and senior officer, I would be left behind, or else sent to scout ahead.

Now, it made my stomach churn sickeningly to witness the cruelty and violence that was dealt to the humble peasants. Prince John would list towns that he deemed behind on taxes. I would then be sent with a band of men to force the villagers to hand over any gold they had, or else take what was owed in material goods. I knew Prince John did this because poor peasants who were barely able to scrape out a living would not have the strength or will to fight back. I hated every second of it.

Surely, my pretense did nothing to improve Laurel's opinion of me as word of my doings spread far and wide. But it did put me in Prince John's good graces, and he began divulging more and more of his plans to me with every cartload of gold and goods I brought back. I kept a running list of which villagers most needed help, and updated James. He and Lincoln would then do their best to bring supplies back to those families, or else rob a wealthy traveler and redistribute their fortune.

ON ONE SUCH RAID, WE WERE SENT TO THE VILLAGE CLOSEST to us. One that I knew well. One in which I had stayed.

"No, no! It is all I have!" one woman begged. Two young children clung to her skirts as I ordered my soldiers to capture the chickens in their small yard. There had been nothing of value in the house.

"You should have paid your taxes then!" I thundered.

She began sobbing. Tears ran down her dirty face and she dropped to her knees. "Please, kind sir! Please! Have mercy!"

"It is merciful that I am not taking your children. Be grateful for that, woman," I spat, then strode away. The men laughed and mocked as they gathered up the few chickens she had and took them away. Her sobs seemed to follow me long after I was out of earshot.

My men and I loaded up our cart with furniture, livestock in crates, and bags of coins. The villagers all cowered in their homes as we passed. Mothers shielded their children and snapped curtains closed as we passed. They were all terrified.

The last home we visited that day was set apart from the others, to the side of the road. It had a distinctive, pointed thatched roof. I walked up the familiar path and pounded on the front door. "Sheriff of Nottingham! Open on behalf of Prince John!"

Sam opened the door. When he saw me standing there, surrounded by aggressive mercenaries, his mouth dropped open into a perfectly round circle. "Wha'- wha' be goin on 'ere?" he asked nervously.

"We have come to collect taxes, old man!" I spat. Inwardly I prayed that Sam would keep his tongue and senses.

Sam's eyes darted from me to the soldiers behind me, then back onto me. "I done paid me taxes, I did, er... Sheriff."

"It wasn't enough!" I roared. "You peasants are always trying to cheat your way out of your fair share of taxes!"

Sam looked bewildered. "I don't 'ave anyfink else in me 'ouse, I don't. Our money is all gone, it is."

"We will see about that!" I gestured my men forward. "Search everywhere!"

All the soldiers shoved Sam roughly to the side as they rushed past me. They began to rip open cupboards, empty drawers, and tore open the straw mattress covering.

Sam looked at me beseechingly, but I ignored his pleading stare. I gave no sign of recognition or pity. James would explain for me later. It was obvious that Sam and his wife were desperate to understand. Last time they had seen me, I had been offered an invitation to join the Merry

Men. They had attended my initiation. Now, Sam looked shocked beyond words that I was ordering his enemies to ransack his home.

Tildy was pressed against the wall, close to Sam. She watched in dismay as my company of men dismantled their home, stole everything of value, and carried their possessions out to the heaping cart.

"Thank you for your cooperation," I said sardonically, and slammed the door in their faces.

As always, Prince John was pleased with what we brought in. He had us inventory everything three times before he was satisfied. "Well done, Sheriff, well done," he gloated. "I knew you were up to the job."

I bowed stiffly. Prince John gestured for me to relax. "At ease, Baron!"

"I am at ease, Your Majesty."

Prince John smirked. "More discipline than your father had, I see. Very well. Keep this up and you will be a general very soon."

I inclined my head. "If it pleases you."

"Come and have a drink! You have earned it."

"I appreciate the offer, but I have other pressing matters that need to be tended to."

Prince John flicked his hand at me. "Very well then, dismissed."

LAUREL

$\mathscr{I}$t was my turn to report to James. I had given him all my current knowledge, but no matter what efforts I expended during the week to glean new information, James had already known about everything from Baron. I was irritated that Baron seemed to be able to give so much more information than I could. I felt useless. If Baron was so skilled at spying, why was I even here?

"Little John planned the annual tournament," James informed me. "It starts next week."

I perked up. That coincided with the festival week, and all servants were given a leave of absence. Maybe this was exactly what I needed to cheer up and get my mind off of... I didn't even want to think about him.

"Who all will be there?" I asked nonchalantly.

James smiled in a way that told me he knew exactly why I had asked. "Mostly the families in Sherwood, myself, you if you come, and Lincoln. Obviously, your father's group is too far away, and Philip's army doesn't celebrate festival week, so that group can't get away. And I believe Baron said he was too busy with work."

Good! I didn't want to be around that blockhead anyway. He would probably criticize whatever I did. He would be too busy- he had to juggle being the Merry Men's saintly informant with being one of Prince John's closest advisors. I didn't need him. Maybe I would find someone new to be with. That would show Baron. Someone who was honorable, untainted by his past, and who treated me with respect.

"He really is doing some noble things, you know," James told me. "He has been sending gold back to the villagers he stole from. He won't even let me tell anyone who it is really from. He always says to tell them it is from Robin Hood. Poor Sam was very confused."

I didn't say anything. James often told me stories of how Baron had made sure a widow had a wedding ring returned to her, or how he gave up his own salary to replace what had been taken from villagers. The stories were painful to hear. They reminded me of what I had lost by ending things with Baron. But I also refused to go crawling back to Baron to apologize. Besides, I also had heard stories from the servants. Stories about how Baron had attacked those who stood up to him. Stories about him stealing everything from poor peasants. All the villagers and servants were terrified of him. I didn't know what to believe anymore. I couldn't tell from one minute to the next if Baron was on our side or not. I wanted something, anything, to take my mind off my current predicament. I wanted to get away.

"I'll go," I told James.

I WOULD NEED A MOUNT TO GET TO SHERWOOD FOREST AND back in a reasonable amount of time. The stable boy, Conrad, the one Aalis was still crazy for, was not a bright lad by any standard. All I had to do was get him out of the way without arousing suspicion. I walked back to my lonely straw tick. All the other servants chattered excitedly about their plans for festival week.

"Isn't it exciting, Isabella?" a perky voice came from behind me.

I pivoted and found myself face to face with Aalis. I hastily rearranged my facial expression into one of eager anticipation. "Yes!" I squealed and clasped her outstretched hands. She even jumped up and down, overcome with enthusiasm. I couldn't match that level of girlish giddiness.

She hooked her arm in mine and began to walk down the corridor to the servants' quarters. "What are your plans, Izzy?"

"I want to go home and visit my family," I said. "They are in Barnsdale."

"And...? Anyone else?" She nudged me in the ribs.

"Who else would I visit?" I asked, confused.

Aalis heaved a sigh of exasperation. "Honestly, Izzy! Sometimes I think you have no interest in boys at all! Is there not anyone *special* you want to see? Didn't you say you had someone back home?"

Oh, right. Cue the supposed obsession with boys. Although, I reminded myself, isn't that what I had been doing? At least until I came to my senses and stopped seeing Baron.

"Oh, yes, there is," I giggled, trying to sound convincing. Aalis raised her eyebrows. Oh no, she expected more information. I cast my mind around and settled on Peter, Little John's son that was my age. "His name is Peter."

Aalis sighed, "Well, it isn't as good a name as Conrad, but it will do."

Conrad... A plan clicked into place as though my brain had been working on it for days.

"What are *your* plans?" I asked Aalis.

She shrugged. "Stay here. There will be minstrels and games and food. One year they had an acrobat who could flip across all the tables!"

"Festivals are more fun with company," I commented lightly. "Do you think Conrad will ask you to go with him?"

Aalis sighed again. "I wish! But he is so shy. And I can't ask him! That would be too forward!"

"He already asked you to the tournament dance, didn't he? What if I happened to mention to him that you were hoping he would ask you to attend with him? Give him a nudge in the right direction?"

Aalis beamed. "Yes! But don't make it sound like I really, really want him to ask. Just slip a comment in really casual-like."

"Don't worry, Aalis," I said slyly. "I think all he needs is a *minor* distraction and he won't be able to resist you!"

BARON

"Sheriff!" A soldier jogged up to the roped edge of our training arena. I struck hard at my opponent, and he collapsed. I tried to wipe sweat out of my eyes, but the perspiration on my arm merely smeared across my face. I turned and marched to where a cloth was draped over a stool. I grabbed it and blotted at my face and neck.

"Sheriff-" the soldier said again.

"What?" I barked.

He flinched. "It is just... your horse, sir."

I furrowed my eyebrows. "What about him?"

"Well, sir... he is gone!"

I vaulted over the ropes and set off toward the stables at a brisk pace. "Did the stable boy say what happened?"

"Ah, no sir. It seems he was preoccupied with, erm... a young lady."

Of course. Everyone was obsessed with pairing off for festival week. I marched into the stable. In my allotted stall, instead of my horse, was a note pinned to the back wall by an arrow. I tore it off.

I thank you, sir, for your fine horse.
It will be returned in due course.
He was taken for a purpose good,
Yours most humbly— Robin Hood

Squeezed into every corner of the paper, double cursive Ls were looped to form Laurel's signature. No one would ever know that it was a signature; it looked like an ornamental decoration. The soldier was watching me apprehensively, anxious to see my reaction. I knew if it had been my father, he likely would have flown into a rage. This soldier expected me to do the same. I shook my head. Laurel and her idea of jokes. She would be long gone by now. Off for a week of tournament games back in Sherwood Forest, no doubt. Off for a week of carefree fun while I continued to slave away on the mission she had tasked me with.

"What does it say, Sheriff?" the soldier asked.

I read the paper aloud, then crushed it in my fist. "Search the grounds immediately!" I yelled at the soldier. "If Robin Hood is here, I demand for him to be brought to me alive! On the double, soldier! Go, go, go!"

He scampered off to fulfill my request. I waited for his footsteps to fade, then slowly opened the note again. Laurel's handwriting stared back at me. It seemed to mock my pain of losing her. Only she would have the nerve to steal the Sheriff of Nottingham's horse right out of Prince John's stables and then leave a note. '*Yours most humbly?*' I inwardly scoffed. The irony! There was not a trace of humility in Laurel.

LAUREL

A gloomy haze seemed to linger over the forest; it wasn't quite as cheerful as I remembered. Everyone greeted me upon my arrival. I bobbed my head and waved in acknowledgement, but my heart wasn't in it. I still felt depressed. No matter, this weekend would be fun! Nothing like a celebration and some good competition to cheer me up... But even so- everything looked dismal and bleak. Even the weather seemed to reflect my current melancholy mood. A grey mist hung under the branches of the treetop canopy and extended all the way to the ground. Everything around me looked dull and muted, not the bright, vibrant, energetic forest I knew and loved so well.

"Nice horse!" Peter Little, John's son, called out to me.

"Thanks!" I swung down from the saddle and tossed him the reins. "It belongs to an old suitor. Take care of his pony for me, would you? I have to return him later."

"*Old* suitor?" Peter asked curiously, but I turned and walked away. I didn't want to discuss it with anyone. Not yet.

~

LITTLE JOHN HAD DONE HIS BEST TO HOST A FUN tournament. But with more than half of the Merry Men missing, and after the grandeur of the tournament in honor of the new Sheriff of Nottingham, this one seemed a little lackluster.

Most of the usual events flopped miserably at the beginning. Without the usual contenders, Little John dominated at the quarterstaff battle, I easily won the knife throwing contest, and Lincoln's son, Louis, who had inherited his father's agility, won all the footraces.

Each day had a packed schedule of events, and after two days, the events became more enjoyable. I slowly forgot about my misery at the castle and began to enjoy myself again. Even the sun seemed to shine more brightly. I relished the competition. The more difficult, the better. I had always loved a good challenge.

During the wrestling matches, everyone was paired off and the winners would move to the next round. I did very well for most of my matches. I was paired against several of the youth in Sherwood Forest, mostly boys. I made quick work of all of them. The boys would wrestle each other often enough, but always hesitated to wrestle a girl. I held no such reservations, and within seconds, had them pinned.

It was only initiated members of the Merry Men who gave me real competition. They never held back and had no qualms about hurting me. I was finally paired against Lincoln. He wasn't nearly as large as Little John or Baron, so I had a chance of defeating him, and we were evenly matched in terms of skill. But Lincoln's long arms and legs gave him a distinct advantage; he had a much longer reach than I did.

When our round began, Lincoln wasted no time. He pounced immediately. He drove his shoulder into my middle to knock me to the ground. I clenched my abdomen just in time to prevent the wind being knocked out me, but still hit the ground with a loud *thud*. Several girls among the onlookers gave a loud groan. I spun on the ground to avoid being pinned and tucked my head into my neck so Lincoln wouldn't be able to get one of his long, thin arms around my throat. I rolled away and leapt back onto my feet.

"Go, Laurel!" cheered a young girl's voice from the crowd. I grinned.

Lincoln was back on his feet too, breathing heavily. "You are getting slow, Lincoln!" I teased.

Lincoln grinned back, and ran at me again. I ducked under his arm, pivoted sharply, and jumped onto his back. I wrapped my legs around his torso, locked my ankles and began to squeeze with all the strength I had. At the same moment, I wrapped one of my arms around his neck and forced his head forward with my other. I could feel him struggling for breath and held on tight.

Lincoln latched onto my arm and attempted to wrest me away from his throat. He twisted and turned, but I clung tight to his back and continued to apply pressure to his neck. He couldn't throw me off, and his strength was waning. He finally did the only sensible thing left and fell straight backward.

His full body weight slammed me into the ground. I continued to hold onto his back, even though my eyes were streaming from the pain. He rolled onto his side and reached over his shoulder to grab at at me. I buried my face into my arms to avoid his hands, and he grabbed the back of my tunic instead. I heard a loud ripping sound.

'There goes another good tunic,' I thought, but refused to yield. Finally, Lincoln slapped the ground to signal that he was beaten. I let go immediately and rolled off him.

"Well done, Lincoln," I said, and dabbed at my streaming eyes.

He massaged his throat. "Same to you." He took a good look at my uniform. "Sorry about that, I will fix it for you."

I looked down. My tunic had torn all up the seams along both sides. I shrugged. "It was worth it to beat you!"

"This time!" Lincoln waggled a finger at me. "I will get you next time!"

Little John gave me a shirt to replace my ripped one while it was being repaired. He said it belonged to one of his daughters, but he didn't like her wearing anything that tight, so he was more than happy to give it away.

I was paired against Little John in the final round and lost spectacularly. For several minutes, Little John just stood there while I tried a variety of attacks and holds. I even tried the same trick that I had done with Lincoln, but I couldn't get my legs to wrap around Little John's torso. Nothing worked. Once he attacked me back, I had no chance. He had me pinned within seconds.

MORE EVENTS FOLLOWED THROUGHOUT THE DAY. SEVERAL of the women had a quilting competition, where they presented different quilts and everyone voted on which was the best. Boring. It was the same with the young girls who showed off their stitched samplers. I examined each one to be polite, I but thought to myself that I would rather gouge out my own eyeballs than have to sit and attend to tiny threaded patterns each day.

I saw a crowd clustered around a table and went to investigate, eager for any distraction from the patchwork quilts. Everyone was watching Peter Little and Dalton, one of Dale's sons, play chess. I smiled as I joined the throng. At least chess was interesting to watch. Friar Tuck had taught all of the youth in Sherwood Forest how to play. It was a popular pastime for the children of the Merry Men, but I was a mediocre player at best; I tended to under-analyze the positions and didn't plan my attacks with as much foresight as I ought to.

My father had lamented this fact, and said it made me a poor strategist for battle plans. My response was always that I didn't need to lead an army. I was a spy, not a commander. But I always enjoyed observing chess games. Peter was an excellent player – the best after Friar Tuck. He slowly whittled Dalton's defenses down and began to take more and more pieces. Eventually, Dalton's king was forced to the side and Peter checkmated him.

Applause broke out from the watching crowd, and Peter and Dalton shook hands. "Who is next?" Peter called.

"He already beat everyone," grumbled Dale's daughter, Teresa, the one with the shorter than normal leg. "There isn't anyone left."

"Laurel, how about you?" Dalton called out. I shook my head, but my refusal went unheard. Hands pushed me down into Dalton's vacated seat.

"I will lose!" I protested.

"You aren't *that* bad!" Peter assured me.

I raised my eyebrow. "I'm flattered."

But people were clamoring for me to play. This was supposed to be a week of games, after all. Peter generously offered me the white pieces, so I could move first.

We began with a standard opening series of moves. I leaned forward to study the board, looking for any weakness in Peter's position. There was none that I could see. I bit my lip and slowly moved a pawn up. If Peter took it with his bishop, my knight would then be able to capture the bishop and fork his king and queen. I knew Peter was too good a player to fall for such an obviously transparent trap. It only worked on more inexperienced players. But I couldn't think of any other strategy to use.

Peter took the pawn. An audible gasp went up from the crowd, and Peter instantly realized his mistake! "No! I didn't mean to-"

"If you touch it, you take it!" I said happily and captured with my knight. "Check."

Peter slowly moved his king out of check, and I captured his queen. Peter's fans groaned. He studied the board for a long time before moving again.

Although I was up in material, Peter was too good a player to lose. No matter what tactics I used for the rest of the game, Peter always managed to evade my traps, and captured the rest of my pieces. He eventually checkmated me, but it was close. The closest I had ever come to beating him. We shook hands, and the crowd cheered again.

"Good game, Laurel," Peter said as the crowd dispersed. I gathered up the white pieces and placed them into a leather bag. Peter did the same to the black pieces, and we began to walk back to return them to Friar Tuck.

"If you hadn't blundered the queen, you would have won much sooner," I told him truthfully.

"I wouldn't have blundered, if you hadn't been trying to distract me with your outfit," Peter returned.

I stopped in my tracks. "What?"

Peter suddenly seemed silly with embarrassment. "I only meant... playing girls is different from playing boys. Not that I pay attention to other girls, of course! I mean..."

I grinned. "So, you are saying you almost lost because you were paying attention to me instead of the board?"

Peter's face flamed red. It gave me a smug satisfaction to know how much I was making him squirm. "I wasn't *trying* to look!" Peter said defensively, glanced over, then snapped his eyes forward again, as though he had been caught in sinful wrongdoing.

"That is what they all say," I laughed. "You do know this is your sister's shirt, right? Do you have a hard time not looking when *she* wears it?"

"No! That would be disgusting; she is my sister! It just... just looks better on you!" Peter's eyes remained resolutely forward.

"Does it? I didn't realize you had been paying so much attention to what I look like." I loved watching Peter's blush deepen and spread to his neck and ears. It made me feel strangely powerful, to know that I had the control to make Peter so intensely uncomfortable. It was a terrible thing to be glad about, and it was made worse when we arrived at the largest of all the buildings- the chapel that Friar Tuck used for sermons. It was a stone building with a bell tower twenty feet tall. Peter knocked, and refused to even glance in my direction, so embarrassed was he from our conversation.

Friar Tuck opened the door, and smiled at Peter, who

wordlessly handed the bag of pieces and chess board back.

"How did it go?" Friar Tuck asked in his jolly voice.

"He beat everyone, but I almost won!" I answered cheerfully.

"*You* nearly won?" Friar Tuck asked in astonishment. "Against *Peter?*" He only had to glance once at Peter's crimson face before he understood. "I see."

"Thank you for the chess set," mumbled Peter, and we turned to leave.

"Just a moment, Laurel!" Friar Tuck called. I wrinkled my nose briefly at Peter, then arranged my facial expression into one of polite curiosity and turned back.

"Yes?"

Friar Tuck waited until Peter was out of earshot. "Don't tease the boys, Laurel."

"I didn't! I didn't do anything!"

Friar Tuck eyed me suspiciously, then sighed in a long-suffering way.

"I wasn't doing anything wrong!" I insisted. "We just played a game of chess and he made a mistake and I took advantage of it! You taught me to do that! '*Punish your opponent's weaknesses,*' isn't that what you told us over and over? I am just doing what you told me to do!"

Friar Tuck shook his head and rubbed his temples. "You and your father are so alike."

I smiled innocently, but Friar Tuck shot me a look that told me he didn't believe my innocence for a second.

I HAD THOUGHT THAT OUR INTERACTION AFTER THE CHESS game would dissuade Peter from talking to me, but it hadn't. After his brief embarrassment faded, he became the same old Peter I had always known- calm, dependable, and friendly. It was easy to talk to him. He was a good listener and didn't ever seem bored while talking to me. It made me feel like we were ten years old again. I didn't have any siblings, but I felt like I could count Peter as my brother.

Though the tournament wasn't exactly what I expected, it was still fun. There were games and contests and dances. My favorite game- Escape and Evade, was always a popular event.

During Escape and Evade, the competitors were split into two teams. The first team would be assigned to capture a designated person from the second team. The second team was tasked with helping the designated person escape from the set perimeter before time ran out. They could tackle and hold any of the enemy team, but nothing that would cause a serious injury. You only had to tag the assigned person for their team to lose. It was a thrilling contest of strategy, speed, and subtlety. I excelled at it and was always unanimously elected to represent my team.

Unsurprisingly, when teams were chosen, I was selected to represent our team of five people. I had remained undefeated for the last three years, and Little John's team was eager to see me fail. The rest of my team huddled around while I used a stick to sketch out a rough map of the playing area in the dirt. "Okay, Teresa, you are lookout. We will put you here and you yell when you see anyone coming. Fredrick, you are the runner. Chase down anyone headed our way. Peter, you and Dalton are the last line of defense. I will be here-" I gestured the garden beside the chapel which served as the starting line for our team, "and will slip past everyone after they come looking."

"Easy as that, huh?" Dalton asked.

"It is Laurel!" Teresa said. "She can do anything!"

I grinned at her and shouldered my arrows. "Let's go!"

BARON

I ground my teeth in frustration. I had just carried out the third whipping that day. I envied all the other Merry Men; they had been tasked with easy jobs. Even though most were undercover and in danger if they were discovered, none had to act the part of a brutal, blood-thirsty savage like I did.

I had hoped to see Laurel, to make up with her, but she was avoiding me. I told myself it was for the best; someone might recognize her if they saw us together. After she took my horse, I forced all the men to search the grounds and castle several times. It was fortunate that Robin Hood really had made fools of my father and Prince John so many times before. No one seemed shocked that Robin Hood could have snuck into the castle grounds and stolen the Sheriff of Nottingham's horse.

It was very beneficial for everyone to think that Robin Hood truly had paid a visit. Now, no one suspected he was really tracking down King Richard in Vienna. Despite the supposed break-in of Robin Hood, Prince John practically skipped down the hallways, so thrilled was he at the potential success of his plan in taking over as king.

And all the while, I was miserable. I hated having to be like my father. I hated being tasked with such a difficult undertaking when I wasn't even an initiated member of the Merry Men. But most of all, I hated being apart from Laurel.

With Laurel and James both gone at Sherwood Forest, I had no one. Festival Week only highlighted how alone I was. All around me, everyone paired off and went to games and events. I had become so notorious for my brutality, people gave me a ten foot radius wherever I went. Everyone was terrified of me.

After yet another day of ignoring happy couples, I sat in my room and stared blankly at the wall. I missed Laurel so much that it was like having a continual stomachache. As I glumly pulled off my boots, a curled and yellowed scrap of parchment fluttered out. Instantly, I knew what it was and felt my heart shrivel. It was one of the notes Laurel left me so often when we were together. There was no telling how long it had stayed crammed in the toe of my boot.

I slowly smoothed out the slip of paper and read,

Surprise! How long did this one take you to find? Can't wait to see you again soon.
Love, LL

I had to see her again. I felt like I would burst otherwise. I was tired of waiting patiently. The time for being long-suffering was over. I was ready to fight for her.

LAUREL

"They're coming!" Teresa's shrill voice split the air. "*Everyone* is coming!"

I hadn't expected everyone to come all at once! The horn had barely sounded! The usual strategy was to send a few runners to scout out the area. That was the strategy I had planned for!

"Go, Laurel, go!" Peter urged in a whisper, and scanned the foliage surrounding the chapel.

Several people burst into the clearing all at once. Dalton and Peter sprang into action, but there were too many for them to hold back. Teresa couldn't help physically, and there were five on Little John's team. My intended exit was blocked. I couldn't retreat- this was the starting line! I was hidden behind several shrubs, but it was a meager hiding place and wouldn't serve me for long. I was cornered.

Blast! I couldn't lose! I had a reputation to uphold! Being caught within a few minutes of the horn would be humiliating.

"Where is she?" Little John called loudly. "She is here, I know it! Fan out, boys! Find her!"

Dalton and Peter grabbed at legs right and left, but both ended up pinned. We were outnumbered. I hardly dared breathe. Then, with a stroke of brilliance, my eyes alighted on the chapel. There was no rule that said we couldn't go inside the church. Technically, the chapel *was* still inside the playing area.

Little John was standing on the steps leading up to the chapel's door and scanning the area. I scurried around the side and vaulted through an open window... and ended up crashing down on top of the table. It had lit candles on it, which toppled over me and spilled hot wax on my arms and clothing. I opened my eyes and saw Friar Tuck, who had leapt back from the cushion he was kneeling on to pray.

"Argh, Laurel!" he shouted, exasperation written all over his face. "This is the house of the Lord!"

I immediately heard shouts rise up from outside. "She is in the chapel! Get her!"

"Sorry, Father!" I said breathlessly, and scrambled to my feet. "I will repent on the Sabbath! I promise!"

I sprinted for the stairs to the belltower, ignoring Friar Tuck's lament of, "You never even attend services!" The front door crashed open and Little John, along with another one of his sons, stood in the entryway. I would never reach the stairs in time.

"We've got her!" Little John roared in triumph.

I skidded to a halt and switched directions. I hurdled over the wooden pews and came to a stop in the empty fireplace. Little John and his son were too large to follow me up the chimney. I placed my hands and feet on opposite sides of the chimney and began to shinney my way up.

John tried to squeeze into the fireplace and reach up after me, but I was too quick. I heard a dull scraping noise as I ascended, and felt my quiver snag on protruding rocks several times, but I never slowed down.

"Paul, take the stairs!" John cried, "Don't let her get away! I will guard here! We will get her this time! She doesn't have anywhere to go!"

Up, up, up I climbed. The smoky scent of the chimney caught in my throat, and the ash coated my clothes in sooty blackness, but I worked my way up the tight chimney. Finally, I reached the top and pulled myself out. I looked back and immediately saw the reason for the scraping noise. One of Friar Tuck's metal candelabras had hooked into my quiver of arrows. I tugged it off. I was going to be in so much trouble. I was sure Friar Tuck would say I had broken the eighth commandment by stealing. From the church, no less.

I saw Paul, but he was struggling to squeeze out of the belltower and onto the roof- the slats around the bell were too narrow for him. He was stuck. For now.

I scanned the area below. The other team had sent everyone to rush us all at once. No one was guarding the outer perimeter. I saw Teresa, still seated on the tall stump we had assigned her. With her oddly short leg, she couldn't move quickly. I hastily pulled the ball of light rope out of the bottom of my quiver, arrows clattering onto the roof as I did so. I held a single arrow in my teeth while the others rolled off the slanted roof and plummeted to the ground below. I knotted the rope quickly around the shaft of the arrow from my teeth, and raised my bow.

"Watch out, Teresa!" I yelled. I sighted and released the arrow. It flew through the air, trailing the rope as it went. The arrow thudded home on the stump where Teresa was seated, just beneath her crossed legs.

"Tie it!" I screamed, watching anxiously over my shoulder as Paul began to extricate himself from between the belltower's slats. I fastened my end of the rope to the cross on the top of the chapel.

Paul had freed himself and was teetering his way across the roof, arms held wide for balancing. I hoped Teresa had had enough time. I couldn't wait any longer. I hooked the stolen candelabra over the rope, and dove off the roof. I held onto two of the arms of the candelabra, and it made a zinging sound as I sped down the track. Teresa had done a good job securing the line. Peter and Dalton whooped gleefully as I flew over everyone's heads. I heard someone yell "No!" from the other team.

As I neared the ground, I let go, hit the ground, and rolled to slow myself down and absorb the shock of the fall. Then I leapt up and sprinted toward the unguarded outside perimeter. Several onlookers cheered as they saw me approach the finish line. I lifted my arms in triumph as I neared, then heard pounding footsteps behind me.

I turned and saw the opposing team thundering toward me, with my teammates hot on their heels. But it was too late for anyone to prevent my victory. I pretended to yawn and walked very slowly, backwards, over the finish line. My teammates all began shouting at once. They ignored the soot I was covered in, lifted me up onto everyone's shoulders, and paraded around our small village center. Another year undefeated.

"Way to go!"

"That was amazing!"

Little John's team shuffled up, clearly disappointed, but showed they were good sports about losing. Paul Little slapped my back. "Well done, Laurel, that was your best escape yet! We will get you next year!"

"You can *try!*" I goaded, but shook his hand.

The other team's gloom didn't last long. Everyone won and lost sometimes. Father had always drilled into everyone that it didn't matter what the outcome of any match was. Most important was that you never stopped trying. Several small children started the chant of "Laurel! Laurel! Laurel!"

"That girl will be the death of me," I heard Friar Tuck grumble, then he called out to me. "Laurel! You owe me a new candelabra!"

I couldn't stop grinning.

∾

FINALLY, AFTER I HAD BEEN SET DOWN AND THE CROWD HAD dissipated, dinner was announced, and most people moved off, still talking excitedly about the games. I wasn't hungry; I was still thrilled with my success. I changed out of my sooty clothes into a clean tunic and leggings, and used one of the rain barrels to splash my face and hair clean.

"Been gone so long you can't remember where we have the picnic?" I heard Peter's voice from behind me.

My face was still dripping, so I kept my eyes scrunched shut. I reached my hand out toward his voice. "No, just not hungry. Lend me a handkerchief?"

I felt him place a cloth in my hand, and I wiped my face dry. "Good game today."

"Yeah, that was brilliant! You should have seen the look on Dad's face when you flew right over his head... They will be talking about that one for years!"

I threw the handkerchief back at him. "Good thing Teresa is handy with knots! And that you can wrestle down my pursuers! I was glad you were on my side!"

Peter blushed faintly again. "So, you don't want to eat?"

"Nah, too many adoring fans over there. I figured I would just go for a walk or something."

Peter fell into step beside me. I wasn't sure if I wanted him there or not. I supposed he could follow along; I was in a good enough mood that I was equally content having company or not.

"Remember that time we tried to dig a bear pit?" Peter asked suddenly. "Just there, wasn't it?"

I snorted. "Oh yeah! We dug for three days then covered it up with sticks and leaves!"

"And caught Lincoln instead!" Peter finished for me. "Look, you can still see a little bit of it right here!"

We laughed together, and sat down in the shallow depression.

"And remember the time that we hid up in the trees and dropped acorns on anyone who passed under us?" I said.

"That wasn't just one time! I think we did that at least once a week for a year!"

We went on trading memories back and forth, recounting all the fun times we had shared growing up together.

"So, who was that suitor you mentioned before?" Peter asked abruptly. The fun mood was instantly killed. All the emotions I had tied to Baron came flooding back in a rush. During Escape and Evade was the first time in weeks that I felt like I wasn't pining after him. And Peter had ruined it.

"Baron Blackwellson," I responded flatly.

Peter, bless his heart, was trying valiantly to act uninterested, but it was obvious that he was painfully curious. "The Sheriff of Nottingham's son?"

"That is the one," I said shortly.

"I heard Dad talking about him," commented Peter. "It is ironic, isn't it? You being Robin Hood's daughter and him being—"

"Yes, yes, it is hilarious."

Peter fell silent and pulled up a few handfuls of grass. I felt bad; there was no reason to be snappy with Peter. He had done nothing but be kind to me since my arrival.

"Sorry," I apologized. "I'm not mad at you."

"It's okay."

We sat in silence for a few minutes.

"What happened between you two?" he asked finally. He kept his eyes resolutely down at the ground, and the words sounded forced.

I shrugged. "We were just too different. I thought I could handle it, but I was wrong."

"Were you the one that called it off?" Peter asked.

I nodded. I hadn't seen Baron since I ran out on him. The look he had on his face when I did... My heart sank. It was painful to think about, and I regretted my hasty decision. Baron always made me feel safe. Now I felt like I was on my own again. Always looking out for myself and my mission, and nothing else. For a short period of time, I felt like I could trust and rely on Baron implicitly. I felt like he would be there for me, no matter what. But not anymore. I was back to my old ways, concerned with no one else, an independent loner. But it felt different now. After being with Baron, it was lonely to be by myself.

"I missed you, Laurel," Peter said suddenly, "when you were gone." I could tell he was watching me closely.

I picked at a hole in my sleeve. I didn't return his feelings. Not even a little. But it would be too rude to say so baldly, so I said nothing. I hadn't missed Peter; I missed Baron.

I pushed out the thought. No, that was stupid. I didn't miss Baron! Not at all! His past repulsed me. He had been raised by his father, who was one of the most abhorrent people I had ever met. Baron held me as a prisoner for months! He tortured people! He had committed some truly despicable crimes. I couldn't be with him. He was a villain! If I was supposed to be with someone, it should be a good guy. A hero. Every girl wanted a knight in shining armor, valiantly riding in on a white horse, right? I glanced sideways. Peter smiled encouragingly. I looked away.

I supposed Peter counted as a good guy. He was Little John's son, and I considered Little John to be one of my closest friends and confidantes. They were alike enough. Surely if I was with Little John's son, it would be like having a constant best friend. Peter was studying to be a healer; that was a noble cause. He was intelligent. We had a few common interests. Not many, but a few.

We had been friends for a long time when we were children. We had even joked about getting married when we grew up. Peter was a comfortable person to be around, and he loved Sherwood Forest, just as I did. He wasn't high maintenance or difficult to please. He helped build shelters for widows and nursed sick animals back to health. He was sweet. I should want to be with someone like him.

I exhaled quietly. There was no reason I had to jump

into any relationship at all. I had been perfectly content to stay single and dedicate my life solely to my work for the last five years. I could go back to that. But as I evaluated that option, I felt as though there would be a gaping hole in my life. Father and most of the Merry Men were away on missions. I was lonely. I had no one to talk to. At the end of the day, I would return to my small, solitary living quarters, all alone. This week had been fun, being able to talk and laugh with someone. There was nothing wrong with wanting a companion, was there? I felt so isolated at the castle, surrounded by people but still so lonesome. I wanted a friend.

Peter reached his hand out for mine. I let him entwine our fingers. I made a great effort to try and create a connection between us. I channeled all my attention into our fingers, waiting for that tingle of anticipation to flood my body. I wanted to feel the same spark that I had with Baron. It shouldn't be difficult to find that with someone else, right? I focused hard and tried to conjure up the emotions that had swept through me when I kissed Baron. But I felt nothing. There was nothing that drew me to Peter. There were no tantalizing thoughts of passion. Not a single trace of desire or breathless excitement. There was none of the wild abandon that overwhelmed me when I was around Baron. Just a placid indifference, no matter what feelings I tried to bully myself into formulating.

Peter squeezed my hand. Maybe I wasn't trying hard enough to create a spark. There had to be some chemistry between us! I knew Peter. I liked him well enough. He was a good, wholesome person. Good and wholesome, not boring. I forced myself to smile at Peter. He smiled back eagerly, then inched forward and started to close his eyes.

Great, Laurel! I told myself. *Now you've gone and done it. What are you going to do now?*

Peter leaned in until he had nearly tipped over. I felt pity for him. Wasn't this what I was supposed to want? To be wooed and sought after by an honorable and upstanding man? I should be enjoying this. But still I hesitated. I couldn't kiss Peter. I just couldn't. He was so close, eyes closed, lips puckered up. Unbidden, my mind replaced Peter's face with Baron's, and I was suddenly able to lean forward, almost eagerly. Peter's lips felt cracked and chapped, and our noses bumped in an awkward way. This was nothing like kissing Baron. I instantly felt dreadful.

I ended the kiss almost immediately then leapt to my feet. "I need to go," I told him hastily, and ran back to the stables.

"Wait!" Peter cried out after me, but I didn't stop.

I didn't stop to pack supplies for the return journey. I didn't even grab my water skin. I just mounted and kicked Baron's horse into a full gallop.

We plunged through the thicket, back toward Prince John's castle. I was sickened with myself. What had possessed me to behave so thoughtlessly? I was leading on someone I had no interest in. Someone I would never be interested in. Was I so desperate to have someone in my life that I would take anyone, regardless of whether or not I was attracted to him? I felt dirty. I wiped my mouth with the back of my sleeve over and over, until my lips nearly bled from being rubbed raw, but I still felt tainted.

Why did you go and do a stupid thing like that? the tiny voice in the back of my head piped up.

Shut up, I argued with myself firmly. I wanted to rationalize my behavior. *I'm not committed to anyone; I can kiss whomever I like!*

What would Baron say?

Who cares? I retorted silently. *We aren't together anymore, remember? It wouldn't matter to him!*

Wouldn't it? quipped the voice.

I clenched my teeth. He wouldn't care. He would probably be glad to be rid of me, glad that I was someone else's problem. I hated how much I still loved Baron. It made me feel pathetic and weak, wanting to be with him again. I wanted to stay angry at Baron, but I couldn't anymore. It had been easier to stay angry than examine the raw pain and loss I felt. I reminded myself what it was that I was angry about. Baron had told me that I was hasty and impulsive. What lies.

If you aren't hasty or impulsive, what was all that business just now with Peter? the voice asked.

"It was nothing!" I screamed aloud. The horse reared in fright and I barely managed to cling to its back and avoid being thrown off. Baron had been right about me, after all. But after these long weeks of me ignoring him, would he be willing to reconcile? Particularly after he found out about Peter?

I didn't want to think anymore. I focused on the wild landscape rushing past and closed my mind to everything else.

BARON

*L*aurel would be back. She wouldn't leave a mission incomplete. It was as though I could predict Laurel's actions perfectly. She always thought she was so clever, but I knew exactly the sort of things she would do.

I waited in a dark corner of the stables for two nights in a row. I had dismissed the stable boy, Conrad, for failing in his duties, and no replacement had been hired yet. Agnes had taken pity on the lad and hired him on to work in the kitchens, much to the delight of Laurel's friend Aalis.

In the middle of the night on the second night, I heard the stable door creak slowly open, then the soft clopping of familiar sounding hooves through the darkness. I had been waiting long enough that the moonlight filtering in through the windows made it easy for me to see everything, dim as it was. I waited until Laurel had barred the stable door and led the horse to his stall before I moved. I stayed hidden in the shadows and crept up until I was directly behind her.

"Glad to see my horse is back."

Laurel whirled around and threw a wild punch. I caught her fist in my hand. "You need to learn how to punch better," I told her. "That was pitiful."

"Be glad it wasn't one of my knives!" she snapped, and wrenched her fist out of my grasp. "What are you doing here?"

"I heard some outlaw named Robin Hood stole my horse and I was waiting for him to return it, as he so kindly promised." I lit a torch. It nearly blinded me with light as it flared up. Laurel held up her hand to shield her eyes.

"Put that out!" she hissed. "What if someone sees us together? You were the one that was all worried about that, *weren't you*? Acting a little hasty and impulsive there, aren't you?"

"Laurel, we are on the same team. We are going to be working together for a long time," I said. "Can't we at least be friends?"

Laurel narrowed her eyes and didn't say anything.

"Look, I can help you!" I offered.

"I don't need your help!" she retorted instantly. "Nor do I want it!"

"I know you don't need help," I said calmly. "But we are part of a team. If we work together, we can get this done a lot quicker."

Laurel folded her arms tightly across her chest, and it looked like she was chewing her tongue. She seemed determined to be mad. I thought her anger would have fizzled out. I had given her space for weeks. I forced myself to look her straight in the eye. She stared brazenly back, her jaw jutted out in her typical, stubborn way. The tension between us built with every second.

"So, what is your grand plan?" she asked, at long last.

"King Richard is coming back." I told her.

Laurel's jaw stayed set, but her eyes softened and grew hopeful. "When?"

"I don't know; the letter just came in yesterday. But he was released, and Prince John wants to meet to draw up battle plans."

Laurel dropped her arms. "And my father?"

I nodded. "He is on his way. It will still take him about two weeks at the earliest. But soon."

Laurel's face broke out into a wide smile. "You are sure?"

"Positive."

For a moment, I thought Laurel was about to hug me. She had raised her arms slightly to do so. I wanted her to embrace me, but she held herself back and brought her arms down rather forcefully and patted her legs. "Good!" Laurel said. "I am ready to be done here!"

"Me too," I agreed fervently.

"After this," Laurel broke off and there was a rather pregnant pause. "Never mind." She looked momentarily torn, but then shook her head slightly. "So, we are supposed to just wait?"

"Ideally, we would find Prince John's battle plans for when Richard gets here," I said. "But he keeps them under lock and key in his desk. He won't even show me yet."

Laurel waved her hand, unperturbed. "Locks are nothing. But even I can't break his lock open while he is sitting right there. It will have to be at night."

"What will be at night?"

"Breaking into his office and stealing everything, of course! He will be sleeping in the next room, but that shouldn't be a problem either. It just makes it a little more exciting."

My stomach clenched horribly. I didn't want Laurel to constantly put herself in danger. But she didn't seem worried at all. If anything, she looked eager.

I heard a clanking sound headed our way. Guards. I quickly doused the torch in a bucket, grabbed Laurel, and spun with her out of sight of the window until I had her pinned against a wall. "Let go of—" she began to say, but I clamped a hand over her mouth. She tried to wriggle free, but I held her so tightly that she couldn't escape.

"Shhh!" I listened hard. "Someone is out there."

Laurel grew still. We were so close that I could feel her hair underneath my chin and heard her quiet breathing. I could only see a sliver of moonlight across her face. We were both motionless as the clanking walk of the soldier on duty grew louder and louder. When it sounded like he was just outside the stable, only feet from us on the opposite side of the wall, he paused. I heard the swishing sound of his water skin being raised, and then several loud gulps. A loud belch followed. I felt Laurel's shoulders shake with suppressed laughter. Now was not the time for jokes! I prayed that Laurel would contain herself. I could just imagine how much she would love the thrill of jumping out and scaring an unsuspecting guard.

I hardly dared breathe. I couldn't tell what the guard was doing that would take him this long to pause during his patrols. I tried to focus all my attention on listening to the guard, to decipher what he was doing, but Laurel pressed against me kept drawing my mind away from the task.

Finally, *finally*, the guard's clanking walk resumed, and his footsteps faded away until they had disappeared completely. For the first time, I noticed that Laurel had been uncharacteristically quiet since I had whipped her out of sight of the window. I slowly released the pressure of my hand on Laurel's mouth, but couldn't bring myself to pull away from her just yet.

Laurel raised her fingers to meet mine, but instead of shoving my hand roughly away, as I had expected, she directed my hand down to her waist. The intensity of her gaze was palpable. Even though the sound of the guard had completely disappeared, we stayed where we were, pressed against each other in the darkness. Laurel ran her fingers lightly up my arm.

I felt my self-control slip away at her touch. I couldn't help myself. She was so close! Being around her was intoxicating. Now that she was finally near me again... it was as though I couldn't control my own body. My hand crept around to her back. I wanted to hold her and never let go. I wanted this moment to stretch on forever, uninterrupted and unbroken.

"Baron?"

"What?"

"I need to tell you something."

"So tell me."

She took a deep breath, held it for several seconds, then shook her head. "Never mind. It's nothing."

If she had wanted me to let her go, she wouldn't have hesitated to tell me. Laurel never held back from stating her opinion. I slid my hand up her back and bent down to gently brush my lips against her neck. She smelled so good. Any moment now, all the restraint I had would break into a thousand tiny pieces. I clung to her even more tightly, and she returned the gesture.

"We shouldn't be together," Laurel said softly. "We're all wrong for each other, you know."

"I know," I said. "We're too different."

I didn't let her go, and *still* Laurel didn't push me away. Was this another one of her games? If it was, she was playing her cards well. It was impossible to think about anything other than her.

"Baron?" I loved when she said my name.

"What?" I murmured. Several long moments followed before she spoke again. I used the opportunity to move my mouth up and kiss along her jaw line. I didn't want to talk. I wanted us to forget about our fight. It had been such a trivial thing. I wanted to return to the way things had been. I wanted to be happy again. I wanted Laurel back.

"We have to stop." Her words came out as a whisper.

"Why?" I asked. "I've missed you."

"I missed you too, but—"

"But what? Don't you love me?"

Laurel's body stiffened ever so slightly. "No."

"You are lying again," I told her.

Laurel pounded a closed fist against my chest. "Stop telling me what I do or don't think, Baron! You don't know!"

"I do know!" I told her. This was my chance to fight to win her back. She was so transparent to me. I always knew exactly what she was thinking! "No matter how different we are, we can make this work."

"I kissed someone else!" Laurel's words sounded forced. I immediately froze. There was no trace of a lie in her voice this time. She was telling the truth. She continued, "I kissed Little John's son during the tournament. His name is Peter."

I wanted Laurel to stop talking. I wanted her to laugh and say it was a joke. But it wasn't. As much as I wanted her, maybe she truly didn't care about me anymore. Maybe I didn't know her as well as I thought. A deep flush crept up my neck and face, and I was suddenly glad that it was night. With a monumental effort, I pulled away from Laurel. I silently cursed how I lost control of my senses every time she was around. "I see."

I had never met Little John's family. But when I imagined Peter, I pictured a younger version of Little John. Probably taller and more muscular than I was. And clearly, this was someone she had known for years. They would have had a long history together, shared memories to reflect on. Peter wouldn't be tainted from the shame of having the Sheriff of Nottingham as a father, as I was. Peter would have Robin Hood's instant approval. I recalled that James once told me that Little John had a son who was aggressive about making a play for Laurel. Peter was probably gloating about his success to everyone. I immediately hated him.

I heard Laurel take several deep breaths, as if she was about to speak, but no words came. I wanted to find out everything that had happened, but at the same time, I didn't want to know any more. It caused me physical pain to think about Laurel with anyone other than me. The part of my heart that had torn apart after Laurel left was ripped wide open again.

"We aren't together," Laurel said defensively. I couldn't tell if she meant that she and I had split up so she could be free to be with Peter, or if she meant that she and Peter weren't together currently. I wasn't sure how to respond. But fortunately, I was saved from having to say anything, because Laurel cleared her throat and continued, "So-about Prince John."

I leapt onto the subject, eager to talk about anything else. "Right. You wanted to get into his desk."

"Tonight." Laurel said.

"Right now?" I asked, slightly panicked.

"No, after today."

"I could do it instead of you," I volunteered. I knew if I tried to dissuade Laurel from going herself based on risk factor, she would get angry and say that she was every bit as capable. "It would be easier for me."

Laurel scoffed. "I can't see you sneaking around without arousing suspicion. You are too conspicuous, you big oaf." I was glad she added the insult on at the end. It seemed like, in her own way, she was extending an olive branch and letting me know that we could continue being friends. I still hated the idea of her sneaking into Prince John's rooms alone. I could only imagine what would be done to her if she was caught. But I knew better than to say anything. "Fine," I agreed. "I was going out to survey the land around the castle tomorrow, anyway. I will be camping there tonight. I will send James to meet you halfway."

Laurel smirked. "I look forward to it!"

She held my gaze for a long time, defiantly staring back at me, as though daring me to criticize her actions. She seemed determined to prove that she didn't need anyone's help. I wanted so badly to warn her to be careful and stay safe. I wanted to keep her away from danger and protect her from getting hurt. I didn't want her to take uncalculated risks. Even if she wasn't interested in me anymore, I couldn't dismiss my own feelings so readily. "Just don't die," I finally told her.

"I'm not planning on it," she said breezily, and walked out of the stables.

"No one ever does," I breathed softly after she was gone.

LAUREL

The following evening, I snuck down to the washing room and exchanged my woman's attire for that of a male servant. It was fairly similar to the Merry Men's uniforms, except that the linen tunic was a dirty off-white color, as opposed to green. I gratefully pulled on brown leggings again, laced up my old boots, and fastened the wide brown leather belt. I braided my hair tightly and wound it up on my head, then pinned it firmly under my cap. Goodbye, Isabella! I dropped the stupid servant dress into a fireplace and smiled as I watched the itchy fabric ignite.

I knew the rotations of the guards well. I easily snuck up to the tower directly above Prince John's quarters. I marveled at how much easier it was this time compared to when Baron and I snuck in to carry out a jail break.

I looped a rope around one of the empty iron torch brackets of the topmost turret, leaned my body over, and slowly lowered myself down the tower, bit by bit. When I had cleaned Prince John's rooms that day, I had unlocked the washroom window. My right leg was coiled around the rope, and my left foot held it firmly in place against the arch of my right boot. The security allowed me to let go of the rope with one of my hands. Once I had descended to the correct window, I carefully pried it open.

I swung my body and grabbed the ledge to pull myself in. I had a brief moment of stomach-lurching tension when my footing teetered on the narrow windowsill where I was perched, but I recovered quickly and leapt down to the floor. I landed silently and held my breath, listening hard for any irregular breathing.

I heard heavy snores, but nothing that sounded abnormal. All I had to do now was make sure Prince John and his wife stayed fast asleep, break open his desk, and steal everything without the drunken guards learning of my presence.

I pulled a damp cloth from the pouch I had attached to my belt. I had soaked the fabric in the narcoleptic juice of stewed King's Wort. Careful not to inhale its scent, I crept into Prince John's bedroom. I moved toward the heavy snores and was amused to realize that it wasn't John that was snoring so deeply; it was his wife. I slowly put the cloth under her nose. She inhaled deeply and rolled over in her sleep. Was it enough?

In any case, her snores subsided. Prince John grunted loudly in his sleep and began to stir. I hastily clamped the cloth over his face. He woke up instantly and struggled, but I pressed so hard against his nose and mouth that there was no way he could avoid the overpowering scent. His struggles grew fainter and fainter until they ceased completely as the drug worked its way through his system.

For a moment, I stared at his sleeping form. How easy would it be to slit his throat now and be done with it. It certainly would save us a great deal of trouble and would protect King Richard against the constant threat of being overthrown. But I hesitated. I reminded myself firmly that I was not ever to take a life unless it was absolutely unavoidable. I wasn't a cold-blooded monster.

It was with some regret that I turned away and moved toward the desk. The lock was a difficult one to pick, but I eventually managed it. A quire of parchment was stacked neatly in many drawers. I dug through the desk, holding up different papers to the moonlight to inspect them, but it was too difficult to analyze each one in depth. But no matter – I would have plenty of time later. I folded and tucked all of them into my belt. There was also a heavy bag of gold stashed in a corner of a drawer. I pocketed that too. So far, so good.

Now to remind everyone who they were dealing with. I smirked and whipped out a blank piece of parchment and quill.

> Dear Good Sir,
> I appreciate your generosity in donating to the less fortunate today. Please note that your locks are of poor quality. Love live King Richard!
>
> Yours sincerely,
> Robin Hood

I sniggered quietly and left the note in plain sight on the desk. What a simple job! And Baron had been worried. How many times had I reminded him that I was experienced in these matters? What a tale this was going to make, and right under Prince John's nose too!

A slight scuffling noise at the doorway to the bedroom made me look up. Prince John's wife was standing there, looking horrified at the sight of me. Before I could do anything else, she opened her mouth wide and screamed. "Help! Thief! Help! Guards!"

I dashed around the desk toward her. She held up her clenched fists. "I'm not afraid of you, you... you criminal!"

I pivoted and administered a swift side kick. My boot caught her at the hip and propelled her back through the bedroom door. I closed and bolted the door.

"Your Majesty! My lady! Are you alright?" a guard called. Prince John's wife continued to scream hysterically from behind the locked door.

A thousand curses!

I heard the guard throw his shoulder against the door, and a volley of loud bangs followed. The whole castle would know that there was an intruder. But they would have to catch me first.

I leapt onto the windowsill and reached for the rope, but my fingers groped into empty space. I couldn't feel it! I began to overbalance. I toppled and tumbled out of the open window. My hands grabbed frantically and, as I began to fall, the fingers of my right hand touched braided twine. I clenched at it, but my weight was too much for a single hand to stop my descent.

I held on for as long as I possibly could in a desperate attempt to slow the speed of my falling body as I flailed my other hand about, trying to catch the rope. I could feel the rope rushing past my right palm, eating away at the flesh on my hand, and I continued to descend at an alarming rate. I finally managed to clench the rope with my other hand as well. It felt like my arms had been wrenched from their sockets, but I refused to let go, and I stopped falling. I hung suspended for a moment. It felt like my hands were on fire.

I heard an almighty crash above me as the guard finally succeeded at breaking into John's suite of rooms. A howl of rage issued up, I heard the window bang open, and a voice issued from above my head. "There he is! Give me your knife!"

Blast. They were going to cut my line. I arched my back and swung my legs, causing the rope to swing again. I had to land on the outer wall. There was a trellis of roses on the other side that would be easy to climb down, if I could land on top of the wall. If I could just reach it...

That was probably one of the worst ideas of my life.

I let go of the rope a half second too late. Just as I was nearing the height of my swing, the guard at Prince John's window cut the rope, and my trajectory was thrown off. Instead of landing on the top of the stone wall, my shins banged into the hard edge. I collapsed onto the top of the wall. An arrow zipped past me, and I quickly rolled across the wide stone and off the other side to avoid any more arrows that could be headed my way.

I managed to grab at the trellis with one hand as I went down, but my other scrabbled helplessly for a hold. My fingers slipped and I fell again. But this time, it wasn't my hand being burned by a rope, it was my entire side and abdomen being shredded by thousands of thorns and the rusted iron claws that formed the trellis. My thin tunic was no protection at all. I would have screamed, but I couldn't find the air to do so. My belt got sliced and fell off. All the papers I had tucked into the belt came loose.

I hit the ground with a thud, and all the wind was knocked from my lungs. I gasped, helpless as a fish out of water, for more than a full minute and watched the precious documents flutter to the ground all around me. Several were lost to the slow-moving, foul contents of the moat.

Finally, I managed to inhale tiny amounts of air at a time, then rolled to my side. My eyes streamed from the pain, but I scrambled to my feet and gathered up all the sheets of parchment I could see. I heard shouting from the castle behind me. I had to leave, now!

I bolted the servant's door from the outside and staggered across the makeshift footbridge. No swimming in that muck for this girl today! Once on the other side, I heaved the planks off the castle's bank so no one would be able to follow me without lowering the drawbridge or swimming across the moat.

I moved toward the northern wood. My entire body ached. With each footstep, my shins throbbed, and a sharp, stabbing pain erupted all over my side and flamed across the entirety of my abdomen. I didn't want to investigate the extent of my injury. But I knew it was bad. Not fatal, and shockingly, nothing seemed broken. I would be fine, just as I always was. Fixing cuts and scrapes was what healers were for, right? Blood was streaming down my side in rivulets, pulsing out of my body with every beat of my heart. The gushing felt unnatural, but I could handle a little blood loss. *One step at a time*, I told myself over and over. *Just one step at a time*. Once I got back to camp, I would need some fluids and a little rest. Then I would be alright.

Despite the adrenaline pumping through my body, I became light-headed and dizzy. The heat of the summer night pressed heavily on me, and it became increasingly difficult to pull enough air into my body to fill my lungs. Nausea started to overwhelm my senses. I felt like I was going to vomit, and darkness crept in at the edges of my vision. *One step at a time*, I drilled myself again. The only thing keeping me going was the knowledge that the parchment I carried might hold the information to change the outcome of our mission. Of our country's future! Everyone was counting on me. I couldn't stop!

I became numb to the pain searing through my body and continued to stagger toward the forest. The forest meant safety. James was waiting for me. I had to get to him. *Step again,* I coached myself. *And now one more step.* No matter how many steps I took, the forest didn't seem to be growing any closer. In fact, it seemed to swirl around me, making focus increasingly difficult.

I fought with every fiber of my being to repeatedly place one foot in front of the other. Blackness clouded in to block out the point I had fixed my sights on. I shook my head, hard, but far from snapping me out of my lethargy, I stumbled and nearly collapsed. The nausea and heat were getting to the point of being overpowering. I couldn't hear the sounds of the night forest, or of the soldiers clanking about in the castle anymore, just an endless rushing noise in my ears. All I wanted to do was crumple to the ground and fall sleep. What was wrong with me? Why couldn't I get a hold of myself? I had to complete the task at hand. I had to make the rendezvous point with James! I shuffled all the papers into my left hand and slapped my own face sharply with my right. It only helped slightly to keep the darkness at bay. *One step at a time.*

I glanced down at the papers in my hands. The light of the moon illuminated my clothing. It looked... different. My head bobbed as I tried to focus, and my brain worked painfully slowly. I hadn't put on anything red today, had I? How confusing. I didn't even own a scarlet-colored tunic.

How was I suddenly wearing one? *One more step.* Was I hallucinating? Every breath was a struggle. Every footstep felt like I was wading through waist high mud. Every thought was sluggish. Keeping my eyes open took a monumental effort for every second, and it felt like my head weighed a hundred pounds. I pinched myself, hard. I *had* to stay awake. *Just one more step.*

Not much further now. I couldn't, *wouldn't* stop! I needed to get to James. He would know what to do. I was so close! Just one step at a time. *Just one... more...*

BARON

*I*t was dawn. Something had gone wrong. I knew it. I paced the perimeter of my tent until a shallow groove was worn beneath my boots. James should have come and gone by now. What had happened? Part of me wanted to leave to go back to the castle and find out if any prisoners had been captured. If James or Laurel had been captured, their torture would be carried out this very moment; I had to prevent it. But an inkling of doubt held me back. James had been waiting for Laurel before he was going to see me. Had she somehow been delayed? If it was merely a delay, I should wait. But if not...

Graphic scenarios sprang to mind instantly. Laurel-imprisoned and beaten. Horrific images swarmed through my mind's eye, and I couldn't push them away: Laurel being whipped and screaming for mercy, or perhaps thrown into that rat-infested dungeon. She could be hanging by her wrists from the ceiling, or maybe both Laurel and James had been taken prisoner and were...

James emerged from the trees. I stomped over.

"Where have you been?" I hissed angrily. "You are hours late!"

"It's Laurel," James said in his quiet, calm manner. Then he finished with the words I feared above all others. I had known it from the second they suggested this hair-brained idea. "She is hurt."

"Where?" I demanded. "Where is she?"

"I left her back here..." James began leading the way to the location where we usually met. "I had to make sure you were alone. I didn't know what else to do for her..."

My heart beat wildly against the inside of my ribcage. "What happened? Tell me!"

"I'm not sure," admitted James. "She fainted the instant I saw her. I just had time to hide her before everyone came searching."

"They knew it was her?!"

"I don't know."

"Who hurt her?"

"I don't know."

"Are people still looking for her?"

"*I don't know.*"

I threw a dirty scowl in his direction but was taken aback by his expression. For the first time, I could tell James was ruffled. He usually seemed so calm and collected. But now, he looked anxious- scared, even. Laurel must be hurt badly to have him looking so worried.

"She is here," James pointed ahead to a dark shape that laid motionless on the ground. "I have no idea how she made it as far as she did."

We both hurried over to where she was laying. As the rising sun poured its rays onto her body, I saw her entire shirt soaked in blood. The servants' tunic she wore was no longer its normal off-white color, but a deep crimson;

Laurel's face was ghostly white. James must have torn off the lower part of Laurel's shirt and bound her middle tightly when he found her, but already the cloth was soaked in blood. I gently pulled back the fabric covering the wound to examine the damage beneath. Blood was still slowly oozing from dozens of deep cuts, and her entire midriff was stained red. What on earth had caused this? Had she been whipped across her front?

Without hesitation, I ripped off my own shirt and tore it into long strips. James copied me. I began to remove the old shredded and stained fabric, intending to replace it with my own makeshift bandages, but her wounds began to bleed more heavily. So instead, I used the fabric from my tunic to bind over the top of the stained cloth, and placed pressure on her side.

I saw that the palm of Laurel's right hand was bright red and still bleeding freely from an ugly gash that ran the width of her palm. "Get water," I instructed James, and he scampered off to find some. I bound Laurel's hand with thin strips from James's shirt.

I continued to apply pressure on Laurel's side, frantic to staunch the bleeding. I bent to listen to her heart. It was pumping feebly. At least she was still alive. And she was breathing. Her chest rose and descended ever so slightly. "Don't die, Laurel, don't die," I repeated the chant over and over, as if by doing so, I could force her to evade death.

Laurel didn't move. In the time it took James to run back to my tent for a water skin, Laurel never even twitched. When James sprinted back into the clearing, he looked positively terrified. "Is she...?"

I shook my head and grabbed the water skin he proffered. I lifted Laurel's shoulders up and coaxed a few drops of water into her mouth. Her head sagged to the side and the water trickled out onto the already saturated shirt.

"Hold her head!" I ordered James. He obeyed instantly. He held her head while I carefully poured more water into Laurel's mouth. This time, her throat worked, and some water was swallowed. We repeated the procedure a few more times.

I laid Laurel back down. She still didn't move. This was a nightmare come to life. I could see Laurel's life slipping away but was powerless to stop it.

Neither James or I spoke. We both just watched Laurel, anxious as we awaited any change in her condition. The sun rose until it was almost directly overhead. James and I forced more water into Laurel several times, but still, there was no improvement.

I wouldn't give up. I rubbed her hands, which now felt clammy and cold despite the warm weather. I dripped water into her mouth as often as I could, and stroked her face, trying to cause her to wake up with the very force of my thoughts.

Hours passed. "Baron," James said eventually. "You should probably go back. Don't worry about Laurel; I can take care of her. Won't your men be wondering where you are?"

They probably were. But I couldn't leave Laurel. I just couldn't. I would willingly let the entire mission fail if it meant saving Laurel's life. Laurel had been right. I cared more about her than the cause I had signed up for.

"I don't care."

"She would want you to do your duties."

"And if *she* tells me to, I will."

Silence again. We waited for hours. It was late afternoon before anything happened. Then for the briefest of moments, Laurel stirred.

"Laurel?" I asked instantly, eyes riveted on her face. But nothing happened. She had gone deathly still again.

"Should we take her back to your tent?" James asked.

I glanced up at the grey cloud cover that swelled across the sky and blocked the sun. I could sense the impending rain. "Yes."

I lifted Laurel easily. She was so light. Frighteningly light. She had lost so much blood already; her small frame couldn't afford any more. James and I trudged back to my campsite. I looked down at Laurel's pale face and had a flashback to the time I had carried her out of that freezing lake. Would I be able to save her again?

I laid Laurel down on my bedroll and draped all the blankets I had over her. *Please live, please live, please live.*

I sat beside her, determined to stay awake all that night to watch her for any sign of improvement. I heard the patter of raindrops start to fall on the top of the tent and felt an occasional drip as the water soaked through the canvas and fell onto my head. I didn't move. I continued to hold Laurel's cold hand and stared at her unmoving face.

As I sat, James pulled a thick sheaf of papers out of his satchel. Many had clearly been crumpled and smoothed out again. I recognized John's signature at the bottom of the top-most one.

"Where did you get those?" I asked.

"From Laurel," James responded. "It is what she went there for, remember?"

I did remember. Suddenly, I wanted to fling all of those accursed papers into a fire. Laurel had risked her life for those flimsy, inanimate objects that wouldn't bring us even fractionally closer to our goal. Those dratted papers were the reason Laurel was laying comatose and bleeding to death. I saw smears of Laurel's blood trailed across some of the sheets. I began to see red. Not from the blood, but from the anger building inside me. I wanted to destroy all connections to the cause of Laurel's injury.

"How can you think about that right now?" I asked indignantly.

"She wouldn't want her work to go to waste."

"Well, I don't want her *life* to go to waste!" I snapped.

He noticed my expression. "You know, I think a walk would do me good," James said hastily. He tucked the papers into an inside pocket of his cloak, pulled the cowl low over his face, and exited out into the drizzling rain.

I returned to staring at Laurel and waited. I rubbed her wilted hand for what felt like an age. The only promising sign I saw was two faint pink spots that appeared on her cheeks. I didn't think I would ever fall asleep with how anxious I was. But eventually, the exhaustion from the day overpowered me, and drowsiness set in. My head began to nod when Laurel finally moved.

"Baron?" her voice was barely a whisper, but I snapped up at once, fully alert.

"Laurel!" I couldn't contain my relief. "You are alive! How are you feeling? What happened? Who did this to you? What went wrong? Can I get you anything? What do you need?" I had so many questions, and they all came pouring out of me at once. It had been nearly twenty four hours since James brought the news. Twenty four long, painstaking, agonizing hours.

"Slow down there, you," she chuckled once, then grimaced. Her eyes clouded over with pain.

"How are you feeling?" I asked apprehensively.

"Fantastic."

I grinned. "Liar."

She smiled faintly. "Okay, a little lousy," she admitted. Her voice was barely audible, and even this little bit of talking had drained all traces of color that had returned to her cheeks. It was frightening to see her so weak. She had always given off such an air of stubborn strength. Laurel gritted her teeth again.

"Rest," I told her. "Just rest." I saw that she had soaked through the bandages I had already applied to her waist and hand. I gently unwrapped her hand and rinsed the wound. I ripped the only other shirt I had and bound her hand anew.

"You need to stop bleeding before I run out of clothes," I told her. She smiled briefly and then gasped aloud as I unraveled the bandages around her middle to replace them. At least the seeping had ceased. I carefully cleaned and re-wrapped her torso, then gently laid her back down.

"The papers..." Laurel began, and it looked like she was straining to sit upright. I placed a hand on her shoulder to force her to stay laying down.

"James has them. Don't worry about anything. Do you want water?"

She shook her head. Her lips were dry and cracked.

"Too bad, drink some anyway. You need it."

"You are such a... mother hen, it is only a s... s... scratch," Laurel grumbled, but allowed me to raise her shoulders slightly to pour water into her mouth. It worried me that she was beginning to stumble over her words, as though fading back out of consciousness.

After several gulps of water, she seemed very drowsy and turned her head away from the water skin. She closed her eyes and her body relaxed. With her last bit of energy, her fingers found mine. I fretted over how weak her grip was, and held her hand tightly to reassure her that I wasn't going anywhere.

"Sorry about what I said before," she murmured. "You were right."

"Forget about it," I responded. "We both said things we shouldn't have. I'm sorry too."

She smiled faintly. "I am glad you are here, Baron," she said softly, and began to drift off into an uneasy sleep. "You make me feel safe."

That was all I needed to hear.

LAUREL

*M*y memories were confused and fuzzy. I had brief spells of consciousness, then would slip back into a haze of pain. I felt myself laying in the back of a cart. The bright sun blazed down on me as we traveled along a bumpy road. I could hear the squeak of the wooden wheels and clop of the horse hooves and felt the surface I lay on rumble. Every time we hit a bump in the road, my entire body would seize from the pain, but I was too weak to push myself up to look around, or even to adjust to a more comfortable position.

Occasionally, James's face would float in from over the side of the short wooden wall of the cart, and he would force liquids down my throat. It was a struggle to keep anything in my stomach, even water. I often saw James's mouth move to form words, but my brain couldn't make any sense of what he was saying. I tried to respond, but my tongue felt swollen and heavy, and I couldn't get any words to come out. James's face looked concerned every time I tried to speak, but before I could think of a way to reassure him, I would fade back into a restless slumber again.

Was this dying? I couldn't tell from hour to hour if I was getting better, or worse. I wanted to sleep, but at the same time, worried that the next time I fell asleep would be the last. But even with that fear, I couldn't prevent myself dozing off again and again. I had never felt so helpless and weak. I wanted to hate the feeling, but couldn't even work up the emotional energy to be angry.

The heat and sunshine on the open road eventually changed to a breezy green dimness. Trees shielded me from the scorching sun, and the air smelled familiar. There was the comforting scent of pine needles, campfires, and tree bark. I didn't even need to open my eyes to know where we had gone. We were back in Sherwood Forest. I was home.

The distant familiar sounds of camp- pots clanking, dogs barking, and children laughing, were welcome. But as we drew closer, I heard James's anxious voice call out to an unseen person or persons, and most of the surrounding noises ceased. I sensed the press of bodies close by, hovering around the cart, but couldn't work up the effort to open my eyes.

I felt myself being lifted out of the cart and carried across camp. The ease with which I was carried and the deep vibrations of the man's voice told me it was Little John who supported me. I was laid down on a bed, and I felt my wound dressings pulled off to reveal the ugly gashes across my stomach. I heard gasps. It must look bad.

Finally, I forced my eyes open. The dark interior of the hut made it difficult to see anything, and it took several moments for my vision to clear. My eyes lit upon Little John and James first. They stood together, staring down at my midsection. Little John's hand was up to his bushy beard and covered his mouth. James was shaking his head. I had never seen him look so depressed. I wished my father was back from Austria. He would want to be there with me. He would know what to do.

I slowly rotated my head to see who else was there. There was one of the healers, a thin, middle-aged woman named Sybil. She was a kind woman that children would run to see when they fell and scraped their knees, and the most skilled healer in Sherwood Forest, and I was glad she was there. Peter stood beside her, a look of abject horror on his face as he stared at my exposed wound. Of course he would be here. He was her apprentice.

Peter and Sybil exchanged grim looks, then began to bustle around the hut, collecting bandages and creams. I didn't need to hear their words to know what they were saying. I was dying. What my chances of survival were, I had no idea. I wished my father was there with me.

Peter held my head up while Sybil forced a bitter tasting drink into my mouth. I coughed once in protest, but when I felt my abdomen clench, decided it would be better to let the drink pass. It would be less painful to suffocate. If I had to contract my muscles again, the pain would be unendurable.

Once the drink hit my stomach, my tongue seemed to deflate a little, and my mind cleared slightly. It would have been kinder to leave me as I had been. I suddenly had full awareness of exactly how much pain I was in.

"Laurel? Laurel! Can you hear me?" Sybil was talking to me. I focused hard on her mouth, trying to force my brain to process her words. At first, her speech sounded garbled and flowed together in a string of unintelligible sounds. She repeated herself until I understood.

"Y-yes," I croaked.

"We need to clean this. It is going to hurt, but it will help, understand?" Again, Sybil had to repeat herself several times before I was able to comprehend. I nodded.

I couldn't imagine that anything would be more painful than what I was already feeling, but then Sybil and Peter began to scrape at my wounds to remove the dirty and inflamed portions. I wanted to scream but doing so would have caused my abdomen to contract again and cause even more pain. Tears welled up in my eyes, and I scrunched them shut tight. I bit my lip until it bled. James gave me a stick to bite down on instead, and Little John squeezed my hands. It only helped a little to distract me from the agony of whatever operation Sybil and Peter were performing.

When the rolling waves of blackness came, I welcomed the bliss of unconsciousness. I didn't want to feel anything anymore.

BARON

So, this was Sherwood Forest. I had navigated around the perimeter of the forest innumerable times, but I had never actually entered before. After James left with Laurel to take her back to Sherwood Forest, I had immediately returned to Nottingham Castle. I was prepared to quit on the spot so I could go to Laurel. I didn't care when I returned to Prince John, if ever. All I cared about was being there with Laurel.

But it wasn't necessary. Before my arrival, several of my soldiers had informed Prince John of my skills as a tracker, and the second he saw me, he insisted that I go after Robin Hood. I assured him that I would not rest until I found the one who had broken in and stolen so many valuable documents.

Once I had traveled into the very heart of Sherwood Forest, a teenage boy appeared. I amused myself momentarily by wondering if he had intended to rob unwary travelers, but he made no such attempt with me. When I affirmed to him that I had come to see Laurel, the boy's face fell.

"She ain't doing too well, me mam says."

Fear clutched at my heart. I instructed the boy to lead me to her, and he turned and trotted off. I wanted to yell at him to run, to hurry up, but he walked with a heavy limp, and I doubted whether he could go any faster. It felt like an age to arrive. We passed tidy little huts, gardens, and a multitude of laundry lines and cook fires. A training area was on my right, and I saw a basket full of the same kind of throwing knives I had seen Laurel use so many times. I felt a pang in my gut. She should be out here practicing and enjoying her life, not wasting away on bedrest.

The boy pointed me toward a small cabin and said Laurel was there. I rushed to the door and flung it open. Once my eyes became accustomed to the gloomy interior, I saw Laurel laying on a stuffed straw bed tick, completely immobile. The hut was empty except for a young man about Laurel's age beside her, a jar of paste in his left hand. He used his right hand to scoop out bits at a time to slather onto his patient. Laurel's shirt was cut short to reveal her midriff, and I could see her stomach half covered with the brightly colored cream.

The healer stared at me suspiciously.

"Who are you?" he asked. I ignored his question and moved to Laurel's bedside. I pushed the healer to the side as I did so, indifferent to his squawk of protest.

Laurel was sleeping. I covered her limp feverish hand with my own and leaned over to listen to her breathing.

"*You can't be in here!*" hissed the healer's voice from behind me. I rose. My head brushed the low ceiling overhead as I stood and rounded on the speaker. I eyed him. Everything about him was average. Average height, average build, average brown hair and eyes, probably average intelligence too. He clutched the jar of salve as though it was a weapon.

I didn't want to wake Laurel. I pulled the salve from his hand, plunked it down on a rickety table, then shoved him through the doorway. "Hey, stop that!" he said, annoyed.

I ducked my head under the doorframe as I left and closed the door quietly.

"Who are you?" the healer asked again, louder now that we were outside. "And what are you doing here? Get lost! I am trying to take care of my patient! She needs me!"

"I am here to see her," I answered. The healer flinched at the sound of my voice. Everyone was always alarmed when they first met me. Laurel was the only one who had never once seemed intimidated. But right now, I didn't care what this healer thought of me. I just wanted to be sure that Laurel would recover.

"How is Laurel?" I asked.

The healer still looked confused. "Who are you again?"

I sighed impatiently. "Baron. Baron Blackwellson!"

The man's eyes widened in comprehension. I saw his eyes quickly take in my appearance as though he was confirming a sneaking suspicion. Then, with unsettling speed, his eyes shifted from curiosity and slight irritation at being interrupted in his duties to blatant dislike.

"I see." The healer suddenly seemed a little bolder as he clenched his fists and puffed his chest up a little. He stepped to the side, barring my path back to the hut. "I know who you are all right. And who *your father* is too."

The insolent little twerp.

"That is neither here nor there. Now, how is *Laurel*?"

"I cannot discuss the condition of my patients with anyone except her family."

This kid was really getting on my nerves, and I fought down the urge to throw a solid punch at his face. "I count as family," I told him. "She and I are together."

He cocked an eyebrow. "Oh really? Seems that, last I heard, she dumped you. Sounded like a good plan to me. We all know you are a spineless traitor. I've heard all about you."

The idea of punching this git was becoming more appealing by the second. "First of all, I am *not* a traitor. And second of all, this is none of your business!"

"*Actually*," his voice seemed shrill, "It is my business. Anything to do with Laurel is my business. Professionally and personally."

"Why is that?"

He just smiled smugly, like he knew something I didn't. My stomach lurched as I realized who I was talking to. This must be Peter. He was smaller than I expected. With Little John as his father, I assumed he would be at least my size. And he wasn't even good-looking! What did she see in him? There was no way he and Laurel were together. This fool wasn't her type at all. Even in her weakened condition, Laurel would want to see me, not him. *I* was the one that made her feel safe. Not him.

I let out a harsh bark of laughter. "Real cute try. What is your name, kid?"

His eyebrows contracted. "Peter Little, son of John Little. I'm in charge of Laurel's recovery, and you need to leave. Aren't you supposed to be off playing Prince John's lapdog, anyway?"

"I don't *play* in the real world, kid. I have real, actual work to do. I don't play hide and go seek in the forest like you, and there's no way I'm leaving you in charge of her recovery!" I said, voice deadly cool.

"Because you can make that decision?" retorted Peter. "If I heard correctly, you may have called the shots back at *your daddy's* camp, but here, you are not in charge. You are a nobody. You aren't even a fully-fledged member! You are on probation. I don't take orders from you. No one does."

This impudent brat was really getting on my nerves. I was used to my orders being obeyed instantly and without question. When they weren't, I was allowed to administer whatever punishment I thought up. The more time I spent with this Peter, the more tempting it was to knock him unconscious. A brief but vivid image of Peter kissing Laurel flashed across my mind.

I swiftly lunged forward, grabbed Peter by his collar and seat of his pants, lifted him bodily into the air, and dumped him into the nearby water trough with a very satisfying splash. He spluttered and gasped as I sauntered past and re-entered the hut, firmly bolting the door behind me as I did so.

"Hey!" screeched Peter as he clambered out of the watering trough, now sopping wet, and pounded on the locked door.

I returned to Laurel's bedside, drew up a small stool and held her hand again. The loud pounding on the door seemed to rouse Laurel. Her eyes fluttered open and, when she saw me, the corners of her mouth slightly turned upward. I had missed her smile. I gently squeezed her hand, and she returned a small amount of pressure.

"Who's a mother hen now?" I asked her.

She let out a breathy exhale, as though attempting to laugh, but was still too weak. "That would be you. No need to fuss. I am fine."

"Sure you are."

She gazed at me as though she couldn't believe if I was real or not. "I didn't think you would come. But you are here."

"Of course! I will always be here for you!" I said emphatically. Whether or not she and I were together, I knew I would always be there for her. The pounding on the door continued. "Peter is here too," I added grudgingly, in response to her puzzled expression.

"I see," she said croakily, and weakly moved her head so she could see past me. I turned and saw Peter's face staring at us through the grimy window. His face was contorted in anger, and water trickled out of the hair plastered to the top of his head. He jabbed a finger at me then gestured for me to come outside. Drops of water splattered against the window as he gesticulated wildly.

I narrowed my eyes at him. I wanted to kiss Laurel in front of him. I wanted to kiss her so badly that it hurt. But I couldn't. Weak as she was, I didn't doubt she would punch anyone who tried to make a move on her. Hadn't I seen what she did to Leopold when he attempted it? And besides, she had rejected my advances the last time I had tried. Now was not the time to make another attempt.

I contented myself to lift Laurel's hand to my lips, staring combatively at Peter the whole time. That would show him. I heard Peter yelp and dash away, probably to get someone to help. Pathetic. He couldn't even break down a simple wooden door.

"You are trying to mark me as your territory, aren't you?" laughed Laurel weakly. "Men are so possessive. You don't own me, remember?"

"I think you made that pretty clear."

Laurel smiled. I could tell it was costing her a lot of

energy to talk. She fell silent, eyes closed. I saw her neck muscles strain and knew she must have clamped her jaws shut against the pain she was feeling. My eyes drifted down to her exposed abdomen. Her skin was inflamed and swollen, with greenish-yellow bubbles of infected pus dotting the entirety of where she had been injured. Scabs were beginning to crust around the edges of the wound. I studied the wound carefully for any blackened skin, but I didn't see any. Thank the stars, the tissue wasn't dying... yet. But I hadn't ever seen such a serious infection before where the person lived through it.

"It looks bad, doesn't it?" my eyes snapped back to Laurel's face. She had opened her eyes again and was watching me intently. "No one will tell me, but I know."

I briefly considered lying, but Laurel would see through it in a second. "Yeah, it looks bad. But you can handle it."

"Never said I couldn't."

She stopped talking and took several measured breaths. I hated seeing her in so much pain. If only she wasn't so bound and determined to single-handedly save all of England!

I tucked a strand of Laurel's hair behind her ear. "I missed you."

"You are ridiculous. We just saw each other," Laurel winced and her hand groped for her side. I gently pulled her hand away.

"Don't touch it. You need to heal."

"That may have gotten more difficult. I think you just scared away my healer."

"I will get you a new healer. A better one!" One that didn't have selfish motives, I added silently.

As if on cue, Peter's face popped back into the window.

This time, he was accompanied by Little John. John rapped smartly on the window with his knuckles. "Open up, Baron!" he called. "You can't lock patients away from their healers!"

"Somebody's in trouble," Laurel said quietly in a singsong voice. She grinned at me and applied a little pressure to my hand, then let go.

I stood and opened the door. Peter pushed past me and went right to Laurel. I made to follow him, but Little John laid a hand on my shoulder. He was one of the few people tall enough to do so. "Let's take a walk."

I looked back at Peter and Laurel. Peter glared at me through narrowed eyes and placed his hand on Laurel's forehead to check her temperature. Laurel gave a shadow of a smile. It was driving me mad to see Peter sitting next to Laurel and touching her. I could tell what he wanted, and it wasn't just to help his patient recover.

"Who has to have their daddy's help now?" I asked Peter spitefully. He bristled, and Laurel's eyes twinkled. Little John's grip tightened on my shoulder, and I was steered out the door.

LAUREL

$\mathcal{I}$ watched Little John guide Baron away. I wanted him to stay but couldn't find the words. I couldn't beg him to stay with me after breaking up with him. My pride wouldn't allow it. Peter kept his eyes narrowed at the open door until Baron and John faded from view into the surrounding forest.

"Sorry about that," Peter said pompously. "Some men just don't know when they aren't wanted anymore."

The irony that Peter was the one saying that to me made me want to laugh. I needed to have a blunt conversation with Peter, but didn't have the energy for heavy emotions. I watched Peter dab more of the cream onto my middle. I felt like I had used up all my energy talking to Baron and now had no more words left for Peter. But I don't think he minded; he was engrossed in tending to my wound. Sybil flitted in and examined Peter's work, then pulled him outside to converse in low whispers.

I could only catch a few garbled phrases that floated in the door like "blood" and "get worse" and "fever." I took a mental inventory of my situation. I couldn't get up by myself. Even moving my hand was painful. I had no idea what looked terrible enough to make Sybil so concerned. She had witnessed horrific injuries on a multitude of occasions. I had been drinking the bitter concoction that Sybil brewed every time she brought it to me, so I was able to talk and think well enough. Didn't that mean I would get better? Surely, I would have a longer-than-normal recovery time, but that was only to be expected. A few weeks, and I would be good as new! Sybil was an excellent healer. I was in capable hands.

I scanned the forest line through the open door for any sign of Baron and Little John's return, but I didn't see them anywhere. I stared up at the thatched roof of the hut. A spider crawled along one of the wooden beams and began to spin a web. I watched it for what felt like an hour. Ever since being injured, time seemed to behave strangely. Sometimes hours would pass in great gallops of time. Other days, the minutes would drag by with agonizing slowness.

Sybil and Peter came back into the hut. They both looked gravely serious. I looked from one face to the other. Peter avoided my gaze. Sybil, however, looked me straight in the eye, and got directly to the point.

"Laurel," she began crisply. "I need to know what happened."

"I fell."

"Onto what?"

"An iron trellis," I said feebly. I felt silly admitting that I had stumbled and been thwarted by an artistic mechanism used to support flowers.

"A *rusty* iron trellis?" Sybil asked shrewdly.

"Probably," I answered. I thought hard. I had seen the trellis before, when I took the ground level chamber pots outside to be emptied into the moat. I scoured my recollections and remembered the reddish-brown crust that had covered the trellis. "Yes. Very rusty."

Sybil nodded, as though her worst suspicions had been confirmed. "I thought as much."

I had never seen Sybil hesitate about giving information to a patient. It made my insides clench horribly. I was going to be okay, wasn't I?

"You have blood poisoning," Sybil said calmly. "It gets progressively worse. You are already weak and your heart is beating rapidly. Soon you will start with chills and a fever, then you will become weak and disoriented. Eventually you will slip into a coma and die."

She stopped talking. I felt like I couldn't breathe. I was going to... die? That was impossible! I would recover! I always did. Was this a joke? It must be an elaborate prank that Little John had cooked up, right? I stared hard at Sybil. There was no trace of a lie in her eyes. Only an overwhelming pity and sadness. Peter dug the toe of his boot into the packed dirt floor and refused to look at me.

"Is there any chance of recovery?" I bit my lip.

Sybil shook her head. "I don't know of anyone who survived an infection this bad. Cuts by themselves can be mended, but once the infection enters your blood..."

"How long?" I asked quietly. I would send word to Father. He would want to be here with me. This would break him, I knew. He had nearly died of grief when Mother passed away. But he would stay strong for me until I was gone.

"You are young and healthy, so I'd say between 3 days and a week," Sybil answered.

I caught my breath. So soon! Father would never get here in time. I blinked back tears. "I want to be alone now," I told Sybil and Peter. Peter immediately left, but Sybil gave me a hug first.

"You holler for me, any time you need me. Day or night," she said sympathetically. "I will bring you something for the pain as soon as I can. You won't suffer after that." She left and closed the door behind her.

I was dying. I stared up at the spider above my head and let the tears fall down my face. That spider would go on living, unaware that directly beneath him, a person was slowly and painfully wasting away. How many breaths did I have left? How many more times would my heart beat before it stopped?

I didn't know what would happened after I died. Would my consciousness, my soul, go to heaven? Would I simply cease to exist? If there was a heaven, I would see Mother again. But far from reassuring me, the thought made my tears fall faster and hotter. I didn't want to die! I certainly didn't want a slow, painful death. I wanted to live. I wanted to have a future.

But now I didn't. I wouldn't ever find out if Father and King Richard made it back to England. I wouldn't ever grow old and tell stories to my grandchildren. I wouldn't have made a single difference in the world.

My heart skipped a beat, and I began to panic. Was that part of my slow progression toward death? What would happen if I simply refused to die, but stubbornly lived on? I tried to sit up and throw off my coverings. I managed to shove the blanket to the floor and rolled to my side. Pain exploded all over my body, but I staunchly refused to acknowledge it. I would live! I chose life!

I raised up onto my elbow and ignored the searing pain that flared across my body. I would walk it off. With immense effort, I swung my legs over the side of the straw tick. By that point, my body was drenched in sweat and I pulled air into my lungs with heavy gasps. I would live; I couldn't die now! I needed to live. I was afraid of death.

I clung to the side table and tried to heave myself onto my feet. My legs wouldn't support my weight. I collapsed to the floor. I was useless. Useless and dying.

I broke down and sobbed.

BARON

*L*ittle John and I took a long walk. He tried to give me a bunch of fatherly advice, but I only half paid attention. Peter was his son, not me. He should be telling Peter to allow Laurel to decide who to be with and not intervene. He should be going on and on to Peter about letting go of what was and looking to the future instead of back at the past. Peter was the one he should tell to not dump people in water troughs, no matter what they say. Though once I thought about it, Peter wouldn't have the strength to actually do so. I stayed for the entire discussion only out of respect for Little John, not because I wanted to listen. It sounded like an eloquent fatherly lecture, but most of his words were blocked out by my own thoughts.

I kept worrying about Laurel. Was she recovering? Would she heal properly? I came to see her, not to listen to Little John prattle on about how to handle relationships as a man. I had known him long enough to respect him, but still wondered if perhaps he was simply standing up for his pathetic son. The son who tried to worm his way into a relationship with

Laurel. Peter, Sneeds, Leopold- there was no absence of men who were willing to try and win over Laurel. Though I couldn't blame them for trying- I was doing the same thing.

Finally, *finally*, when we had arrived back at the hut, Little John clapped me on my shoulder and left. I made a beeline for the door, but I was stopped by a thin woman who came around the corner and held up a hand to forestall me. I recognized the woman as the healer Peter was apprenticed to.

"How is Laurel?" I asked anxiously.

Sybil's mouth set into a firm line. She glanced at the door. It was shut.

"Please tell me," I begged. I needed to know.

"She has blood poisoning," the woman said.

"But it can be cured, can't it?"

She shook her head. "Laurel doesn't have more than a few days left. It spreads and gets worse very quickly."

I froze. A few days? That was it? She was going to die?

"Can't you *do* something?" I demanded.

The healer shook her head sadly. "I can give her a little for the pain to keep her comfortable until the end, but that is all. I don't have any training to do anything else."

"Well, who does have that training?" I said loudly. The woman flinched and retreated. Without realizing it, I had stepped closer toward her and was towering over her. I really needed to stop intimidating people.

"Maybe the village physician. Maybe. But he doesn't treat people from Sherwood Forest... I doubt he would even see her."

"So, you are just giving up? You aren't even trying?" I fought to keep my rage in check. "Maybe none of the rest of you care about Laurel, but I do!"

I pushed open the hut door. I found Laurel huddled on the ground. She was asleep again, and her face was puffy and red. I could tell she had cried herself to sleep. I hurried to her side and lifted her gently back onto the lumpy straw tick.

Laurel's eyes fluttered open. She saw me and she let out a shaky breath. "I'm dying," she whispered.

"I won't let that happen!" I told her forcefully. "I'm taking you to the village physician. He is going to treat you."

"He doesn't like me," Laurel lamented. "He won't help."

"Let him try to tell *me* no."

Laurel's chin began to quiver. "Thank you."

I HURRIEDLY COLLECTED A FEW THINGS FOR THE JOURNEY, got directions to the village, and bullied Sybil, the healer, into giving me medication for Laurel. Several people tried to talk me out of my plan, but I ignored them all. Sybil said that my moving Laurel would only hasten her death. Little John told me that I needed to accept the inevitable. Peter told me he wouldn't allow me to move his patient. After a few more comments, I began to rebuff all contact with people.

The last person to talk to me was James. When I saw him approach, I prepared a snarky comment about how I didn't need anyone else telling me I was wrong in my decisions. But that wasn't his intention. Instead, he handed me a leather pouch of coins. "Good luck, Baron," he said simply. "I would have done the same thing if it had been my wife in Laurel's position." He vanished as quickly as he came.

Transporting Laurel in her weakened condition was difficult. James had brought her in on a cart, but it was currently dissembled for repairs. Laurel couldn't sit on a horse; she was too weak. So I carried her. It would take hours to walk back to the village. I set out in the late afternoon and traveled all night. It took me longer than I expected, burdened as I was with our supplies and Laurel. I didn't want to hurry; Laurel would moan in pain if I stumbled or had to readjust my grip. I arrived in the village mid-morning.

I pounded on the first door I came to. "I need the doctor!" I burst out when the door was opened. I was directed to one of the larger buildings. I walked as quickly as I could and kicked on the door so I didn't have to adjust Laurel's position.

A plump man with greying hair sprouting in a half circle around the back of his head answered quickly. He spotted Laurel, and it was obvious that he recognized her. "I don't serve members of the Merry Men," he said haughtily, and began to close the door.

I jammed my foot into the threshold to prevent the door shutting, then shouldered my way inside and laid Laurel on one of the beds. The man was watching me, mouth open. "Did you not hear me?" His voice had a singsong quality, but at the moment, it came out as a squeak. "I don't treat people from Sherwood Forest! Get out!"

I crossed the room in two long strides. In one fluid movement, I grabbed the man by the front of his tunic, lifted him bodily into the air, and slammed him against the wall. His eyes bulged and his mouth flapped open and closed, gulping like fish out of water. His feet worked in a circle in the air, desperate to be back on the firm ground again.

"You will treat this woman to the best of your ability, or so help me I will pull all your teeth from your head one by one," I snarled. So much for my resolving not to intimidate people.

His eyes darted to Laurel and back to me.

"I am the Sheriff of Nottingham. You will treat this woman or I will have you arrested here and now!" I yelled. "And you will speak of this to no one. Understood?"

His head bobbed up and down. I placed him back on the ground, and he scuttled over to Laurel. I hovered over them both. Laurel stirred, and her eyes half opened. The physician tried to get her to move her arms and legs, but she could barely get them to twitch when asked.

"Hmmm..." the physician inspected Laurel, and gently began to prod and poke all over. Laurel's face was flushed from the fever, and beads of sweat poured off her body. Her face was deathly pale.

"There is an infection," the physician said in his singsong voice, "but that is easily remedied."

Relief swept over my body. An easy remedy! Sybil didn't know what she was talking about! She was just going to let Laurel die. I caught Laurel's eye and nodded encouragingly.

"Can you do it now?" Laurel panted. Her throat sounded parched, and every word cost her a great deal of effort.

"Why, certainly! Certainly, I can!" the physician answered, then with a quick glance at me added, "my dear lady." He scurried over to a corner and picked up a large kit. Tension was draining out of my shoulders and neck now. It would all be over soon. Laurel would be fine. "Now don't look, my dear, don't look," he told her in a calm, comforting tone. Laurel turned her head away.

Then the physician opened the kit.

Inside the kit were an assortment of scalpels, tubes and a large jar with leeches crawling all over each other inside. The physician took hold of a large scalpel in one hand and reached out for Laurel's arm with the other.

"Wait just a minute!" I thundered. I knocked the scalpel from the physician's hand. It wasn't just the scalpel that went flying. The physician did too. I hadn't intended to be so forceful. The physician crumpled to the ground, and there was a *ting ting ting* as the scalpel went skittering across the stone floor.

"Sir! I must ask you to restrain yourself!" shouted the physician from where he was now spread-eagled on the floor.

"What do you think you are doing?" I roared.

"It is customary to bleed the infection out of the patient!"

"She will DIE if you do that!" I bellowed. How could anyone possibly think that losing more blood would help Laurel? Only a few days ago she had nearly died! She didn't have any more blood to give! Couldn't the fool doctor see how pale Laurel already was? Any more blood loss and she would never wake up again.

"No, she will die if we don't get the infection out!" the physician retorted. His voice no longer sounded singsong, but nasty and guttural, and an ugly look had come across his face. "This is why I hate treating people from Sherwood Forest! All of you want help, but none of you heathens like my methods!"

I pointed a finger threateningly at the physician, and

he curled into a protective ball. "Don't take any blood from her," I warned.

The physician's eyes darted all over the room as if looking for a way to escape.

"Baron," Laurel's weak voice came from behind me. I dropped down beside her and clutched her hot hand. The fever Sybil predicted was already raging. "Maybe he knows best."

"No! There has to be another way."

Laurel's eyes looked glassy. She struggled to form words. "I don't think there is. I don't have long."

I rounded on the physician, still cowering on the ground, and bellowed, "What other options are there?"

"None!" He squeaked. "I don't know any other way."

I cursed and kicked a stool. I refused to accept that answer. I would not let Laurel die, either by infection or bleeding to death. This couldn't be the end. There had to be a different way, there *had* to!

"But-" the physician sounded hesitant.

"But what?" I demanded.

The physician licked his lips nervously. "There is someone else who might be able to..." his voice died. "But... But the thing is..."

I waited impatiently. Laurel didn't have time for this idiotic man to talk slowly. "Well?"

The physician's eyes darted around the room again, as if making sure we would not be overheard.

"*Well?*" I asked again and stepped aggressively toward the cringing man. He quailed before me.

"It isn't a physician." The man looked very nervous even mentioning it. "Or a healer."

"Who is it?"

"Some people say... there is a woman... They claim she

can heal people without bleeding them. Just potions and herbs. But I don't feel like I can in good conscience recommend-"

I crossed the room and scooped up Laurel. She had faded off to sleep yet again. My stomach clenched horribly. She needed help. Fast. If she slipped into a coma, there would be no saving her. "Where do I find this woman?"

The physician licked his lips again and his eyes flicked toward the windows, as if expecting to see the villagers with ears pressed against the glass.

"There is a path in the woods. It is the cottage with the crooked tree out front," he pointed the way.

I was out the door in a flash, hurrying as I carried Laurel toward the woods, and didn't listen to the physician's parting cry, "You didn't hear it from me!"

LAUREL

*N*o matter how hard I struggled, I could no longer prevent sleep from overpowering me. All my recollections became muddled and foggy. I tried to form one cohesive thought, but even that was too much. I couldn't hear anything. All sounds were blocked out as if pillows had been gently pressed over my ears. I couldn't open my eyes. I couldn't feel my own body. I could barely even breathe. The all-encompassing pain I had felt was slowly fading away into black nothingness. Perhaps, if death was painless, I should embrace it. I didn't have the energy to fight it anymore. I was ready to die.

BARON

The part of woods we were in was dark and foreboding. Moss draped down from trees, and cobwebs stretched across the abandoned path. It took half an hour of walking before I reached the cottage. At first, I had worried that I wouldn't see the crooked tree. How was I to know which tree he meant? Every time I passed a tree that had the slightest bend in its trunk, I strained my eyes to see any sign of a cottage.

But as soon as I saw it, I knew. There was a blackened tree that grew at a forty-five degree angle from the ground, then completely switched directions halfway up, and continued to grow along that trajectory for nearly ten feet before growing straight upward. If this wasn't the crooked tree, nothing was. Dead branches hung sadly off the trunk, and a massive vulture was perched at the top. It stared down at my approach with wide, hungry eyes. I shifted Laurel's weight, trying to wrap her more securely in my arms. I would not let anything happen to her.

The cottage beyond the crooked tree was spooky. Foul-smelling contents of a large iron pot boiled over a cook fire outside, and a flock of ravens clustered on the boughs of the forest surrounding the cottage. Their cawing grated at my ears. Even though it was a cloudless summer afternoon, the small clearing seemed cast in shadows, as if not even the brightest sunshine could permeate the gloom around this small shack. With each step I took toward the cottage door, I felt an unsettling disturbance close in around me. It felt as though I was being watched by thousands of unseen eyes, and a thousand unheard voices were crying out at me to run away.

Blue-tinted smoke curled up out of the chimney. The roof was missing several shingles and the shutters on the windows hung limply. I could only assume the walls had been white when the home was first built, but now it had been overwhelmed by thorny vines that climbed up the green, mildewy sides. Weeds grew unrestrained everywhere I looked, and I heard snakes slither through the tall grass at my feet. When I looked down, I saw bones scattered about among the moss-covered rocks lining the faded dirt path. There was even a cracked and yellowed human skull.

For the briefest of moments, I wanted to turn and leave this hair-raising place. But I shook off the feeling. If this was where I could find help for Laurel, I would stay.

As I neared the front door, it creaked slowly open. An ancient, hump-backed woman emerged. She was the oldest person I had ever seen. Wispy white hair streamed behind her as if in a high wind. She wore ragged and patched clothes, and clutched a heavy black shawl around her bony shoulders with one knobby hand while she hobbled toward me, stooped over a thick cane.

"Baron, do come in," the woman hissed. She smiled, but the effect was far from comforting. To the contrary, I felt hair stand upright on the back of my neck and her very appearance made my skin crawl. She had broken, crooked, yellowed teeth, and large warts dotted her face; one on her cheek had a small tuft of hair sprouting from it.

The use of my name disturbed me. "Do we know each other?" I asked as I stepped over the threshold.

"I know all about you, dear boy. But alas, you do not know me. You may call me Mother Margarite."

It didn't matter what she knew about me, or what this old woman looked like. All that mattered was that Laurel got better. The old woman gestured for me to lay Laurel down on a wooden table. Symbols and ancient writings were carved into the table, which reminded me of a sacrificial stone alter I had seen once. I hesitated. The table seemed to emit a dark, unsettling energy and I didn't want Laurel anywhere near it.

"Mother Margarite, then, can you help my friend?" I nodded my head toward Laurel, still in my arms. Her breathing was shallow, and she was as white as a ghost. I didn't know how much longer she had. She had stopped making sounds, even when I had to move her. Was she so far gone that she could no longer sense how much pain she was in?

"I could..." Mother Margarite seemed unwilling to commit. "I have everything I need here," she waved her hand at the walls behind her. Guttering candles illuminated them with a dim, flickering light. I lifted my gaze to the odd things suspended in solutions in all the jars that lined the dusty shelves along her home. One jar contained something that looked horribly like human eyeballs, which stared back at me.

Mother Margarite placed two wrinkled fingers onto

the side of Laurel's throat. "I would say she only has a few hours left to live, if that. You brought her just in time. I am the only one who can save her now."

"Then please help her!"

Mother Margarite merely gazed at me, waiting. Waiting for what? "*Please*!" I begged. "Please help her!"

"Only the truly desperate come to me," observed Mother Margarite mildly. "Do you feel desperate, Baron Blackwellson?"

What did that matter? "Yes!" I answered quickly. "Yes, she will die soon!"

"And you don't want her to die, do you?" Mother Margarite seemed unruffled by my hasty answers and peered at me with those sunken eyes. I got the distinct impression that she would be impossible to intimidate. "She is more than just a friend to you, yes?"

How much did this old crone know? "It is complicated."

"What will you give me in return?"

I fumbled for the heavy pouch of money James had given me and held it out to her. Mother Margarite shook her head and chuckled, "I don't deal with things as trivial as coins, boy. You will need to do better than that."

"I will give you anything! Anything you want!"

Mother Margarite smiled again, an evil leer that never reached her sunken eyes. It showed every one of her broken, yellowed, and crooked teeth. "I have your word, Baron Blackwellson, that you will give me *anything* I ask for in return for healing this girl? You swear it?"

I had no other choice. "You have my word. I swear it on my life. Now, *please*."

"Do you swear it on *her* life?" Mother Margarite pointed a gnarled finger at Laurel.

I hesitated. I felt like I was being set up. But if it was to save Laurel... of course I would be willing to do whatever I needed to.

Mother Margarite seemed to sense my apprehension and added with an air of immense generosity, "I know you are a busy man, Sheriff. I will give you a year to fulfill your oath."

A year would be plenty of time to do whatever she wanted. I was more than willing to work night and day for a full year if it meant saving Laurel. "Yes, yes, I will do whatever you want IF you heal her! I swear it on her life. Just help Laurel, now!"

Suddenly, Mother Margarite seemed full of vitality. She dusted off a spot for Laurel on the table and bustled about, collecting bottles, herbs, powders, and potions. I gently laid Laurel down and checked for a heartbeat. It was very weak. I could hear her heart fluttering as if it was only remembering how to beat properly. She was barely breathing. I lifted one of her eyelids and saw only white. Please live, please live, *please live*. I couldn't go on without her.

I didn't care that we fought sometimes. I didn't care that we were so different. I didn't care that Laurel was impulsive and impatient and could be more difficult than a mule with a headache. I just wanted her better. Even if she didn't want me back. I could be happy just knowing she was alive and well. But I would not be able to survive her death. I was sure of that.

Mother Margarite lifted her shawl to cover her head and began to chant in a foreign tongue. I felt a chill breeze sweep through the house even though the door was closed and the day was warm. The air seemed to swirl around Mother Margarite, which disheveled her appearance even more. She moved her bony hands over Laurel's limp body, and I saw a bluish light emanate from those wrinkled, crooked old hands, as well as from the symbols carved into the wooden table under Laurel's body.

Black magic. The thought pierced my mind and made my blood run cold. I had heard rumors about people who made deals with the devil, stories of black magic and ancient myths. But if it worked, it would be worth it. I would give up anything I owned, do anything I was capable of, to have Laurel back.

I watched Mother Margarite work for about an hour. Sometimes she traced herbs in circles around Laurel's body, other times chanted while she poured the dark contents of a bottle into Laurel's mouth. She unwrapped the bandages that were tied around Laurel's middle, and I saw how the infection had spread. Most of the skin was inflamed and hot to the touch, stretched tight over the deep gouge marks in her abdomen. Along the ugly gashes, more bubbles of greenish-yellow pus had popped up, and some of the scabbed skin was blackened and dead-looking. Sybil had been right. Laurel was dying.

Mother Margarite seemed at ease and hummed a ghostly melody while she drew symbols onto the wound site with a harsh-smelling liquid. To my amazement, the infected boils and necrosis seemed to dissipate before my very eyes and vanished into thin air. The swelling went down and soon, all that remained were the red slashes across Laurel's abdomen from where the claws of the iron trellis dug into her side, and even those seemed to be thinning out and fading. Mother Margarite slathered Laurel's middle with a thick green paste and rolled thin black bandages firmly around everything.

At long last, Mother Margarite was finished. She rolled

up the herbs into a tight bundle, replaced them on her shelf, and handed me the large jar of green salve. "She will come around in another hour or so. Keep washing the wounds, change the dressings twice a day, and apply this paste each time. She should be all better within a month. Don't let her do any work at all. She is to lay in bed. Nothing else. Even when she starts feeling better, she is not to get up for at least four weeks. Preferably six. Start her out with gruel and porridge, and lots of water."

I stared at Laurel. Sweat was no longer beading off her forehead. She was breathing more freely now, and color was returning to her face. When I bent to listen to her heart, there was a stronger beat. Relief flooded my body. She was recovering.

"Thank you!" I said sincerely. "I don't know how I can ever repay you." I held Laurel's hand and felt warmth radiating from it. Who cared that Mother Margarite's house was a little creepy? She had saved Laurel! All my apprehension about Mother Margarite disappeared as quickly as Laurel's infection had. I scooped up Laurel and prepared to leave. As I reached the door, I remembered I now owed a debt as payment for Laurel's treatment.

"What do you want in return?" I asked as I exited, turning back to look at Laurel's savior.

Mother Margarite smiled that sinister smile again. "I want you to murder King Richard."

LAUREL

*W*hen I finally became conscious, I wished I could slip back into my painless slumber. The agony was inexpressible. It felt as if every inch of my entire body had been beaten with clubs. Perhaps all the skin on my abdomen had been ripped brutally away. It certainly felt that way. My head was throbbing as it never had hurt before, and my throat felt like it was bubbling with acid. I gasped for breath and let out a tiny squeak. I couldn't even work up enough air to properly cry out. I felt a hand press onto my shoulder, and I was forced to stay down. I wouldn't have been able to get up by myself anyway.

I opened my eyes and Baron's concerned face swam into view. "Ow," I croaked.

Baron opened a jar and began gently dabbing some paste onto my exposed torso. "Take it easy," he said.

"Ow," I repeated. I tried to look down at my body, but I couldn't contract my abdominal muscles enough to lift my neck. My head flopped down to the side. "Ow."

How long had I been out? The only thing I had to go

off of was the length of the stubble on Baron's face. At my last clear memory, just after I stole the papers, he was clean shaven. But now, there was scruff all over his chin and jaw. It looked like several days' worth of growth. I couldn't have been unconscious that long! A few vague recollections floated into my mind. James transporting me back to Sherwood Forest. Sybil and Peter telling me I was going to die. Baron taking me to the village physician. But the memories were like a dream and slipped away faster than I could hold on to them.

"Am I... alive?" I asked.

"You are." Baron gave me a half-hearted grin. "I found someone who could heal you."

"Who?" I asked. I was surprised. Even though I was in a significant amount of pain, it was far less than I had expected, and I was able to think clearly. I must be recovering. But if Sybil and Peter couldn't help... who else could it have been?

"The village physician tried. But he wanted to bleed out all the infection, and that would have killed you. You had already lost so much blood."

"Pompous prat," I groaned. "I blacked his eye when he tried to put leeches on me when I was twelve and he swore he would never treat anyone from the forest again."

Baron should have laughed. Most people did when I recounted that tale. But he only nodded solemnly. Maybe my storytelling abilities weren't back up to my usual level yet. "Who was it?" I persisted.

Baron sighed. "There was an old woman in the woods."

I gasped. "Not the wicked witch?" I had never seen this legendary woman. I heard ghost story after ghost story when I was a little girl about an evil witch that lived in the woods and preyed upon the souls of those who sought her dark powers. The stories went that she had the mystical abilities to change forms, that she could transform people and things, cast magic spells, and never die. But anyone who requested her services had to pay a heavy price. I was far more afraid of those stories than I was of any of Prince John's dim-witted henchmen.

"I don't know if she was a witch, but she healed you." Baron sounded dejected. If the stories were true, what had she demanded of Baron?

"Did she ask you for anything in return?"

Baron looked up sharply. "What makes you say that?"

I was taken aback by his suspicion. "Nothing, I just heard stories about her is all. That she usually expects payment. But I've only ever heard stories. I didn't know anyone that has actually met her."

Baron's face relaxed, but he still looked preoccupied. "Yes, she asked for something."

He didn't elaborate.

"What was she like?" I asked, painfully curious. All the haunting tales from my youth suddenly seemed real.

Baron considered for a long time before answering. He half-glanced at me, then said casually. "Just old. She is just a really old woman with a lot of experience. She knew a remedy no one else did is all. Some potion."

"What did she ask for?" I pestered. It hurt to talk, but my curiosity was greater than the pain. It looked like Baron chewed on his tongue momentarily before responding.

"I offered her money."

"And she accepted?!"

"What, you think someone would turn down money?"

"No, it is just... all the stories I heard about her made

251

me think that people sold their souls in exchange for a magic spell. I had never heard of her accepting money before." Truth be told, I was scared of stories about black magic and witches and all the rest. I couldn't fight magic.

"Well, rest assured that I didn't sell my soul. And you are getting better, so there is no need to worry about it."

Baron went back to dabbing salve onto my midriff, but his mind seemed a million miles away from what he was doing. I didn't have the energy for whatever was troubling him. All I could do was gasp quietly for breath. Baron was a competent person. He could handle whatever was troubling him. If he wanted to let me know, he would.

Sybil and Peter and all the rest had been astounded beyond words when Baron carried me back into the heart of Sherwood Forest, alive and well.

He didn't leave my side in all the time he was in camp and refused to let me do anything other than lay in bed. He seemed somewhat distant, but as we had broken up a few weeks earlier, I wasn't shocked by that behavior. What was concerning was how much the distance bothered me. I didn't want to be distant with Baron. I wanted the closeness we had shared before. I wanted to tell Baron everything. He understood me in a way that no one else did. I didn't ever have to explain myself to him.

Peter was highly displeased to see Baron staying so close to me. He often tried to banish Baron from the house I was in, but I always refused to have him sent away. I wanted Baron with me. He was the only one who had refused to accept the possibility of my death. He was the one who had kept me safe when everyone else gave up hope. Now, after his help, I was healing with almost impossible speed, which mystified Sybil and frustrated Peter, who wanted the credit for healing me.

Even when I was feeling completely better, Baron staunchly refused to allow me to get out of bed or do any work and gave strict orders to everyone in our tiny village to not allow me to. Everyone was so in awe of his miraculous ability to save me that they obeyed him without question. I again marveled how Baron had the ability to command people without even trying.

"I OWE YOU MY LIFE, YOU KNOW," I TOLD BARON A FEW DAYS later, just before he was due to return to Prince John's castle.

"You don't owe me anything," Baron said right away. "You have saved me before. We are even."

"Everyone else gave up. But you didn't."

Baron smiled. "I will never give up on you."

I reached my hand out for his. Just as always, the second he touched me, my heart began to flutter wildly. I didn't want him to leave. I wasn't lonely when Baron was around. I clung to his fingers and pulled him closer. "Stay with me."

"What do you think I have been doing?" Baron asked softly and smoothed some of my hair out of my face. I didn't want him to stop touching me. I wanted to block out the rest of the world. He and I had completed our part of the mission; there was no need for either of us to return to the castle.

As valuable as Baron could be staying undercover, I didn't want to be parted from him again. It had been a mistake to push him away. I felt the same irresistible draw toward him that I couldn't ever explain or wish away. He was the one I wanted. I was sure of it.

"Kiss me," I told him.

Baron's fingers tightened over mine. He started to lean forward but then stopped almost immediately. I saw conflict raging in his eyes but couldn't understand his hesitation. I knew he wanted to be with me just as much as I wanted to be with him. What was holding him back? I tried to pull Baron closer to me, but he resisted.

"Baron, I want to get back together."

He closed his eyes, and I hastened on. "You were right- I am impulsive. I was impulsive when I called things off, and I was impulsive when I kissed Peter. I was wrong to do those things. I am sorry. I still love you, and I want to be with you."

I had expected Baron to be overjoyed. I had expected that he would eagerly accept, just as he did months ago when I suggested we run away together. I certainly hadn't expected him to look conflicted and upset. "We can't," he said quietly.

I caught my breath. "What... what do you mean? I am sorry about before, I am! With Peter- it didn't mean anything!"

"It isn't that."

"Then what? What did I do?"

Baron shook his head. "It isn't about you! I'm not the person you think I am."

"But I know about-" I began, but Baron forestalled me.

"It goes beyond Walter and his hand, Laurel. It goes beyond my parentage and what I've done in the past. You wouldn't understand."

"I am a pretty smart person. Explain it to me."

"I can't."

I was stunned. I knew about Baron's past, or at least enough of it. I had accepted that he had to act the part of the Sheriff to maintain his image, whatever distasteful tasks he had to carry out. I was willing to look past all that, but he was refusing to let me back into his life. I didn't understand it. He had immediately come to my aid when I needed it. He must care about me. But then why would he refuse my offer? I had never been rejected before. The hurt went deeper than any other injury I ever had, right down to my very core. I had heard that love could hurt, but until this very moment, I hadn't understood it. Now I did. It was as though my very soul was being cleaved in two.

"Baron, what I did- I am sorry! I don't know what else I can say. I am sorry about everything! I choose you!"

"This isn't about anything you've done!" Baron said irritably. "You don't need to be sorry!"

"Then what is it?"

Baron ran his hand through his hair and blew out a sharp puff of air. "I can't tell you."

I was utterly bewildered. "I thought you loved me."

"I do!"

"Well?" I waved my arms as if to say, *Then what is the problem?*

"We just can't! I want to. I do! But it is impossible right now. I don't have an answer for you." Baron rose abruptly. "And I don't know when I will."

He ducked out of the hut and, a few minutes later, I heard the heavy hoofbeats of his horse gallop out of camp. I didn't understand. If he loved me, why didn't he want to be with me? Was he with someone else? I had kissed Peter, had he gotten together with another girl but didn't want to tell me? Baron had just saved my life yet again, by finding someone to heal me when everyone else had given up hope. He wouldn't have done that if he didn't care about me. And I had even apologized! Was Baron aware of how infrequently I apologized? To *anyone*? I never allowed myself to be vulnerable and open up to people, and this was why. I sat, trying furiously to dissect the problem as dusk faded into a dark, velvety night.

I couldn't understand the issue. If we loved each other, that should be enough. We could work things out. But now, Baron was saying he didn't want to. At some point, I had ruined my chances of a future with Baron. If only I knew how.

BARON

I needed to see Mother Margarite again. She must have misunderstood me. Perhaps she knew of me from my former life, when I would not have hesitated to kill King Richard. My allegiances had changed. If I killed King Richard, I would never be accepted into the Merry Men. I would lose Laurel forever. She would hate me until the day I died. I couldn't do it. And beyond that, killing King Richard was a death sentence for the one who committed the crime. Everyone knew that. I didn't want to be a murderer, I didn't want to forfeit my life, but nor could I lose Laurel. It was an impossible task that I had been set.

And now Laurel had come back and said she wanted to get back together... She must know how badly I wanted to. But how would it be for her, to be with the treasonous murderer who was destined to kill the king? I couldn't do that to her. I couldn't kill King Richard. But if I didn't, would Laurel really die? Mother Margarite must have been joking. Or bluffing. But until I was sure... I couldn't promise Laurel anything. I had to know. Tonight.

I went to find Mother Margarite. I had been so relieved that Laurel was healed that I hadn't clarified any of what I had been asked to do. I must have been confused because I was so worried about Laurel; that must be it. Maybe I had heard wrong. The second I had seen Laurel looking better, I just grabbed her and ran, desperate to get her out of there. My mind must have been playing tricks on me at the time.

The moon was a sliver of a crescent. It cast a very faint glow over the path. I tied my horse to a tree on the outskirts of the forest and began the journey to Mother Margarite's derelict hut. The area had been unsettling before, in full daylight. But now, in the pitch dark of night, any slight noise sounded sinister and ominous.

The broken-down cottage seemed even eerier than when I had first visited. The darkness seemed impenetrable- thick and unnatural, even though I could see the moon. Skeletons of small rodents crunched under my boots as I walked up the path, and a cold draft washed over me as I neared the door. No lights shone out of any of the windows.

I knocked on the door and waited. A light flared inside and I heard shuffling footsteps. I squared my shoulders to appear as intimidating as possible. I was prepared to say that I needed to renegotiate the terms of our contract. I would offer something else. The wooden door creaked open.

There stood Mother Margarite, just as ancient and hump-backed as ever. Her skin hung off her, nearly transparent with how thin it was, and she was so old that her wrinkles seemed to have wrinkles. Maybe she would die before my year was up, and I wouldn't have to do anything. I would be freed.

"I knew you would come," Mother Margarite said with an evil grin. "Everyone does."

"I need to renegotia—" I began, but she was already shaking her head.

"Baron, Baron. We made a deal. I can't go back on that now. A life for a life."

"But you don't understand!" I said desperately. "I can't! It is impossible!"

"I never set impossible tasks, boy," Mother Margarite hissed in a low, ominous whisper. "Difficult, yes. But impossible, no."

"I *can't!*" I insisted. "If anyone found out…"

"I never said you had to tell anyone." A wicked smile split Mother Margarite's face. "Do it discreetly and you will be able to stay with the woman you love. You will be able to join her little band and no one would ever know. It will be our little secret."

I couldn't think of how I would ever be able to accomplish that. In every situation I could think of, my involvement would be discovered. Laurel would die, or else hate me forever. Either way, I would lose her. My mind reeled. I couldn't give up Laurel. I couldn't. What if Mother Margarite died instead? That would break her spell, wouldn't it?

It was as though she read my thoughts. She leered and revealed her yellowed, crooked-toothed grin. "You aren't the first one to want to kill me, Baron. But you won't succeed if you try. My spells won't die with me. They never do."

"I refuse!" I stated firmly. "I won't kill him!"

Mother Margarite shrugged, indifferent to my threat. "If you choose that, then Laurel will die exactly a year from when I healed her. She will start to get sicker the longer you wait. That is why I had you swear on her life instead of your own. If you don't complete the task, she dies. Who do you care more about, her or Richard? The decision is entirely up to you."

"You're bluffing," I accused.

Mother Margarite laughed. It was an unearthly, spine-tingling cackle that made the hair on my neck stand on end.

"You don't have to take my word for it, boy! Wait and see for yourself! In about six months, Laurel will become ill with a mysterious disease. She will grow weaker and weaker until either she or Richard dies."

"But you said a year!" I said, aghast.

"Oh, did I? Oh, and of course, you need to kill Richard in the same way Laurel was destined to die, or else the spell won't work."

I felt blood pounding in my ears. This was becoming more impossible by the second! I was destined to fail. "Give the king blood poisoning? I... I can't!" I croaked.

"You can, and you will. You will see. Good night, dearie." She shut the door in my face. I heard her footsteps shuffle away from the door.

I stared, dumbfounded, at the door for a long time. The flickering lamp light behind the grimy window was extinguished. I pounded on the door again. I would not leave until we reached an agreement. If I needed to, I would arrest her and keep her in prison until she agreed. Mother Margarite didn't answer. I continued to pound for several minutes. I grabbed the brass handle and to my surprise, found that it swung out easily; I was about to kick the door in.

It was pitch black inside. I lit a torch, then gasped aloud. The interior looked entirely different than what I had seen only moments before. No potions nor powders lined the walls anymore. All the aged shelves were broken and cracked. Cobwebs and dust lay thick over all the surfaces, except for the carved wooden table in the center of the room. The symbols seemed to glow blue-white in the torch's glow.

I lifted the torch higher and moved slowly from room to room. In the bedroom farthest from the entryway, a skeleton wearing the same outfit Mother Margarite had been wearing sat in a weather-beaten rocking chair, it's mouth agape as if laughing. It felt as though I had plunged into an icy lake. My mouth went dry, goose-bumps erupted all over my skin, and my insides felt hollow.

I approached it cautiously. This was impossible! I had spoken with Mother Margarite only minutes before! The thought of 'black magic' flew through my mind again, and it was as though a cold hand was squeezing my heart. Suddenly, I wanted to flee. To run and never look back. But I couldn't turn my back on the skeleton. I wanted to tear my eyes from the gruesome sight, but it was though I was hypnotized. The empty eye sockets stared back at me as I backed slowly out of the room.

Was this all in my head? Was I going mad? My eyes fell upon the wooden table carved with symbols, then to the torch in my hand. There had to be a way to break the spell, there had to be! I held the torch to the table.

In an instant, the symbols all flashed fiery red. The flame from my torch went soaring away from the table, flew around the room, and descended onto my hand. I shouted and whipped my arm away. I studied the table a moment more, then hit it as hard as I could. Far from breaking the table, I felt a searing pain erupt in my hand,

and I saw that a symbol had been burned into my skin. The symbols on the table glowed brightly, as if mocking my feeble attempt to destroy it.

A whine of panic entered my brain. How could I save Laurel? I had no one to threaten. I couldn't challenge a spell to a duel. I had no way of protecting her. I stumbled backward out of the hut and stood, staring at it. What else could I do?

I held the torch to the ancient woodpile leaning against the side of the house. The flame wouldn't catch. I tried to light the house on fire any way I could, but the fire refused to ignite. The shack had looked like it should have been easy to destroy, but nothing I did made any difference. I couldn't destroy the house. It was impossible. Just like the task I had been set.

I couldn't bear any more. I turned and ran through the blinding darkness.

With each of my pounding footsteps, the thought drummed through my head. *Laurel or Richard? Laurel or Richard?* How could I ever possibly choose? My initial reaction was immediately to choose Laurel and, if it was a simple choice between her and any other commoner, that would be easy. But actually plotting to assassinate the king? The knowledge that I would be personally responsible for the murder of England's ruler, and for the kingdom being passed to Prince John... It was repugnant. And even if I did choose that option, how on earth would I ever be able to give Richard blood poisoning? And to do so without my involvement becoming known?

I was so sure that joining the Merry Men would be a turning point in my life. No longer would I be a villain. I wanted to be the hero. But heroes don't make deals with the devil. I cursed under my breath. I had no future, just a bleak wasteland ahead of me. My father's voice floated into my mind, jeering, '*You thought it would be that easy, did you? You thought could just walk away from who you are, from your past, and be free? You will never be free. You will always be my son. You thought you would be accepted as a member of the Merry Men. Ha! You don't deserve it. You don't deserve to be with anyone like Robin Hood's daughter. You are nothing. You always will be.*'

How had I been so desperate that I accepted a deal without knowing the price? I vowed that, somehow, Mother Margarite would pay for the agony she was causing me. I clenched my teeth furiously. All my frustration seemed to well up to a breaking point, and I punched a blackened tree to the side of the path. It cracked satisfactorily, but still did nothing to alleviate the helplessness I felt.

Richard or Laurel. One of them had to die. And I had to choose which.

TO BE CONTINUED...

TO MY READERS

Thank you for reading! Yes, I know I was an evil author for leaving it on a cliffhanger, but I promise the conclusion is coming soon!

If you would like to receive updates and sneak peeks into upcoming books, please go to my website and sign up for my newsletter at MaryMecham.com, where you can also download a free copy of my Rumpelstiltskin retelling, *A Curse of Gold and Beauty*.

You can also follow me on Instagram, Facebook, or TikTok at @MaryMecham_Author

Happy Reading,
   Mary Mecham

ABOUT THE AUTHOR

Mary Mecham is a born and raised Texan. She has always loved fairy tales, and as a child, carried books everywhere. When she wasn't curled up with the latest recommendation from the local librarian, she was often found in theaters, acting onstage in musical theater productions. Her favorite role was the Wicked Stepsister in the play Cinderella, which inspired her first novel, *Ugly: The Stepsister's Story*.

As an adult, Mary still haunts the libraries of Houston, but is more frequently found doing disability advocacy work. Mary is the Founder and President of Advocates for Disability Inclusion in Literature, as well as the Director of Disability Book Week, and holds multiple leadership roles with various disability related organizations.

ALSO BY MARY MECHAM

Becoming Hook
A Villainous Retelling of "Peter Pan"

Hunting Sirens
A Gender-Flipped "Little Mermaid"

Poisoned: Snow White's Story
A Disability Inclusive Snow White Retelling

Ugly: The Stepsister's Story
Inspired by "Cinderella"

A Curse of Gold and Beauty
Inspired by "Rumpelstiltskin"

Laurel of Locksley
Inspired by "Robin Hood"